THE RIVERSEDGE LAW CLUB SERIES

Easy Street

"This third installment in Impellizzeri's Riversedge Law Club series is a standalone narrative that eschews courtroom drama for a compelling story of secrets and lies. Membership in the Law Club should get a boost from this well-told, character-driven story."

KIRKUS REVIEWS

"Fans of 'Suits' will find themselves at home—but with a far more sinister twist. A legal thriller that feels all too real."

REKTOK ROSS, bestselling author of *Summer Rental*

"Intrigue, secrets, corruption, and scandal. Impellizzeri's newest installment in the Riversedge Law Club Series absolutely thrills. Told through multiple points of view, *Easy Street* is a case you won't be able to put down until you've cracked it."

TOSCA LEE, *NYT* bestselling author of *The Line Between*

"An old building has a dark history—but not nearly so dark and destructive as its residents' secrets. In the vein of Highsmith's *The Talented Mr. Ripley* and Grisham's *The Firm*, Amy Impellizzeri's gripping, suspenseful thriller explores the oft-blurred lines between friendship and betrayal, reality and lies. The tension mounts from page one and doesn't let up until the shocking conclusion. Masterful!"

ROBERT ROTSTEIN, *USA Today* bestselling author of *A True Verdict*

"Masterfully plotted and utterly addictive, *Easy Street* sizzles with gripping legal drama and crackles with explosive secrets. With betrayal, scandal, and suspense at every turn, this fast paced thriller proves sometimes the most dangerous cracks are the ones you can't see."

LINDSAY CAMERON, Author of *Just One Look* and *Biglaw*

THE RIVERSEDGE LAW CLUB SERIES
In Her Defense

"A gripping legal thriller that will grab readers from the get-go."
KIRKUS REVIEWS (STARRED REVIEW)

"Impellizzeri delivers in *In Her Defense,* intricately weaving a psychological suspense and a gripping legal thriller into one bang of a book. A twisty, winding road of deceit, betrayal, and the extent to which someone will go to conceal the truth. I gobbled it up."
KIMBERLY BELLE, internationally bestselling author of *Dear Wife* and *Stranger in the Lake*

"Courtroom dramatics, corrupt judges, blackmailing and backstabbing lawyers, and a legal cat and mouse between a lawyer and her own client. Add in an affair between a lawyer's husband and the client, a soon to be demolished strip club, and a string of murders and you have the makings of an on-the-edge-of-your-seat, can't-put-down-read! In between all the legal maneuverings, Impellizzeri's characters are flawed and poignant, their relationships are multi-layered, and the end is truly both tender and surprising."
KATE MORETTI, *New York Times* bestselling author of *The Vanishing Year*

"*In Her Defense* is an intricately plotted, compelling legal drama with heart-and a twist ending that you won't see coming!"
KATHLEEN BARBER, author of *Truth Be Told* (formerly published as *Are You Sleeping* and now an Apple TV+ series)

"Finally—the female-driven, character-rich, John Grisham-style legal thriller I've been waiting for...."
EMILY CARPENTER, bestselling author of *Burying the Honeysuckle Girls*

THE RIVERSEDGE LAW CLUB SERIES
Barr None

"Impellizzeri's prose is shrewd and evocative"
KIRKUS REVIEWS

"Razorsharp, Fierce with a capital F and with breathtaking twists, *Barr None* is a force to be reckoned with. Netflix, are you listening?"
BARBARA BOS, Managing Editor, BooksByWomen.org

"*The Firm* meets the *Devil Wears Prada* in former attorney Impellizzeri's newest novel, *Barr None*, about the sacrifices required to succeed as a female attorney at New York City's most prestigious law firm. A smart and thrilling page-turner you don't want to miss."
DANIELLE GIRARD, *USA Today* bestselling author of *The Ex*

"Dark, disturbing, and constantly unsettling. Amy Impellizzeri's deep understanding of the perils of lawyering comes through in this cautionary tale about power, ambition, and the soul-crushing effects of stress and desire. Uniquely structured and instantly cinematic, *Barr None* is endlessly thought-provoking."
HANK PHILLIPPI RYAN, *USA Today* Bestselling Author

"A twisty, jaw-dropping look at the rotten underbelly of a prestigious Manhattan law firm, Barr None's tantalizing secrets unfold like the best true crime case. With the deftness and expertise of a former lawyer, Impellizzeri nails every hairpin turn with authenticity, telling a mesmerizing story where corporate law intersects with the darkest of human instincts."
EMILY CARPENTER, Bestselling Author of *Burying the Honeysuckle Girls*

EASY STREET

THE **RIVERSEDGE LAW CLUB** SERIES

EASY STREET

AMY IMPELLIZZERI

Wyatt-MacKenzie Publishing
DEADWOOD, OREGON

ALSO BY AMY IMPELLIZZERI

Lemongrass Hope
Lawyer Interrupted
Secrets of Worry Dolls
The Truth About Thea
Why We Lie
I Know How This Ends
In Her Defense
Barr None

Easy Street
Amy Impellizzeri

ISBN: 978-1-954332-48-5
Library of Congress Control Number on file.

Wyatt-MacKenzie Publishing
DEADWOOD, OREGON

Wyatt-MacKenzie Publishing, Inc.
www.WyattMacKenzie.com
Contact us: info@wyattmackenzie.com

DEDICATION

To Heather, for every single AH-HA moment …

THE RIVERSEDGE LAW CLUB SERIES

Meet the Characters of Easy Street

Felicity and Archie—lawyers at Rogers Hawk and lovers—Felicity is harboring secrets from her past and running up incredible debt that Archie knows nothing about. Archie has reasons for wanting this building that will threaten to tear everyone apart.

Holly—former Rogers Hawk lawyer—left the law and returned to her first love—cooking. Holly connected with Daniel—personally and professionally—to start a clean living catering biz. Her entire POV is sworn testimony from a deposition in an insurance fraud case.

Ava and Roan—practiced law together at Rogers Hawk until Ava left to become a writer—Ava ends up taking on a ghostwriting job for a client who is suing Rogers Hawk in a sexual harassment lawsuit that names Roan as a defendant.

Sara—the 4th unit owner. Sara only interacts with Archie, but through Sara, the group learns that Easy Street has an underground tunnel. The tunnel previously led to the long closed Riversedge Asylum across the street. Agnes, Sara's grandmother, was a patient of the Asylum and was accused of murdering her husband, Jasper, whose body was never actually found.

Nola Dyer—the fierce new lawyer—previously of BARR KNOLL—who is representing the host of plaintiffs suing Rogers Hawk Law Firm for sexual harassment.

Everyone will be shocked when all the secrets buried under the floors of EASY STREET come into the light.

"Three may keep a secret, if two of them are dead."

–Benjamin Franklin, *Poor Richard's Almanack*

PROLOGUE

Agnes stands on the window ledge of the top story of the building located at 724 East Street.

The road runs north and south and it isn't east of anything except this old building that her dead husband has started renovating. But will never finish. The street name makes no sense to her. It's one of many things that makes absolutely no sense to Agnes, even though other things have become crystal clear.

Have people just run out of names for streets? Agnes wonders.

One foot dangles over the edge. *It would be easy to do it,* she thinks.

Construction debris fills Agnes's nostrils. The air is thick with it even though all work was halted and, without funding, may not begin again until someone else buys this old building.

But who will buy this building now?

Every day since she unraveled the depths of Jasper's unforgivable secret, Agnes has been coming up to this floor and standing on the ledge, measuring the distance to East Street below with her eyes and her grief.

It's like an itch that's taken hold over her entire body, and Agnes scratches it incessantly by her daily trips to the ridiculously mis-named East Street that inevitably finds her standing in this precarious spot. She's hoping the wound muscling around her heart will scab over before she gives in.

It would be easy to jump. So very easy to jump, she concludes each time.

Except today.

Today Agnes feels something very different as she looks down at the street and then back over her shoulder at the room behind her.

It will be much much easier to stay now, Agnes thinks as she pulls her dangling foot back, conceding that it was a test. Just a test to see if things feel differently finally. And they do. With the drugs finally weaned from her system, and her mind clearer than ever before and her love waiting for her down below, she feels ... safe. Finally.

Agnes takes a step back from the open window and exhales loudly with a hope that the wound has finally healed over.

724 East Street has represented nothing but chaos and pain ever since she first set foot in it. But that all changes today. Agnes looks down at the East Street sign again with disgust.

I'll petition for it to be renamed, she thinks.

And why not? She will fix a great many things now. It's been glorious to discover finally just how strong and powerful she really is.

As Agnes leaves the half-finished apartment, she looks back over her shoulder. She pictures a thin stream of gasoline leading across the freshly sanded floorboards stopping in the middle of the room. One match and the whole thing would go up in smoke. But, no, what justice would there be in that? This building should stand. If nothing else, as a monument to the pain and terror that it has inflicted.

For now, at least. Agnes thinks, with her freshly healed heart and her invisible cloak of power.

For as long as I am living. Or until I figure out who else I can entrust my secrets to.

Until then, I'll simply leave those secrets buried inside this building where they belong.

PART I

CHAPTER 1
Felicity

Archie glances at the bill over Felicity's shoulder. "Jesus. We really outdid ourselves this time."

"No kidding," Felicity grimaces. "We should just stay in one of these nights, and play board games or something."

Holly hits Felicity's shoulder a little too hard. "Girl. You're hysterical. What are we? Our parents? Are you suggesting some Friday night Scrabble, maybe?"

Felicity caresses her shoulder gingerly and laughs at Holly's bad joke a little too loudly. She wonders if anyone else notices how loud she is laughing. No, they're all too drunk. No one notices that Felicity ordered seltzer water, no appetizer, and the cheapest entree on this obscene restaurant's menu in which the portions were the only thing small about the night. Egos, prices, and tales have all become inflated as the wine glasses multiplied.

Felicity is starting to feel invisible to everyone. Even Archie.

It's my own fault, she reminds herself as she stares again at the numbers on the dinner bill. *How could just three couples rack up a bill of this magnitude?*

Across the table, Roan and Ava are leaning into each other, whispering and kissing. As Roan interrupts their intimacy only long enough to slide a credit card across the table, Felicity feels a jealous tug at her heart. And her wallet. "For me and Ava," Roan says unnecessarily. It's always for him and Ava. This whole

1

thing is a well rehearsed dance and Felicity looks around the table for all of her friends to take their marks on the stage. The performances never waver from script.

Soon, Holly and Daniel will throw their American Express cards in the middle, yelling, "Split it 6 ways, of course," and then Archie will slide his platinum card at her like a peace offering and a, "What do I owe for me, darling?" and then Felicity will do all the math and throw her own beleaguered credit card on the top of the pile and split the bill 6 ways but charge Ava's share to Roan, and give the server a generous tip that will total more than Felicity's actual mathematical share of the bill.

And then Felicity and Archie will go home and have perfectly good sex in a newly redecorated bedroom Felicity still hasn't finished paying off and Archie will go home before the morning because they both have to go into the office at some point this weekend.

Archie likes to have Saturday mornings to himself to "regroup" from the stress of the week and to plan the new week ahead. Archie has figured out how to juggle it all. The money, the spending, the workload, the ridiculous Manhattan cost of living. He does it all with seeming ease. He's in great shape and everyone loves him. He does yoga almost daily, and as far as Felicity can tell—and she's looked—Archie doesn't have an ounce of excess body fat on his whole person. Archie doesn't lose his temper, his keys, or his clients.

Archie is perfect, and that's why Felicity feels like a jerk every time she gets offended that he doesn't offer to pay for her meal, or buy her presents, or even ask her to sell her expensive condo and move in with him.

But she does get offended. And she does feel like a jerk more often than not these days. She expected to be so much farther along by now. In work and finances and her relationship. In life.

As Felicity looks around the table at her friends, she hears her own voice loudly yelling inside her head, and she closes her eyes, hoping that will quiet it, or at least keep the voice from seeping out of her. Because the voice is angry. The voice has in fact, been getting angrier and angrier lately. Felicity is worried the voice is going to get so loud one day that it takes over completely, and she's not ready to ruin everything. Not yet at least. The last time that voice took over, Felicity barely survived it. That was the year she lost what seemed like everything she had at the time. She's learned since then she can have more—so much more—and she is constantly in danger of losing it all again. Felicity is worried about burning her life down and so she keeps stifling the voice deep inside her, coiling it back down as if she's rewinding a toy jack-in-the-box, back *into* the box. The toy is not a figment of her imagination, entirely. There *was* a jack-in-the-box. It sat on a shelf in her childhood home, a nearly discarded remnant from her childhood that she'd saved from a Goodwill bag one summer as her mother was cleaning out the closets. Felicity was seventeen at the time. Far too old for kiddie toys, but she wanted that one. She wanted to keep a piece of her childhood intact, and her mother let her. With sadness in her eyes, Marilyn Huck had let her daughter, Felicity, retrieve the jack-in-the-box from the donation bin. She had let Felicity carve out a small piece of her childhood, place it on a bedroom shelf and keep it on display, despite having crossed over into adulthood far too early.

Sitting in the restaurant over a decade later, Felicity imagines herself, pressing, holding, pushing, a squishy bouncing emotion back into its container. She almost has to sit on the lid in her mind to keep it all contained. She knows—from the past—that this is a temporary fix at best.

Felicity steadies her breathing and her emotions as she stares at the exorbitant dinner bill her 5 friends have rung up without her, and reaches out her hand for Archie's card, but Archie does something incredible then—something unexpected. Something off script. He grabs the bill from Felicity, and takes the credit cards and flips them back around the table to their respective

3

owners like he's dealing a deck of cards.

"Dinner's on me," Archie says. Felicity looks at him stunned.

He reaches over and pats her hand. "Yep, that's right darling. I have a surprise for you. For all of us actually. So grab your jackets and follow me to the Uber outside. I'm about to change all of your lives."

CHAPTER 2
Holly

Archie Bello can be a *little* bit of a showboater, so that dinner time gesture wasn't exactly the craziest thing I've ever seen him do. At first, I wondered if he was going to propose to Felicity, and the look on her face was sufficiently surprised that I knew, whatever was going on, she wasn't in on it. So, in hindsight, the proposal thing was a good guess.

All I know is that there is no way I could have *actually* guessed what he had planned for us. None of us could have.

We took an Uber across the river and at first we thought maybe we were going to the Riversedge Law Club, but that didn't seem like a very big surprise.

Why not? Well because Riversedge Law Club has always been an extension of the Manhattan legal scene, and we'd all spent plenty of time there. Listen, you must know all about the Riversedge Law Club. You're lawyers, right? It's a place where the real action of the New York courts takes place. Judges dining with attorneys, prospective clients wooed by law firms large and small. It's just a place where we have all spent a lot of time. Archie taking us over the river to have a nightcap at the Club? That wouldn't have been very strange at all.

However, when the Uber pulled up in front of an old industrial building around the corner from the Riversedge Law Club, well, let's just say, that *was* a surprise.

Later, we'd argue about who went into the building first.

That's because we all wanted plausible deniability when we started fighting over whose idea this whole thing really was. But I know *for certain* who went in first.

I did.

Archie fixed the key in the door and I pushed past him, anxious to see what was inside.

"What is this place?" I remember Daniel asked, suddenly inside and next to me.

"I have no idea. We're about to find out," I answered, even though it was obvious that Daniel's question wasn't for me.

I was so bull-headed that night. I *could* blame it on the wine, but that's not right. I was in a weird place. My confidence had been shaken recently and only Daniel knew why. I guess in a way, I was punishing him for knowing too much. Yes, I know, I can admit that it was very juvenile behavior on my part, but certainly not criminal.

Really? Objection?

Yes, of course I understand. I *was* a lawyer once, you know? Taking depositions like this one, before trial, was a common occurrence back then. I understand the rules. I'll keep talking. The court reporter over there will keep typing up every single thing I say. You'll ask some questions and make a few objections. All of this is really to help us get ready for the eventual trial you all are insisting on having, but mostly we're just trying to get to the bottom of what happened on Easy Street, right?

Good luck to all of us.

Ok. Where was I? Oh yeah, so Archie followed in behind us holding up the keys and jingling them loudly. I think he stepped into the building last. That fact would also be the subject of much debate later on. But that's how I remember it. Hand to God.

In the dark, the keys in his hand glowed like fireflies. Something we didn't see much of in the city. Me? I grew up in the suburbs of New York and fireflies were a summertime staple for me. They were a forgotten childhood memory that I suddenly missed as I watched Archie. An unfamiliar and painful home-sickness took hold of me as we stood in the darkness. *That* I'll blame on the wine.

Anyway—all eyes were on Archie and the keys now. And he loved it. He took a deep, loud breath before exhaling the news. "This is my newest due diligence case. And maybe my next home. Maybe all of our next home?"

"What are you talking about, Archie? What due diligence?" I asked the question for all of us.

"Lou and I have been looking at this file since Monday. A developer wants to buy it and Lou and I are doing a quick search on prior owners to see if there are any red flags that should keep them from buying the place."

Lou was the infamous partner that Archie worked for. Most everyone at the firm feared him and hated him, although not necessarily in that order. But not Archie. Archie gave everyone some incredible benefit of the doubt, and as a result he had become Lou's favorite. It didn't shock any of us that Lou would turn over a plum assignment to Archie. Or that Archie would try to turn it into gold. Back then we just—well, *believed* Archie.

Most of us anyway.

"Ah, so that's why you have the keys? But why would you bring us here to this creepy building? To scare the shit out of us, or something?" Daniel's voice caught a little. I remember thinking I'd never heard him scared like that. It should have served as a warning, but it didn't. It fueled me like a dare instead.

"Well are we going to just stand here in the dark?" I asked, annoyed at Daniel's palpable fear.

Archie brushed past us with a confident "*Follow me*" and led the way down a long corridor to a staircase and we all climbed it in the dark. The six of us moved in surprising silence but the building? It was noisy. The steps creaked and there was a soft hissing noise behind the wall that grew louder as we climbed the steps. In the distance, I heard a knocking sound but I convinced myself that it was coming from the outside. How else can I explain why I kept climbing the steps?

Two flights up, a door was propped open and Archie marched us all through it. He turned the flashlight on his phone and spun around like a disco ball. We all gasped. Well I did at least. I can't have been the only one. Along the far wall was a row of windows floor to ceiling with a view of the River that gave the town—Riversedge, New York—its name. A few cargo boats were visible in the distance and further still, Manhattan, in all its glory. I squinted to see if I could make out my old law office, Rogers Hawk, in the nighttime skyline across that iridescent river.

On that night, it had been over a year since I left Rogers Hawk, and up until that moment, if you'd have asked me, I'd have told you I really didn't miss it. The hours, the backstabbing, the to-go meals, and the exhaustion. I had had enough by the time I traded it all in for my chef's apron and a Culinary School Certificate. Which you might think is a big step down from practicing law, but I assure you, it felt just as rewarding as passing the Bar Exam. The *New York Bar Exam*, at that.

Yes, yes, Counselor. Ok. You don't care about anything other than that night right now. Well, on *that* night, the catering business Daniel and I had started together was growing steadily and fairly quickly. Daniel and I were actually turning a profit. Just the month before, we'd made enough to pay ourselves for the first time. We'd even hired an employee.

"We need to be cautious," Daniel had warned as we hit confirm on the banking transfers and while I felt his tone was just north of patronizing, I knew his message was correct. We'd been working on this idea together for only a short time. The business and our relationship were both fragile. How smart we were with money could make or break either one. Of course, on *that* night, I thought money was the least of our problems. I was much more concerned with other things. But, I guess, now I'm getting ahead of myself.

Right, right.

Ok. Let me back up.

On *that* night—the one where the six of us all first went into the building together, Archie, Felicity, Roan and Ava were still gainfully employed at Rogers Hawk with varying degrees of satisfaction. Ava hated it and Roan tolerated it. Felicity seemed to be steadily, quietly climbing a ladder built only for her. She was working on a very niche set of cases with one of the only female partners at the law firm. If I was a betting woman, I'd have put all my money on Felicity. But Archie was the one who still seemed to love being a New York City lawyer back then. He kept his membership at the Riversedge Law Club current, and dined there flamboyantly at least 3-4 nights a week. Even when I was still practicing law, I let my Riversedge Law Club memberships lapse, citing long hours at the office and less available hours outside the office to use the membership. But Archie always said that was precisely *why* he kept it up.

"The real work happens behind those pillars at the Riversedge Law Club," he'd say. "The real deals are closing inside those walls every single day. If I were you, I'd never give up that membership."

Intellectually, I knew he was right. But that just wasn't my world anymore. Now I was in the food business. The business of food and fuel and nurturing, more specifically. I wasn't doing the firm's dirty work anymore. I was all about clean and healthy living. I'd met Daniel a few weeks after leaving the law, and it seemed like fate had brought us together. He was just as passionate as I was about food and health and cooking. Daniel and I were on the same page about becoming food-as-our-cleanest-fuel ambassadors and that's why we'd started "FREE TO A GOOD HOME"—a private chef business catering exclusively to the busiest (and wealthiest) residents of Manhattan (and even nearby Riversedge!). Our clients all had one thing in common. Well—three things. They had a plan to start a cleaner lifestyle, and the money to fund it but no ability/cooking talent to execute on the plan.

"What are the odds that you'd be friends with not one but *two* Rogers Hawk lawyer *couples*?" Daniel asked soon after we met. "Actually pretty damn good," I'd responded. And I meant it. Rogers Hawk was one of the biggest law firms in the city, and its lawyers did little more than, well, work. So there wasn't exactly time for extracurricular activities like romance outside of firm hours. You either dated people you worked with. Or you took a lot of cold showers.

"How about you?" Daniel asked early on. "Ever date anyone you work with?"

"God, no," I lied.

Um. Shit. Can you strike that last sentence? No? You have to type everything I say. Yes, of course, I remember that rule. Ok, I'll be more careful. I guess it's been longer than I thought since I had to think like a lawyer.

Anyway. On the second floor of what I believed then was Archie's new due diligence assignment, I pressed closer to the window wall, leaning my face against one of the panes, the cold seeping into my pores. The rest of the group lined up next to me and I spun around to see where we were.

The room was now backlit by the city sky and with my eyes a little more accustomed to the dim light, I focused in on the exposed brick lining all the walls not covered by windows.

Across the room, I could see a floor to ceiling fireplace and a sleek shiny new kitchen next to it, appliances and granite glimmering even in the dark. My hands itched to touch them, and try them out. Next to the kitchen, a black spiral staircase that gleamed like patent leather wound its way from the middle of the wood floor into some dark space above us.

"Interesting. On the outside, it still looks like a 1950's era industrial building. But on the inside, just wow. Has the whole building been renovated into modern duplexes like this?"

That was Roan. The rest of us were quiet, serene and surveying. Roan never did know how to be quiet.

"No, not yet. That's the beauty of this whole thing." Even in the dim light, you could tell Archie looked pleased as he answered. Like Roan had asked exactly the right question. Archie moved to the center of the room, grabbed a hold of the winding bannister, and continued on, his face animated and lit up still by the light on his cell phone.

"So the building was bought by a Miami-based developer ten years ago in a short sale. The previous owner was some obscure LLC, apparently a holding company, but I can't seem to find out too much about them, other than the fact that they were in dire financial straits by the time they had to dump the property. At least one of their subsidiary companies was a medical center that went belly up after a lawsuit was filed against them. Apparently they settled the lawsuit in terms that are under seal but it must have been a big enough hit that they couldn't hold onto this property and so they dumped it. This place had been mortgaged and re-mortgaged several times over, but the bank approved the sale and the LLC sold it for less than they still owed. As far as I can tell the holding company dissolved shortly after the sale to the Miami developer."

"Jesus, Archie, you sound like you're dictating a memo to Lou, not talking to your inner circle here."

That was Felicity. I think we all kind of flipped our gaze to her at that point, because it was so shocking to hear her snap at anyone, least of all Archie. Felicity was always so cool and even-tempered before—well, anyway, just before. But you know, now that I think about it, that was probably the beginning of a real awakening for Felicity because she didn't know anything about the building. She didn't know what Archie had up his sleeve. She was as much in the dark as the rest of us. At that point anyway. And maybe, I can't be sure, but maybe that really ignited something, um, *dark* in Felicity.

I know, stop getting ahead of myself, right?

Ok. On *that* night, Archie looked a little startled by Felicity's tone and accusation too, but then he just grabbed her by the shoulders and laughed and said, "Yes! You're right! But I'm just so excited about the possibilities here. The developer that bought this place in the short sale wants to sell. They finished renovations on this one unit and ran out of cash so now they want out. So badly in fact that they're willing to sell for a loss. And remember they bought it on the cheap a decade ago. They're entertaining an offer that is a fraction of the market price. Even with all the work that still needs to be done, this place has tremendous potential. I mean, come on—look at it." Archie spun Felicity around and I got a little dizzy just watching them.

"Well from what we can see anyway. Feels like all the potential of a haunted movie set, frankly." There was that hitch in Daniel's voice again. *Fear.* I'm ashamed to tell you I didn't find it all that attractive in the moment. I realize, in hindsight, I should have thrown my arms around him and thanked him, but I did the opposite. I scolded him.

"Daniel. Come on. It's an old, half-renovated building. You're being a little ridiculous. It's not haunted. It's romantic. I think I sort of see what Archie sees." I turned back to the river view.

"So what, Archie, you want to buy the place?" I told you. Roan could never be quiet.

"Not me. We. I want all of us to buy the place. Turn it into something amazing. We could flip it and sell it. Or better yet— we could live in it. Come home to *that* very view every night. There are four duplex units, stacked on top of each other, just like this one. And each one has this view. Each one has *this* potential."

Archie let go of Felicity's shoulders then and I watched her face change. Transform. "Us? You want to buy it together?" Felicity asked him.

Archie leaned his forehead into hers and nodded.

I mean, everyone knew Archie was talking about all of us, not just him and Felicity, but we all let her have that moment.

And truth be told, things get a little fuzzy for me then. We started talking over each other. It was a ridiculous idea. It was an amazing idea. We all took turns trying out both sides. Come to think of it, I don't remember Ava saying a whole lot, but she was the one who sort of broke up the party by reminding the group that a bunch of them had to work in the morning and she's the one who summoned an UberX to cart us all back across the river. So, I don't know where she stood on the whole thing at the outset. I only know she went a little loony later on.

Yes, yes. Of course, objection. Don't use words like loony. Even if they *are* descriptive. Wink, wink.

At any rate, Ava was the one who broke up the party that night. And as she did so, I had another little unfamiliar pang of missing the Rogers Hawk Saturday mornings. Weird but true. I followed the group out of the unit toward the staircase, doing a quick double take and shuddering hard as we walked out, just before scolding myself that I was getting as bad as Daniel.

Later on, I'd wonder—how could I not—if it was the wine, or the fear in Daniel's voice, just my eyes playing tricks on me, or something else altogether, that made me see things. But, obviously, now, I know I didn't imagine a thing. Just before Archie pulled the door shut on the 2nd Floor that night, I saw something.

Not a what. A who. A woman facing away from us with jet black hair cascading down her back, dressed in a shimmery white gown, and she was standing in the darkest corner of that unit not far from where we had all been standing just moments before.

CHAPTER 3

Ava

Ava slammed the door behind her as she arrived in Roan's office.

Roan's head jerked up in response.

"Babe! What was that for?" Roan started to get up out of his chair, but Ava held her hand up pushing the air back toward him in response.

"I can't believe you! When were you going to tell me?" She barked loudly as she turned the lock on the door and headed toward him. She watched Roan relax as the lock clicked. He nodded, suddenly in on the secret.

Ava whispered, "I figured your admin would leave us alone a little longer if she thinks we're in here fighting, so we could, you know?"

"You know, *what*?" Roan asked needlessly, smirking, as Ava straddled him in his chair, her legs hooking around the ergonomic cocoon Roan had negotiated for himself in addition to a world class corner office, partnership, and a roster of the firm's easiest clients. Roan represented wealthy widows and millionairesses who wanted their estates and their egos well cared for by the handsome, incredibly successful Harvard law grad with "humble beginnings."

Ava leaned into Roan and kissed him softly. When he responded, she bit his bottom lip. He flinched, then recovered, and wrapped his arms around Ava's back, devouring her lips hungrily. Ava leaned into him slowly and self-consciously. She was distracted by the fervent hope that she felt small in his arms. She wanted to be lean and toned and small and youthful. She hoped that even with his eyes closed, he could pick out her body among a lineup. Ava hoped Roan Knight knew exactly who was straddling him and knew that unlike most of the other women who ended up in his lap lately, this one would *not* be paying *him*.

It had started with Tully, a woman whose husband dropped dead during an Ivy League building naming. Well, not the naming itself. But rather, the reception afterward. Just hours after Howard Cross's huge name, in a row of gold block letters the size of a Volkswagen, was unveiled on the side of a new lab building at the prestigious medical school, Howard collapsed into the table of crudites and strawberry-lined plastic champagne flutes. He'd suffered a heart attack that his doctors would later tell Tully was indeed, the infamous "widow maker" that had killed both his father and grandfather before him. Tully knew Howard's heart had endured more than its fair share of a beating. The Cross men were not known for their prudence. They were known for their money and their egos.

But Howard had believed that maybe, just maybe, purchasing naming rights of an ugly building filled with microscopes and 3D printers would create some kind of immortality that had eluded his father and grandfather who were largely forgotten not long after their deaths.

Howard was sure he'd be remembered after his death by the golden, sleek letters adorning the newest building on that Ivy League campus. Of course, he also hoped he'd get to enjoy the imminent legacy during a few more "alive" years but alas, that was not to be. Howard enjoyed the letters on the building for exactly 2 hours and 37 minutes before dying, and Tully enjoyed them for another 35 days and 18 hours before marching into Roan Knight's office to ask how to have them removed.

"It's a ludicrous expenditure of money. He spent $20 million on the naming rights without even consulting me. I want that money back. I want to argue that Howard wasn't in his right mind.

Roan was an Ivy League grad himself, with a complicated relationship with his prestigious alma mater. After all, he'd gotten into college and law school on his own merit, scraping together the pennies to afford the bill that came with the honor. He had no pedigree or familial connections to the Ivy League institutions he'd attended. Only a rockstar application, a gruesome work ethic, and as a result, he'd left that time of his life with gold-embossed degrees and monthly loan payments that still felt stifling a few years out of law school. By the time Tully Cross ended up in Roan's office, Roan had expected to be successful by some objective measures. Three years into his gig at Rogers Hawk, he was still working like a dog and watching the compounded interest on his student loans multiply.

Tully represented something interesting to him. A chance to be a rainmaker and impress the partners at his new firm: but also, a chance at revenge against the system that had lured him in and then charged him handsomely for the alleged rewards.

A few months after Tully came to Roan to ask him to help her remove her late husband's name from the side of the medical school building, Roan had won. On all fronts. Armed with a brief that Ava had written for him, about the contractual obligations of philanthropy and the obligations of the non-signing spouse, Howard Cross's legacy became a legal decision decrying the shady tactics of philanthropy officers in Ivy League Institutions and the naming rights of the newest building on campus were once again, for sale to the highest bidder. Roan's name was included in the newest list of partners during the annual partnership announcement. He paid off his student loans with one lump sum payment, and then he took Tully out to a lobster dinner at the Riversedge Law Club to deliver the good news.

Tully Cross showed her gratitude by paying Roan handsomely. She sent friends and acquaintances and other widow friends to Roan to re-work their late husband's murky estate plans. And then she demanded Roan repay her for the referrals.

She wanted him on her arm for (ironically!) fundraising dinners and benefit lunches. He was on call for nine and dines at the country club, and countless other arrangements. It started innocently enough, but then Tully started calling him "her Roan" when introducing him at events, and Roan told Ava one night as he arrived in her condo, collapsing onto her couch after a late night with Tully, "I think she thinks I'm her boyfriend."

"Don't be ridiculous, Roan, she's 73! What's she going to do next? Ask you to be her gigolo?" Roan laughed, but then Ava noticed the self-conscious tinny sound of his laugh, and she wasn't sure if she should be horrified or jealous. She picked all of the above the next time Roan canceled yet another date night with Ava for one of Tully's referrals' events.

Roan Knight, it seemed, was hot in demand among the wealthy millionairess set and all it required was for him to be their pretend boyfriend on demand. Only lately, Ava thought as she coaxed Roan out of his tailored Italian silk pants behind his closed office door, she wasn't sure he was clear about whose boyfriend he really was and Ava Simone was determined to remind him.

Less than a half hour later, they were parked on the expensive leather couch in Roan's office sipping mineral water and catching their breath. Ava's legs draped across Roan's lap as she buttoned her silk blouse and fanned emerging sweat marks growing under her arms.

"Oh, Jesus. I'm going to have to change," Ava exhaled.

"I'd be insulted if you *didn't* need to."

"Well, you hardly broke a sweat. It's like an ordinary Tuesday at the office for you these days."

"Ava, don't do that."

"Blech. I know, I know." Ava pushed herself off the couch

and got up, embarrassed. She hated herself like this. Needy and jealous of Roan's wealthy female clients. She smoothed her suede skirt down over her hips and stepped into her knock-off Chloe heels. She was, she knew, *beautiful*. She was young, vibrant, sexy, and attractive.

But she wasn't rich. And she wasn't powerful. She was at the bottom rung of the firm, still fighting and clawing her way up a ladder that seemed greased and oiled from her perspective. Ava hadn't found a niche or a sponsoring partner. She was still stuck in some limbo of boring cases and all-nighters while Roan was rocketing ahead of her. They'd started as summer associates at the firm together, four years earlier, but Roan had jettisoned ahead of her while Ava lagged behind.

Especially recently. With Tully Cross's help.

Ava was starting to wonder if she could stay in this place of Rogers Hawk stagnation much longer, with Roan moving so quickly ahead of her. She was starting to think about leaving the firm. And maybe even the law. A proposition that had once been unthinkable was suddenly all that was on her mind these days. In her spare moments, Ava schemed and worked on business plans that had nothing to do with law. She had kept them all to herself, but she was starting to think it was time to try out some of her ideas on Roan.

Archie's proposal the Friday before had been, sort of, timely, from Ava's perspective. Still fanning her blouse on Roan's sofa, she waded in. "So, that building field trip Friday night of Archie's was wild, wasn't it? Is he serious, do you think? Would it be, you know, crazy, if we did it?"

"Buy into an old industrial building with unknown origins and likely a whole host of code violations and hazards yet to be discovered?" Roan laughed. "Yes, it would be absolutely nuts. Archie was just drunk."

"Still," Ava stood up and paced Roan's office, buttoning and unbuttoning her blouse manically. "There's something exciting about it. And I do have some money left over from my college-slash-law school fund. I was going to save it for my kids, but let's face it, I'm probably not going to get around to having any kids."

The irony, Ava thought often, is that she started out on a path to be one of those rich women who courted and swooned over Roan Knight of the humble beginnings. Ava had grown up wealthy, with a trust fund and a hefty college fund. Her parents were well known socialites. Her dad was a successful lawyer and a member of the Riversedge Law Club back in the day. Her mother was a sought-after interior decorator to Riversedge and Manhattan's best and brightest. But when her parents got divorced during Ava's middle school years, they ran through all the money trying to outdo the other spouse in venom. They pillaged Ava's trust fund, and stopped just short of her college fund. After years of fighting and draining Ava's financial future, they retreated to their respective corners, within five miles of each other in Naples, Florida. Every time she called one or the other, Ava half expected her parents to report that they were getting back together. Anger, Ava had learned from her parents, was not the opposite of love. Instead, it was a close cousin, related by passion.

No, cold apathy was the opposite of love, and that was something Ava often feared she was learning from Roan Knight.

After her parents emptied everything but her college fund, Ava managed to get a nearly full ride to college on a field hockey scholarship, saving the balance of her fund for law school. But because of her prudence—a lesson learned by necessity rather than from her parents—there was money left over, and lately, Ava was thinking, maybe an investment or two was in order.

"Ava, the tax ramifications would be ridiculous. You don't want to drain that account for Archie's pipe dream." Roan was already at his desk, looking at his pile of papers. Treating her more like a client than a lover a mere half hour after they'd been wrapped up together on his leather office couch. Ava tried to lure him back into the mood she'd created when she walked in unannounced. She sat on the edge of Roan's desk, playing with the buttons on her thin blouse.

"I don't know, Roan. It might actually be worth it. I mean, maybe I could take a leave and manage the renovations. Really put some sweat equity into the whole project and then we could flip that building and make some real money. We're lawyers for God's sakes. Don't you think together we could all figure out some ways to make a grand investment out of this?"

Roan shook his head and looked up at her. "You? You're going to leave the law? Tell me Ava—what would Daddy say about that decision?"

Ava felt her back and fists clench in a familiar fight response to Roan's ribbing. These were the moments she felt her mother's influence profoundly in her body, ready to strike back. These were the moments that almost derailed her every time. That Roan inspired them made her hate him temporarily, but she reminded herself that she wasn't certain Roan was the fuel for her fury rather than her own flawed and diseased DNA.

Ava exhaled and counted to ten before she responded. She wished Roan would notice the delay and even apologize, but he didn't. He was still paying more attention to the files sprawled across his desk, than to Ava.

When she caught her breath, she continued on. "I'm just saying, Roan. Maybe we should meet with Archie. You and me. See what his plan really is, and evaluate whether there's a place for us in it. Or maybe, who knows—there could be space in his plan just for me..."

Bingo.

"Just you?" Roan stood up quickly and walked over to Ava and wrapped his arms around her. "It's *us*, baby, you know that."

She didn't of course, which was why she'd baited him. It was a familiar line of his and she wanted to hear it. He didn't ever call Ava his girlfriend or talk about the future, but he was always quick to call them an "us." Even though she didn't believe a word of it, Ava *needed* to hear it.

"I'm just thinking that it could be a really interesting project. We could, all of us, chip in and renovate the place together. Shared risk. Shared expenses. Shared profit. You've got to admit—there's some potential here if nothing else. You saw what that developer did to the one unit they finished. We could probably negotiate some sweet deals. Use our lawyer skills to renovate the place in record time and with a lean budget. Don't you think so?"

Roan looked pensive for a moment and then he said the words that warmed Ava all over.

"You know what, Ava? You might just have a point there. What could it hurt? Let's you and I at least talk to Archie and see if there's any room in this crazy plan of his. For us."

Ava continued fanning her wet blouse as she walked confidently past Roan's admin assistant. If Ava would have bothered looking down, she'd have noticed the warning look in the admin's eyes. But Ava did not. She just barreled down the hallway into the next chapter of her life, determined to outrun her parent's legacy. At any cost.

CHAPTER 4
Sara

Archie left a text on my phone. It said *I need you. It's about Easy Street.*

It's unusual for Archie to break away from the "threesome" as I think of them—the three couples that include Archie and Felicity and communicate with me. But every once in a while he does and when he sends a text, I have no idea what to do with it.

On that occasion, I just ignored it and went back to the journal.

When my grandmother died, my mom brought a thick burgundy leather-bound journal to me like it was some kind of amazing gift. I wasn't so sure.

The journal wasn't what I wanted from my grandmother's small final collection of possessions. Her artwork was largely gone, so I wanted the signed copy of Shel Silverstein's *Where The Sidewalk Ends* that she used to read to me at those long ago sleep-overs. I couldn't even think about those poems without hearing them in the voice of my grandmother, and I wanted that book. My mother said she had no idea where it was, and that if it existed at all, outside of a figment of my memory, it would probably be worth a lot of money. That "worth a lot of money" comment made me wonder if maybe my mother's conclusion that the book didn't really exist, was some kind of gaslighting meant to make me forget that the only thing of value my grandmother actually left behind was intended for *me.*

Not dollars and cents value the way my mother thought of it. No, real value. "Internal revenue. The real kind." That's what my grandmother used to call it. We'd joke about the IRS collecting taxes every single April 15, on my grandmother's birthday, like some cruel joke, and she'd say, "Well the joke is on them. Because I know about internal revenue. The real kind. And don't you ever forget it."

My mother worked hard to try to make me forget everything my grandmother said. In hindsight, she had her own wounds from the things that happened to my grandmother and to my mother while those things were unfolding. But it took me a long time to understand the shape and temperature of those wounds. If I'm being honest, I don't think I understand them fully even today. But my grandmother—I always understood her. Deeply. Truly.

I related to her even before I knew about the scars hidden under her skin. The ones buried in her veins and in her brain. The ones that eventually killed her way too early. The ones that made her exactly as perfect a human as I'd ever known.

Sleepovers at my grandmother's were unscheduled and full of games and laughter and poetry. Shel Silverstein volumes to be exact. We read those books over and over again.

So the leather-bound pages my mother presented me with after my grandmother's death felt like an insult, not from my grandmother, of course, who I'm sure would have *also* wanted me to have the Shel Silverstein book had she actually had the wherewithal to make a will or something. Instead, I got only the scraps. Literally, scraps of paper torn and scribbled, bound between thick leather casings. It was the only thing left, after my mother cleaned out her room in the assisted living facility where my grandmother, Agnes, had been spending the last years of her life.

One glance inside revealed nothing of note. Recipes and med lists and notations about nurses she loved (*Ella smells like lemons*) and nurses she did not (*Joan has hands like a cactus. I've refused a bath for 4 days and counting now*). My mother could have easily thrown even that journal away had she been feeling callous that day. Sure it had a taped label on it, printed painstakingly in my grandmother's handwriting, that by the look of its shaky broken curves, had been added only recently. But I didn't know it existed. My grandmother had never told me about it. And yet, when my mother went to clean out the room, there it was. And my mother brought it to me, like it was a real inheritance.

"Your grandmother wanted you to have this," she said as she passed it to me.

"What's inside?" I asked tentatively.

"What's inside?" my mother repeated, quizzically, as if it had never occurred to her to look inside until that very moment. One thing my mother always specialized in was denial. She paused and pulled the journal back to her and for a moment I thought maybe she wouldn't give it to me at all.

She opened it and flipped through the pages quickly.

"Just some writings. Nonsense mostly. It looks like most of it is just sketches and doodles and grocery lists." My mother held the splayed open book up to me so I could see that she was right.

"But it's got your name on it, so clearly, she wanted you to be the one to have it."

I could tell as she flipped through the scribbled pages in front of me that my mother hadn't previously looked through the contents at all. That she believed my grandmother's thoughts and reflections were simply irrelevant. The musings of a mad woman. Not worth her time. And so in that moment I realized that the leather-bound book was the absolute *best* thing my grandmother could have left me. She'd disguised the whole thing as something my mother wouldn't be interested in so I could have the very first eyes on what lay behind the doodles and scribbles. My grandmother was a genius, and I was her willing student. Even in death. The minute my mother left the room,

I sat on my bed, and pored through the pages, trying to figure out Agnes's message.

To me.

And listen, it's true that I never stopped wishing she'd have *also* left me that signed Shel Silverstein book. But if I had to pick between the two, I was certainly grateful for that burgundy leather journal.

When I lost my grandmother, I gained her history. The journal became a solemn but steady companion during the sharp detour my life took after she died. When I lost my grandmother, a jagged fissure ran through me, top down, separating me into two halves—the me before my grandmother died and the one after.

The journal caused it, yes. But the journal healed it as well.

That rag-tag book with Agnes' words and confessions buried hiding deep within, has changed my life in ways I didn't fully understand back then.

For good and for bad.

CHAPTER 5
Felicity

After the building visit, something is ignited in Felicity. While everyone else is mulling over whether Archie is serious or not, Felicity knows with certainty—that he is. And she isn't in doubt about wanting in. She does. Watching Archie's eyes light up as he describes the plans—the hope that everyone will want to *stay* in the building—renovate and move in *together*—is intoxicating. It is all Felicity can do to remember to breathe after that. Here is the answer she's been waiting for. She'll buy this building with Archie. She'll sell her Manhattan condo for some meager profit, move in with Archie, and stop hemorrhaging money faster than she can make it.

Ever since Felicity arrived in Manhattan following law school graduation, she's been waiting for a sign that she made the right decision. Her mother had squirreled away a small savings account to help Felicity pay for law school starting right after Felicity first mentioned out loud that she might want to try law school if she could figure out the finances. Felicity's waitressing tips and her mother's sacrifices had financed her law school tuition in north Jersey, a stone's throw and an inconceivable distance from New York City.

Make the most of your opportunities. Felicity's mother would say to her often.

You've been through so much. And you've worked so hard. You deserve this.

Her mother's words rang like a refrain in her head the whole time Felicity was studying in college and later in law school. She rose to the top easily. A big fish in a small pond and when it came time to interview for the Manhattan law firm positions, Felicity did what she knew best: she twisted herself into a pretzel in order to become what she thought the hiring teams were looking for. Life had taught Felicity to be skeptical and at times inauthentic. She decided she had no choice but to use those lessons to her advantage.

Felicity studied recent case wins of the firms and researched social media for interesting tidbits on the teams she was interviewing with. She landed a coveted position at Rogers Hawk early on in the process, and dropped out of the later rounds of interviewing at other firms her law school career center had set up for her. What point was there to looking elsewhere? Rogers Hawk was the best of the best and represented everything she and her mother had longed for Felicity to have.

So Archie's performance in the dim lighted loft on Easy Street feels like the sign she's been waiting for ever since accepting the Rogers Hawk offer and moving into oh-so-expensive Manhattan .The sign that she's made not only the best decision, but the right one. She wants to sign her name on whatever dotted line Archie is offering. As soon as possible. And she wants to buy into Archie's version of Easy Street.

The only question is how. Felicity is certain her own credit score is shot and she has no reserves. The sale of her condo will indeed yield some money in her pocket, but who knows how long it will take to sell, and it won't really net enough to cover a down payment on the Easy Street building, or even one of its unfinished units, for that matter. She can't ask her mother for any more than she's already given. Felicity is concerned her mother has given her literally all of her savings just to get this far.

So how to afford Easy Street? Even if the current owners are willing to take less—they are still going to require *something*.

But Archie is all in. And Felicity decides she can tag onto that momentum.

After the dinner that Archie bought—uncharacteristically—they go home to Felicity's condo and make love in a way that is new for both of them. Felicity is uninhibited and free from distractions. Archie is zealous and generous. With his mouth between her legs, Felicity lays her head back deep into the pillows and cries out with joy. With hope.

Afterward, with the kind of deep contentment that only comes with full release, she lays her head on Archie's chest, and murmurs, *thank you*. Archie is silent. Pensive. Felicity assumes he is thinking about the building and how to convince the others to collaborate on a sale. So she isn't surprised when he breaks the post-coital silence with a: "We should really get everyone together to talk about Easy Street again. I don't want to let too much time go by."

"Absolutely," Felicity says with enthusiasm. She is as anxious as Archie to get the ball rolling on buying the building at 724 Easy Street.

Only, as it turns out, for very different reasons.

CHAPTER 6
Ava

Ava brought a tray of bacon and prosciutto-wrapped appetizers out of Roan's Manhattan apartment kitchen into the living room, where Roan and Archie were already sitting. Reviewing a pile of papers that represented the title search apparently. They were waiting for the rest of the group—Felicity, Holly and Daniel—who were due any minute. Ava had offered to pick up some appetizers for the group, as a gesture of good will and to give Holly a night off from cooking, but as she looked at the tray coming out of the warming oven, it occurred to her that no one was as good at this sort of thing as Holly. And Holly probably wouldn't even eat anything Ava had brought as it was neither vegan nor healthy nor even aesthetic looking.

As Ava placed the tray down in front of the boys who scarfed down the food, meat and toxins notwithstanding, with questionable manners, Ava surveyed the room. She couldn't help but notice there was something a little *Mad-Men*-esque about the scene.

Gross. I should have put on a French maid's outfit and cooked, instead of picking up a tray at the deli on the way over here.

The thought made her chuckle.

"What's so funny, Babe?" Roan looked up from his place on the couch, chewed-up bacon fat visible on the side of his open mouth.

Ava just shook her head at him and looked away, revolted

with a, *"Nothing, hon."* She tried to imagine what this scene would look like—what it would *feel* like—if she and Roan were living together in one of those floor-to-ceiling windowed units in Archie's new-found project. The building was situated in the very place where Ava grew up. She never imagined she'd come back there to invest in a Riversedge property after she actually found her way out. Sitting in Roan's Manhattan apartment, across the river from her hometown, Ava wondered—would Roan and she really go through with this? She was already sold, but would Archie be able to sell Roan? And if so, would she and Roan settle into Easy Street like lovers in a romance novel? Would they fight nightly the way her parents did? Would she ever really escape that legacy of her parents if she came back home to Riversedge? She shook off the host of questions burrowing into her brain.

"Hey, isn't it funny that the street is called Easy Street?"

Archie looked up at Ava with an expression she couldn't read. "What do you mean by that?"

"What do I mean by that? Archie, my God, why are you looking at me like that?"

"I'm just curious why the street name caught your eye? Why it's so perplexing to you?"

"Sheesh, Archie, you're working too hard. It's just funny, is all. Easy Street. Odd name for a real street. It feels like something made up, that's all."

Archie looked back down at the prosciutto and title documents and Ava caught Roan's eye with a raised eyebrow and an expression meant to say "What the actual hell?"

Roan shrugged and shook his head and Ava thought it was over, but then Archie looked back up. "No, you're right, Ava. I'm sorry. It is funny. I get it. From your perspective, it all probably seems a little outlandish. It's just that apparently—from these documents—the road was called East Street. A few decades ago and a few owners ago. Someone in the chain of title was able to change it. Who knows why?"

"Hunh. Well you never really think about these things. Why streets get named or renamed. It's clever, that's all. East Street would have been very boring. I doubt we'd be talking about buying the building at all if it was still called East Street."

"Really, you think not?" Archie looked at Ava quizzically and she laughed in response.

"No, not really, Archie. I'm just kidding. Seriously, what's with your mood today?"

Archie didn't have time to respond because Holly and Daniel arrived then, loudly, with Felicity right behind them. Ava grabbed a napkin and a bacon appetizer and took a seat in the corner of the room, anxious to cede the spotlight to one of the evening's newcomers. She had to move a scarf that was draped on one of Roan's leather chairs in order to sit on it. An expensive silk scarf Ava recognized as belonging to Tully Cross. It was as if the millionairess had marked Roan's place with Hermes.

Ava looked around at the group—newly expanded—and listened to Archie talk about all the potential of the place on Easy Street.

We can do something really creative here, he said.

I mean, yes, we're lawyers, but do we really have to give up every last creative bone in our bodies to Rogers Hawk? We can create something beautiful and special in that space. We can take control of our money and our futures and inspire some real change in the town of Riversedge. The Law Club doesn't need to be the prettiest and most impressive building in Riversedge, does it?

Archie winked at the group and there was a loud, "Here, here!" with raised glasses and flushed faces and happy optimism all around the room.

Meanwhile, all Ava could think about was that she was in desperate need of a change. She popped the salty, greasy, store-bought appetizer into her mouth and subtly wiped her fingers clean on the scarf she'd moved to the corner of the leather chair.

After the cheers and the toasts, and more soliloquy by Archie, Roan interrupted with a "What do you think, Ava? Is this anything we'd be interested in exploring further?"

"Well, the timing couldn't be better, as I'm just about to announce my sabbatical at the firm," Ava piped up, drunk on prosciutto fat and jealousy.

"You are, are you?" Roan looked at her with a smirk. Like she was a child who'd just said something precious.

"I am. I'm going to ..."

The room looked at her expectantly and Ava took the scene in. Felicity looked pale and tired across the room having come straight from the office and Holly and Daniel looked giddy and well-fed having come from some business meeting or coffee date or who knows?

What do people do when they are no longer working on Rogers Hawk?

Ava didn't realize she'd asked the question out loud until Holly piped up, "I'll tell you what they do, sunshine. They live. Why don't you go ahead and try it out with us. I can find some work for you in the catering biz if all else fails." Holly winked at Ava and Ava felt something warm come over her. She reached down to take another sip of her drink, testing the feeling. It stayed.

"Yep. I'm going to live. I'm taking a sabbatical—so this whole proposal comes at the perfect time."

Ava sat back in her seat and stuffed the swatch of greasy Hermes silk out of sight, deep under the cushion she was sitting in, spitefully. Resolutely.

"Hunh." Archie nodded at Roan. "Looks like she'll have lots of time for a whole host of things, Roan. Maybe even you." And Ava pretended not to notice that everyone in the room laughed then. Everyone *except* Roan.

CHAPTER 7
Holly

Building inspection? Well, I guess you could call it that.

We all went back to look at 724 Easy Street in the daylight a few weeks after that first night, but we didn't have professionals with us. No one who might actually know what they were looking for. It was more celebratory than cautionary. We'd already made up our minds we were doing this over the days leading up to the visit. Retirement funds and savings accounts and Ava's college fund for heaven's sake—all drained with one goal. Grab that building off the market for dirt cheap and turn it into paradise. Or at least *home*.

Sure, sometimes in the very beginning, we talked about flipping it—but I don't think anyone really believed that was the goal. Not when you stood at those windows and looked out over the dominion below. I know, corny, right? But those were Archie's words when he talked about the building, and on that visit as well, damn if he didn't sell us all.

So, no. No professional inspection at least. Archie said he'd had the building checked out by an environmental engineering firm during the due diligence review and that there were some yellow flags, but nothing of note. When I asked to see an actual copy of the engineering report, he grew a conscience suddenly saying something about privileged information. Never mind that every bit of information he had about the building at that point was allegedly privileged. That was the point. Archie was using insider info to put together a proposal that the current owners wouldn't be able to turn down.

In a zoom call with the six of us (me, Daniel, Ava, Roan, Archie, and Felicity) the day before that second building visit, someone floated the idea of creating an anonymous LLC to bid on the property so that Archie wouldn't be implicated in the sale. We also talked about paying for an environmental consultant *after* the sale, which seemed backwards to me. Roan explained that if the inspection yielded anything serious before we bought the building, then legally, the owners would have to pay for repairs, and they might pull out of the sale altogether. And so yes, then the plan *really* seemed backwards to me.

Oh, you know what I just remembered? On that same call, Roan—yes, now that I think about it—it was definitely Roan who said, "Once we buy this building and finish the renovations, we can have it appraised for real. Not based on the short sale, or the bank ownership or the holding company plagued by malpractice lawsuits. No, we can get a real, genuine appraisal and have the building valued at its true cost. And given its location and potential, who knows the real value—4, million? 5 million? Maybe even more."

Suddenly a building we were all planning to buy together for barely a million dollars started to look like a nest egg. Our retirement fund. Our security.

If Archie's words and mood revved us up, Roan's sent us into overdrive. Even in that virtual zoom space, we were toasting and hooting and hollering and just going plain crazy at that point. No one talked any more about risks or environmental consultants or due diligence reviews once Roan started planting the seeds for insurance appraisals.

We walked through the building and everyone was picking out their respective units. Discussing which local architects we'd solicit bids from. Where closets would best be located. Where artwork would go. We stepped over rotting wood and peeling plaster and ignored it as if it was completely irrelevant rather than a glaring, beaming red lit flag placed there by the real estate gods to shake some sense into our naive heads. We were lawyers, but we were acting like our worst clients at that point. No one could have talked any sense into us.

The bottom line is this: we went into the whole thing knowing the risks of environmental trouble and the likely need for remediation. No one could claim surprise later about the flumes of asbestos dripping off the ceiling or the mercury hidden in the door jambs. Yes, that's right. There. I said it. But that's not what this is about, is it?

Because your appraisers saw the same freaking thing we did. Pure potential on top of location for miles.

The asbestos and the mercury and the other environmental hazards? That's not what matters, is it? What matters is that the building was an open book and we all had the chance to inspect it. Us, and your people, and we all came to the same conclusion. It was worth a *lot* of money.

Easy Street.

In fact, only one of us knew about the murder. And then you might ask, if we had all known about *that*, would we have bought the damn building anyway?

In a word? *Maybe.*

But what if we'd known about Archie? About his—*secret*?

No. I don't think any of us would have gone through with it then.

What do you mean, objection?

I absolutely *can* speak for more than just myself.

I mean, if Archie can, then I certainly can, too.

CHAPTER 8
Sara

The morning after I first read my grandmother's journal cover to cover, I woke up, still dressed in clothes from the night before, face down in my bed with the journal cover stuck to my cheek. I felt like I'd just gone on a bender and woke up in someone else's room.

I reached for my cell phone to check the time, and the screen lit up with a warning that startled me.

Stop, Sara. Don't go back there. You don't want to go back there. You might not be able to come back this time. From, Archie.

I deleted the message immediately. Angrily. I've always hated when he treats me like a child. I turned back to the journal and flipped to the last page I'd been reading before I passed out from exhaustion and grief.

It wasn't that my grandmother described the details of the shock therapy so vividly. It was that she remembered anything at all after such a harrowing experience.

She was admitted to a hospital—hardly a hospital—more of a soulless institution. A place where she was shocked and experimented on, and eventually discarded. She was treated inhumanely, when in reality she probably just needed her humanity honored and nurtured by someone who loved her. I wished I'd been alive back then.

It started postpartum.

According to the notes, she'd been struggling as a new

mother. In the margins of grocery lists, bible verses, and Yeats poems, she recorded her fears and insecurities.

I feel sometimes like I'm keeping this baby alive just by the sheer force of my own breathing. But what if I stop? I hold my breath sometimes for long stretches at a time and watch my baby girl to make sure. Mostly, she looks the same, but sometimes she hiccups or startles while my breath is sucked in and I'm sure I've killed her and the feeling is so powerful in the moment, that I can't tell if I'm relieved or devastated.

I read these words with awe and wonder. They hold promise and possible answers. In the time I'd known her, my grandmother had been a self-proclaimed kook. An eccentric. But also an accused murderer. No one ever talked about the murder and so everything I pieced together came from news clippings and gossip and my wild imagination. My grandmother, in all the years I knew her, was as gentle a soul as I'd ever met. She hummed softly while she did dishes and refused to swat flies in the kitchen or install mousetraps. She wasn't violent or angry. Except for that one time, I guess.

And no, she didn't kill her baby. That baby was my mother. My mother was the one who Agnes was keeping alive or killing at any given moment in her imagination, according to those scribbled words in the leather-bound notebook. While she never mentioned the baby by name, the timing lined up. A few entries were dated, including one just before she was admitted to the hospital with depression and one just after she arrived home, months later.

So, yes, despite my grandmother's apparently homicidal recorded post-partum thoughts, my mother in fact, survived. She lived long enough to give birth and marry not one, but two deadbeat dads and create for me a childhood built on the rockiest of terrain.

My mother lived long enough to save up her money to buy a floral shop in Riversedge, New York, and die inconveniently of metastatic breast cancer during my third year of law school. My grandmother was gone by that time, preserved only in the words and notes and clippings of my inheritance.

My mother survived Agnes. But my grandfather, Jasper, did not. Jasper died barely a year after my mother was born, and his was the untimely death that led to my grandmother's arrest—and trial—for murder.

One of the many wild things about my grandmother's arrest and trial for the murder of my grandfather, is that Jasper's body was never found nor was a murder weapon. Frankly, from everything I read about the trial at the time, it sounded like it was a pretty shoddy case by the Riversedge District Attorney. I'm not saying my grandmother was innocent of Jasper's murder. I'm just saying she got kind of lucky at the actual trial.

I lived thirteen years without ever knowing that my grandfather, an ambitious welder's son from North Jersey, died under mysterious circumstances after marrying a young girl from a wealthy family in Riversedge, New York. That in fact, he went missing one day, leaving behind a young wife and a small baby and a mound of debt. That his blood was found on the old floorboards of an industrial building he owned and which he was renovating at the time he went missing. And that fibers of my grandmother's hair were found mixed in with the blood. The police arrested my grandmother pretty quickly, but a slick defense attorney hired by my grandmother's wealthy Riversedge family was able to show that Jasper had a lot of debts, and that if he was in fact killed, it was much more likely he was dragged across those old floorboards by a sturdy loan sharking male, rather than a young and frail 25-year-old woman who'd been in and out of the hospital for psychiatric care recently.

Jasper might just have up and left when life got a little too heavy for him, the defense attorney told the jury in closing statements three hours before they acquitted my grandmother. While my grandmother's trial took place nearly three decades before the OJ Simpson trial, it appeared to be just as sensational in the small Riversedge community in its time. A news reporter for the *Riversedge Chronicle* named Jay Finley took copious notes and published excerpts of the trial testimony daily. Now defunct, the *Chronicle's* back issues are only available on Microfilm and CD-roms in the back rooms of the majestic Riversedge Library. And I've read every issue that pertains to my grandmother's murder trial.

Not Guilty of Murdering Her Husband the headline read on the day the trial ended. Finley included quotes from the local residents in the wrap-up of the trial that had consumed the community for about 18 days that August in 1966.

That poor woman! What she's been through!

Well, it sounds like maybe she got away with murder. But after everything that happened to her, how can you blame her?

That's justice for you. A man's dead and his murderer goes free. What else can I say?

Maybe now that horrible place will finally be shut down! It's a blight in our beloved Riversedge community!

The lawyer that my grandmother's family hired for her not only got her acquitted, but they put on trial the medical clinic that was performing experimental surgeries on Agnes's brain. They were carving Agnes's brain into rivers with her husband's consent, but without Agnes's consent. Places of the likes of Riversedge Asylum were starting to gain disfavor in popular opinion, and Agnes's trial all but sealed the fate of Riversedge Asylum. It closed down a year after Agnes's trial ended.

All was not exactly well after the acquittal. From what I could piece together, later—much later—my grandmother turned inward, expressing all the pain and fear she'd experienced over the last few years into art. She enjoyed some modest commercial success with her art—enough to support herself, subsidized in part of course by her family money. My mother, Delilah, had been taken in by my grandmother's family—as a baby—after the arrest, and they held onto her until she became an unruly teen. Then they unceremoniously dropped Delilah off at her mother's art studio one day with a *good luck* and a shared trust fund. Delilah and Agnes had to get to know each other for the first time during those years. That cannot have been easy, I'm sure. And it does explain their sort of remote, cold relationship all throughout my own life. All of this, of course, was never told to me when my grandmother was still alive.

In fact, I might never have known about any of it if I hadn't gotten curious one day and googled my grandmother's name looking for press pieces about her early days as an artist. I found an old cached newspaper report of the arrest and trial. It wasn't exactly the trial of the century and the *Riversedge Chronicle* readership was genteel enough at the time to demand the coverage remain fairly light and airy. But there she was, in black and white, with her dark hair falling wild around her face and a caption: *Agnes Carson, arrested in the case of the mysterious disappearance of her husband, developer, Jasper Carson.*

Propelled by thirteen-year-old arrogance, I felt certain my mother would love nothing more than to fill in all the details, so I went to her with the printed out newspaper page and asked her for more. Her face turned red with rage or embarrassment I'll never know, because she just left the room, and when she came back, she informed me that we would not be addressing that subject of ancient history ever again.

Given my mother's reaction, I was afraid to ask my grandmother, and so before I got a hold of that journal, my only real information about my grandfather's death came from the back issue newspapers I pored through at the local Riversedge Library. I liked seeing my family's name engraved in the bronze bar in the entrance way of that library in the middle of a whole host of donors. But let me tell you something. If my mother knew they kept those old issues so easily accessible for all to see, I doubt she'd have contributed any of her family inheritance to the capital campaign to restore that old Riversedge library.

My mother seemed to assume that the whole sordid mess was ancient history. That my grandmother's secrets would die with her. Whatever they were. Neither she nor my grandmother ever spoke about Jasper, the trial, or that old building where his blood had been found in the 1960s.

And so, I feel certain that if my mother knew exactly what my grandmother confessed to in coded prose and cryptic snippets in that burgundy bound journal, she'd have burned it to ashes instead of giving it to me.

Over the years, I've had to forgive my late mother for a lot of transgressions, but the easiest one was treating my grandmother's journal like something that didn't matter.

And handing it right over to me when Agnes died.

CHAPTER 9
Ava

Ava scanned the conference room at her Farewell lunch. She was taking it in. Trying desperately to live in the moment, but also, admittedly, looking for *him*. They had barely said hello to each other in the last year. She couldn't help but wonder if he'd at least show up to say goodbye. He'd been such a big part of her life when she first arrived at the firm. It seemed ridiculous that he wouldn't be there in the end. But he wasn't. Of course he wasn't. Jason McKoy had a fiancé and work to do and a bitter chip on his shoulder that was Roan Knight-sized.

Jason McKoy had been Ava's first friend at Rogers Hawk. She'd met him on that very first day, when she arrived at the firm hyped up on caffeine and ambition. He was the paralegal assigned by Ross Martin, the head of the litigation department to show Ava "the ropes." Jason's phrase. Ava had laughed when he said it. She laughed at nearly everything he said back then. He always said her laugh was more endearing than annoying.

Jason and Ava worked side by side with each other night after night, reviewing documents and spilling secrets about their lives. Their dreams. Their ambitions. Their connection was fast and organic. During late night work breaks, Ava found herself revealing things to Jason she'd never revealed to anyone. About her parents' vicious divorce. How she'd gone to law school to spite her father. She wanted to be a better lawyer than him. And a better human.

"Well, I don't know what kind of human he was, but you are one incredible lawyer," Jason winked at her.

"What about you, Jason? You have aspirations of turning this glamorous gig into a law school application?" Ava waved her arm around the room filled with files and laptops and emptied coffee cups and cardboard take out trays.

"God, no," Jason laughed. "This is more like a stop along the way for me."

"Oh? What do you mean?"

"Well, I've been here five years, and I make good money. The work can be somewhat interesting, let's face it. But I watch all the lawyers burn out one by one and I find myself wondering, what the hell are we even doing here? Why aren't we making something or creating something or fixing a problem in the world?"

Ava laughed. "Yeah, it's the proverbial fodder for lawyer jokes, right? We're just plain useless."

"Well, I don't think that's exactly right. I think the law attracts incredibly creative people and then places like this suck that creative juice right out of them. You for example. The way you craft briefs and arguments? It's brilliant. I haven't seen anything like it in the five years I've been working alongside some of the allegedly best minds in the business."

"Oh, Jason! That's so kind. You're trying to butter me up."

"All those things can be true, Ava." Jason smiled at her in a way that warmed Ava from the toes up.

He leaned over then and took her shoulders in his hands. Gently. "You just do me a favor and promise not to sell out like the rest of these clowns, ok?"

"Deal." Ava pulled away from him reluctantly.

They chuckled and clinked coffee cups and a spark passed between them that Ava tried unsuccessfully to ignore.

Long hours and sleep deprivation continued to fuel the relationship. Clouded their minds. Made them feel things that weren't real.

Ava said exactly that to Jason one morning as they were curled up in his full-sized bed in a rent controlled loft in Brooklyn. She had a bigger apartment in Hell's Kitchen and a queen-sized bed with a warm down comforter and framed art on the walls. But she also had a roommate back then so more often than not, they found themselves in Jason's apartment that, on this particular morning, smelled faintly of roach spray and day-old garbage. Ava hadn't noticed it when they'd tripped into the apartment the night before, drunk on sushi and some expensive cab blend expensed to the firm and the client to celebrate a brand-new settlement in the case they'd been working on together for the last four months.

"We can actually sleep in tomorrow," Jason hiccupped as they tumbled into bed fumbling and giggling and passing out before they could even have sex.

In the morning, they finished what they'd started the night before, effortlessly and without giggling. Afterward, Ava lay on Jason's chest, rising and falling with his breath, planning how to leverage the newly settled case into something bigger with Ross Martin.

"You know what? I'm going to ask Ross to put me on that new class action suit. I'm going to tell him I want the corner on all the expert prep and all the expert depositions on that case. And why not? I just settled the biggest fucking case this firm was working on—in record time and for an amount no one believed possible. I'm going to tell him I want it. I've earned it. What do you think of that?"

Ava looked up at Jason from her perch on his chest and saw his serious expression. She was concerned instantly, before she even knew just how concerned she should be. "I think I love you, Ava Simone."

Ava bolted up from Jason's chest and gasped.

"What?" he said. "Why are you so surprised? You didn't know?"

"Of course, I didn't know. And of course you don't. You're

hung over. Maybe even still drunk. It's just the long hours and sleep deprivation talking. You don't love me. Don't be so hilarious, Jason McKoy."

Ava put her head back down on his chest and caressed him slowly, twisting the tufts of chest hair between her fingers for a few minutes, before Jason reached down and grabbed her hands. Stopping her. He lifted her off him roughly. It was the first time she'd seen Jason angry or sad or hurt, and now she was getting to see all three. A perfect trifecta.

"I'm sorry, Jason. I can't be who you want me to be."

"Well, that's a shame isn't it?"

"Time to go?" Ava whispered sadly.

"Yeah," Jason got out of the bed and headed to the bathroom. Ava left in silence and the next day she was reassigned to a new case by Ross. She didn't bother asking if Jason could work with her on the new assignment. A paralegal named Renee was assigned to her and Ava heard through the grapevine that Jason was assigned to a new litigation matter for another partner on a different floor.

"I guess you and Jason will have to get a divorce now," Ava's secretary joked. Ava tried laughing at the words to prove they were funny. She tried really hard.

Over the next few months, Ava replayed that moment in Jason's apartment over and over again, trying to figure out why she'd been so surprised at his words. Trying to remember why she'd rejected him. It wasn't until she started sleeping with Roan Knight, the handsome Harvard Law grad who had started at the firm at the same time as Ava, that she realized, or rather, admitted to herself, that it was her elitist bullshit keeping her from doing anything more than sleeping with her paralegal. He had been beneath her. In every way. Ava knew she didn't have very much to her name, after her parents had done their best to strip her down to the studs, but she was determined to rebuild a legacy that had been meant for her. Whatever that meant. And no good could come from falling in love with her paralegal,

Ava told herself.

The night before the Farewell Party, Roan proofread Ava's resignation speech with a chuckle. It was full of subtle self-promotion, talking about how much she'd miss working on some of the most successful litigation cases the firm had handled recently. Also full of not-so-subtle jabs at the long hours, and the lack of work-life balance. *It's time for me to take care of myself. Stop neglecting my gym membership, roots, and annual mammogram.*

At the Farewell party, she scanned the room, knowing even as she did that Jason wouldn't be there. As Roan draped his arm around her and held up a glass overflowing with Vueve, he bellowed, "To Ava, may you find the happiness you deserve outside of these walls, even though, let's face it. It's going to be hard to top anything you've found right here at Rogers Hawk."

As the room laughed and clapped and toasted, and clinked, Ava stopped looking. She was no longer hoping Jason would pop his head in. She knew enough to be embarrassed at the show Roan was putting on. She felt complicit as she raised her glass and her head to Roan for a long passionate public display of affection.

A new life was waiting for her outside these walls. Even though Roan was right. It was indeed going to be hard to top anything she'd already found.

CHAPTER 10
Holly

The short answer is no. We had no business driving that night. We had all been out late celebrating Ava's retirement from the law. It was funny, really, celebrating a friend's retirement at age 30. We leaned in. Way in. Roan, Felicity and Ava had come straight to the bar from the firm where they'd been drinking buckets of fancy champagne. Daniel and I were drinking more-budget-friendly IPAs but yes, in pretty rapid succession. Archie had stayed behind to get some work done and when we got the call from his paralegal that he'd been rushed out of the firm via ambulance, well, there was not a designated driver in sight, and the Uber wait was 20 minutes, so we all piled into my car parked on the street outside and headed to the hospital.

We fought our way into the hospital, HIPAA be damned. Archie didn't have living parents or siblings that we knew of. But we weren't allowed to see Archie for over an hour. We argued with the late-night hospital staff who were suddenly more impenetrable gatekeepers than any judges we'd ever argued in front of. Felicity was Archie's family. His next of kin. What more did they need? Hell, we were all each other's next of kin, we argued as we waited to get in to see Archie.

A small nurse with wiry glasses and a stern expression insisted that we were not on any approved visitor list and that Archie was asleep, highly medicated, and unable to approve us himself. As we sat tear-stained and confused in the waiting room, the champagne and beer metabolizing slowly into all of our bloodstreams, we couldn't imagine who *was* on the list.

Sometime after 3 am, the small nurse summoned us into Archie's room. We rushed in like overgrown, clumsy children, bumping into each other as we went into his room and needing to be shushed.

Archie looked so frail in that hospital bed. I don't think of myself as a worrier but I sure was worried about him that night. I could tell Felicity was too. The sight of him sobered us up real fast.

All we knew was that he'd had some kind of episode. Heart racing. Sweating. Dizzy, passed out in his office according to the paralegal who'd been working with him that night. He'd had to be revived by an EMT worker who had treated him on the scene.

And I mean, I remember a few things from that night, despite how much I'd had to drink. I remember how terrible Archie looked. He was gray and thin in that hospital bed. And yes, I remember how territorial he was about his medical chart even in his weakened state. He didn't want any of us to look at it. Not even Felicity. He made it a joke of sorts. When the small nurse came in, he told her he was not waiving any of his rights. That she was not to show his medical chart to any of his lawyer friends who would most certainly find ways to sue everyone involved, and he was simply doing everyone a favor by keeping his chart to himself.

Was that a red flag? In hindsight? Well, sure. But at the time, there were nothing but green lights everywhere. The room was full of love and friendship and discussions about the future. As Archie's IV bag dripped electrolytes back into his pierced arm, we all made a pact right there in that hospital room. While we were already in the process of writing up the proposal for the Easy Street building, it was there, at Archie's bedside, that we all agreed that time was nothing but an illusion. It was on that night under the influence of various cocktails, some of which were hospital prescribed, that we decided we wanted to buy that building on Easy Street and renovate it and live together and that we wanted to do it *now.*

Roan offered to finalize the papers forming the LLC and Archie's color came back at the prospect. "You won't be sorry," he said. And honestly, as I think back on it, I'm not sure who he was talking to when he said it.

CHAPTER 11
Felicity

"It was just stress, sweetheart. I've been working around the clock and taking lousy care of myself. I don't think I've been to Yoga all week. And I haven't had a decent meal in longer."

"But, Archie, you jog up the stairwell instead of taking the elevator. You eat kale smoothies for breakfast. You're in perfect health. How could this have happened? Are the doctors doing more tests? Is there anything you're not telling me? Archie, really, I can handle it. I can. Tell me the truth."

Felicity is pacing in the hospital room pleading with Archie. Their friends have all left to get showers and go to work, but she's stayed behind and now Archie is trying to tell her that she is free to leave also. She isn't convinced.

Archie seems to be hiding something from her. Felicity knows a thing or two about secrets, after all. Hospitals remind her of that one fateful day, even all these years later. She cannot escape her memory. Her choices.

When the nurse comes in to take Archie's vitals, Felicity excuses herself to make a run down to the drug store in the hospital lobby. She buys a candy bar, a few trial-size toiletries and a toothbrush and heads back up to Archie's room, where she finds him sound asleep.

Lining up the new toiletries in the blue tiled bathroom in Archie's hospital room triggers something, more feeling than memory, but Felicity ignores it. She climbs in bed next to a snoring Archie waiting for the small nurse with the wire glasses to come in and yell at her but the shift must have changed, and no one comes in. Soon Felicity drifts off to sleep and now the feeling transforms into a hazy, dreamy memory.

In her dream, Felicity sees her toiletries in a row on the powder blue bathroom sink of a motel. Shampoo, conditioner, and toothpaste all stand at attention like soldiers on watch. Felicity leaves them behind as she opens the motel door and lets the salty air whip at her face, landing on her lips. She licks them clean and steps out of the motel door. It slams shut behind her, and Felicity jumps. Her body lands with a thud on the stiff hospital mattress.

"Felicity, what's wrong?" Archie's voice is raspy and tired, and Felicity feels badly for waking him. For disturbing him with her stubborn need to lay next to him. She kisses his forehead and concedes that she'll go home and get cleaned up and come back rested.

"You get some rest, Archie. I'll come back later today."

He nods drowsily and is snoring again before she leaves the room.

Felicity walks home because she's too broke to pay for a cab and she's too sad to walk underground to the subway. During the long walk home, she thinks to herself, *This new project of ours will solve everything. I just know it. The answers will find us on Easy Street.*

CHAPTER 12
Ava

Walking up the steps of the Riversedge Law Club always made Ava feel like a real lawyer. Sometimes she would catch herself narrating the scene like she was a character in her own life story.

The dusk sky reflected against the marble columns flanking the heavy wooden doors that led inside the Riversedge Law Club like a watercolor painting. I was breathless with anticipation of what lay on the other side of those doors but paused at the threshold for a moment longer to enjoy the pastel-colored view.

Ava shook off the melodrama and chuckled as she walked inside. The Riversedge Law Club was the pride of Riversedge, a small community separated from Manhattan by a river and about twenty percent of the real estate prices. Give or take.

While the rest of the friend group was from parts all over, Ava and Archie had both grown up in Riversedge. Of course, being "from" Riversedge was not as common as Riversedge realtors would lead you to believe. Riversedge wanted to hold itself out as a small town with all the trappings of a small Americana town, complete with generations of residents who'd grown up in the area and then stayed to raise their own children as well. But the truth was, its population was mostly transient. Riversedge was only impersonating a small town, with its tree-lined main street and one each of a police station, firehouse, and a post office. At first glance, Riversedge looked like a place where everyone should know each other and should know each others' secrets. But even Ava, born and raised in the town, knew very little about the inner monologue narrated by the others around her.

In reality, very few people were *from* Riversedge originally. Instead, Riversedge played host to a number of people who had come for the pretty views of Manhattan and the better cost of living. Most of the transplants to Riversedge, were, of course lawyers. Riversedge was to lawyers what Boston was to the biotech industry and what California was to Silicon Valley entrepreneurs.

Riversedge was a magnet and a teacher. And the Law Club was a group circle for the men and women of New York who were interested in proving themselves in the courtroom. Well, yes, mostly men, but that didn't make it less interesting or exciting to Ava even though her feminist self acknowledged— dismissively—the problem presented by Riversedge Law Club.

It was, at its core, an old boys' network, founded by some of the earliest settlers of New York. Its marble-lined steps and pillared doorway had been built by men who had Wall Street money to burn, and wanted to protect it at all costs. It was a place where the real business of the American legal system could take place outside of the prying eyes of, well America. In this little cocoon a stone's throw and a river away from America's financial capital, deals were made, lawsuits were settled and power was traded. The mission of the place remained largely intact two centuries later.

Inside the Club, Ava inhaled the smell of greed and power as she approached the concierge to be seated. She had let her own membership to the Club lapse soon after joining, and not long after getting the first monthly dues bill. Roan had suggested she hang on to it longer, but Ava politely declined. "No thank you, darling. It's not like I have to entertain wealthy clients as often as you do." She winked to mask the snark but Roan had rolled his eyes anyway with a *"Don't do that, Ava,"* and never brought up the subject again.

Now that she had taken a sabbatical from her law gig, she couldn't afford the membership dues even if she wanted to rejoin. Ava hadn't been to the Club in years and she was missing the buzzy atmosphere. When she got the invitation for lunch, Ava jumped at the chance. She hadn't even delved too deeply into the motives for the invitation and instead, just quickly responded "accept" to the calendar invite.

Ava announced herself to the ageless concierge at the podium. Ava made the mistake of referring to her as a "hostess" only once—the first time she'd been to the Club as a new associate. She was quickly corrected by the other attorneys at the table.

The concierge was tall and leggy and dressed head to toe in couture. She glanced at Ava with a frigid smile before letting her know the member host was already seated at the table. "I can have someone escort you—"

"No need," Ava brushed past her and entered the loud dining room, glancing around for her lunch date. For a moment, Ava regretted her decision not to be escorted, as she had forgotten just how large and crowded the Club was during weekday lunch hours. In far corners of the room, she recognized a few judges she'd appeared before during the years she'd practiced at Rogers Hawk before she'd left on sabbatical. There were also a few attorneys scattered about the room that she'd tussled with—both inside and outside the courtroom. She tried not to make eye contact with them as she scanned and then finally—

"Ava!" Nola Dyer was standing up at a nearby table, waving her over, and Ava walked briskly, uncomfortably, to greet her.

Nola seemed at ease as she hugged Ava hello. Ava thought briefly how one would never know from her demeanor that Nola was relatively new to the Club, and to the bar. In fact, Nola just passed her bar exam the year earlier. But Nola was a rising star in the New York legal scene, having cut her teeth as a paralegal at the now defunct, but prestigious in its time, Barr Knoll

Law Firm. The firm, named for its larger-than-life founder, had dissolved spectacularly following the mishandling of the biggest sexual discrimination class action case in history but not before churning out Nola, its star paralegal, and transforming her into a top-of-the-class Columbia law student. Now Nola had done the unimaginable—shunning several BigLaw offers, choosing instead to hang out her own shingle. Ava had heard she was handling several high retainer, confidential legal matters representing various A-listers and public figures with a lean staff, all the while creating a killer resume. When she got the calendar invite, Ava couldn't imagine why Nola wanted to meet with her, but she figured being seen with Nola Dyer at the Law Club could only be a good thing these days.

Little could she have known.

As Ava sat down across from Nola she studied her. Nola had deep lines under her eyes and circles that seemed almost outlined in charcoal. Nola waved down a server and ordered a bottle of wine for the table without consulting Ava. Ava decided not to be offended.

When Barr Knoll was still in operation, Ava remembered hearing her father tell tales about the firm and its notoriety. Barr Knoll, the man and the firm, were both known for walking a thin line between advocacy and criminal behavior. There were rumors about sex trafficking and prostitution and even murder allegations relating to three women who'd all died the same night working for Barr Knoll. Ava had always wanted to know more about the place, and she thought about asking Nola for some of the juicy dirt, but Nola looked closed off. Like she was all business and not open to gossip at all. So Ava shook off her curiosity about Barr Knoll and pivoted to trying to learn the reason for the lunch invitation instead.

"You look wonderful, Nola," Ava lied. "How's work?"

Nola nodded perfunctorily. "You, too. It's good. Busy. Uncomfortably so at times. But I'm thrilled at the cases that have been finding their way to me already. How about you? I heard you hung up your litigation bag?"

"Not exactly. It's a sabbatical. A time of reflection and recharge. It was long overdue to be honest, and I'm filling my time with pro bono work and writing. I feel so grateful for the support of the firm to allow me this time," Ava said with practiced polish.

The server arrived with the wine just then and while he uncorked it, Nola leaned into the table and lowered her voice. "Ava. Cut the bullshit." Ava cleared her throat uncomfortably and waited for the server to offer Nola a taste of the wine. "I'm sure it's fine. Go ahead." The server poured two glasses and left quickly, seemingly anxious to get away from the brewing mood at the table before him.

Nola sipped her wine and grunted at Ava. "My God, Ava. You're entitled to leave Rogers Hawk without apologizing for it. The place is a farm. I've turned down a dozen offers from places just Rogers Hawk, because I don't want to live like that. I certainly don't want to work like that. I give you a lot of credit for leaving it all behind. Embrace it. Lean in. You don't have to put on an act for me."

Ava raised her glass and pressed her back into the chair, creating some necessary distance between Nola and herself. The last time Ava had seen Nola was during Nola's interview at Rogers Hawk. Ava was asked to join in the interview, ostensibly to show Nola that other young beautiful women had made a home at the firm, a notoriously transparent boys' club firm like so many others in New York City. Ava agreed because it was Roan who made the request on behalf of one of the hiring partners, and really, she could never say no to Roan. But also, she had heard about Nola. Her reputation preceded her. Nola hadn't even begun practicing law in the city and people already knew her name. Ava wanted to put a face to the name. She wanted to see if the legend was real.

It was clear to Ava from the moment Nola sat down in the Rogers Hawk conference room on the day of the so-called interview that Nola wasn't there to get a job at Rogers Hawk. She was there to get information. She turned the tables on the interviewers, asking questions about the maternity leave, and the female equity partner data and other questions that seemed more likely to set up a grievance claim *against* the firm than an associate position *with* the firm. Ava felt like she was being interviewed by Nola, not the other way around. That familiar feeling settled over Ava again at the Club table as she slowly drained her wine glass.

Discomfort heated her neck and back, and then, suddenly, a question arose. Maybe if Nola was so uncomfortably busy, she was thinking about hiring associates to join the brand-new firm. Ava wondered if Nola was going to ask her to come work for her. The thought gave Ava a jolt of confidence and she sat up a little straighter.

"Well, since you didn't really summon me here to talk about Rogers Hawk, why did you summon me, Nola? Need some help with something?" Ava chuckled but Nola didn't.

"I do. Sort of. I'm hoping you'll be willing to talk to me freely about your experience at Rogers Hawk now that you've left. I'm also hoping you'll keep this whole conversation confidential."

Ava looked around. The din around her was deafening. In theory nothing was private in this room, but at the same time—everything was. In the cold subway-tiled room, the conversations overlapped each other until nothing was discernible but the emotions.

"What is it you want to know, Nola?" Their server was back then, dropping rolls on the women's bread plates. Ava had just started buttering hers as Nola waved him off with a brisk "No gluten please," and Ava looked down at her plate like she'd accepted a bomb she wished she could throw away. As she nibbled on her glutinous roll, she thought about how little sleep Nola must be getting to yield those charcoal eyes.

She can't possibly be happy.

"Front page news."

Ava jolted out of her daydream about gluten and charcoal eyes to come back to the conversation.

"I'm sorry, Nola. What do you say? I forgot how hard it is to hear in this place."

"Ava, you're hilarious. I said, I'm representing several clients who are going to be bringing a significant claim against Rogers Hawk. The papers are being filed as we speak. By this time next week, it will be front page news."

"Front page? Of the *Riversedge Chronicle*?" Ava teased.

"No, dear. Of the *New York Times*." Nola practically rolled her eyes and Ava startled at her words.

Rogers Hawk on the cover of The New York Times?

For a lawsuit?

What on earth was Nola up to?

Should I warn Roan?

A parade of thoughts flooded her mind.

"My God. Nola. What are you working on? And how can I possibly help?"

"Well, my clients are bringing a sexual harassment claim against Rogers Hawk, and I'm hoping you can give a little insight into the culture of the litigation department as a young, beautiful, smart female associate. Did the sexist culture factor into your exodus at all?"

"Exodus? No. Nola, I told you. It's a sabbatical. That's all. I have nothing bad to say about Rogers Hawk."

Nola nodded at Ava like she'd just agreed with her. Ava replayed the last few minutes of the conversation to ensure that no, she had *not* just agreed with Nola.

There was a long pause and then Nola said "Ava, I understand you've been sleeping with Roan Knight for some time. Did you feel pressured into that relationship at all?"

"What? Of course not. Roan and I are—"

Ava searched for the right word. They weren't necessarily exclusive. They weren't living together. But she was his girlfriend. Wasn't she?

"Roan doesn't have anything to do with the lawsuit, does he?"

Nola didn't answer. She looked down at the menu soundlessly.

"Roan doesn't sleep with female associates."

"Other than you."

Ava choked on her wine. "You're barking up the wrong tree there." Nola sat silently as Ava coughed and recovered. The silence made her uncomfortable and she found herself babbling. "I mean, really, if anyone is saying they slept with Roan as an associate—they're lying. His clients—that's another story, but not the associates."

Nola jerked her head up at Ava. "His clients? Jesus, Ava. What kind of place are you protecting after all?"

"No. I mean. It's not like that. A lot of people misunderstand Roan's relationships with his clients. They assume there's something going on because he's often on the arms of wealthy women at charity galas and things like that. But he's just doing his job."

Nola laughed. "His job. Dear God, Ava. Listen to yourself. Sounds like you got out of that place in the nick of time. Just before you started drinking the Koolaid. She waved down the waiter. "I'll have the crab cake salad please. How about you Ava?"

"Yum. That sounds good. I'll have the same," Ava smiled politely at the server as he jotted down the order.

"Oh that's right," Nola folded her hands in front of her face and stared at Ava coolly.

"What's right?"

"I've heard that Roan has a seafood allergy. I guess you don't get to eat much crab cake salad when you go out to dinner with him. I take it you're not seeing him today. Or you wouldn't, you know, indulge?"

Ava felt sick. She squirmed in her seat uncomfortably. No, she wasn't seeing Roan tonight. He had a charity event out of town with Tully. They were staying in Boston for a few days together. An all-expense-paid business trip. But Nola was making her feel like it was a romantic getaway.

"Well, Nola, you seem to know almost as much about Roan's whereabouts as I do."

"*Touché*. I have been keeping tabs on him. I am thinking about deposing him, frankly, among other things. Anyway, let's change the subject. How's your pickleball game? I have a regular court time at 8 am on the Upper West Side on Thursdays. You up for a game sometime?"

Ava looked at her questioningly, trying to figure out where the conversational whiplash was heading to. There was some more light banter about pickleball courts and the weather and then the server was placing crab cake salads in front of them and Ava asked for a glass of iced tea.

"Sure. Bring the iced tea," Nola said to the server without taking her eyes off Ava. "But also, pour us two more glasses of wine, please. We're just settling in here."

CHAPTER 13
Felicity

Felicity sits in the bathroom stall refreshing her phone. Denied. Denied. Denied.

There is a soft buzzing in her ears and she glances up at the blinking light fixture in the ceiling. She watches it for a few seconds until her eyes burn a bright orange and she has to look away, shaking her head furiously.

Her latest batch of loan applications have all been denied. Felicity had hoped to pay off her enormous credit card balances with a high interest loan, but even that avenue is unavailable to her. Every bank sends her the same response.

Sorry. We cannot approve your loan application. Your debt to income ratio is too high ... your credit score is abysmal ... you're broke.

Denied.

Felicity feels the wave of panic start at her feet and travel up to her hair. She can't afford the minimum payments on her credit cards, and she can't afford her mortgage this month. Things have hit rock bottom and she knows she'll have to take drastic measures. But what?

Bankruptcy? Foreclosure?

She puts her head between her legs on the toilet seat and takes deep breaths that hurt her lungs.

How? How has she let it get this bad? She has a good high paying career. A level head on her shoulders. But living in Manhattan is just so much more than she'd ever bargained for.

It's the life she and her mother had wanted for Felicity. The life they'd both worked so hard and sacrificed so much for. And yet, this wished-for life was sucking her dry.

Felicity leaned into the lifestyle at first, charging sushi dinners and expensive Hamptons timeshares and new suits with abandon. She bought a two-bedroom condo on the Upper West Side and agreed to a jumbo mortgage with a high interest rate. Her Rogers Hawk salary seemed like more than enough to afford it all. After all, it was more money than she'd ever made. More money than her mother had ever made.

But Felicity never really was good at math, and suddenly, her salary paled in comparison to her monthly expenses. She opened credit card after credit card, trying to figure a way out of the debt that was amassing, but every month's end, she was deeper and deeper in. It was embarrassing. Too embarrassing to mention to anyone. She certainly doesn't want her mother to know. During weekly check-ins, Felicity's mother, Marilyn, talks repeatedly about how proud she is of Felicity's hard work and perseverance.

And Felicity certainly can't share any of her struggles with the Rogers Hawk friends. They all seem completely capable of balancing it all—even Archie. Especially Archie. What would he say if he knew how deeply in debt she was? That she was two months behind on her mortgage? That her credit card balances were dancing precariously close to her six-figure annual salary.

Would he leave her? Or would he help her find a way out?

Each time she nearly works up the nerve to talk to him, she weakens. She can't even imagine bringing this all up to Archie. She wants to figure it out on her own. She has always been able to handle the hardest decisions on her own.

"You know what I love about you?" Archie asked the first time Felicity invited him over to her place for dinner after work.

"My billable hours?" she joked.

"Your fierce independence. God, it's sexy as hell. I've been with women who could never hope to afford a place like this, and look at you. You did it. All on your own. You're self made. God, it's amazing."

They'd tumbled into bed after that and had the most amazing sex. Sex that hadn't exactly been replicated since. Well, there was that one time after Archie showed them all the Easy Street Building.

Easy Street.

The building has given Felicity new hope that she and Archie will find magic again. That she'll crawl out of debt and regain some self-control and dignity.

But the looming prospect of the Easy Street proposal is making the financial situation feel even more urgent. Felicity wants in with Archie. She wants to sell her apartment and move into Easy Street, sharing a home and expenses with Archie, and some security once and for all. But every real estate agent she's met with recently has told her there is very little equity in her condo bought at the height of the market. Not even enough to take out a home equity line of credit. Felicity is out of options. She might just have to come clean to Archie that she can't afford to go in on Easy Street with him and the rest of their friends. What will Archie say? His health hasn't been the greatest lately. Will this news cause added stress? Will he leave her to avoid the stress at all costs?

Felicity is still in the stall refreshing her latest loan application denials, when she hears two women come in laughing. Felicity knows her eyes are puffy and her face is blotchy from crying so she stays in the stall hoping to wait them out and fix her face after they leave. She lifts her feet up off the floor and props them against the door so the women won't even know she is there. Her legs fall asleep as the women linger at the sinks for a long time commiserating about a new partner in their department.

"God, he's awful."

"Girl, what do you expect? I'm pretty sure it says in the manual—make sure to hit on as many female associates as you can within your first month of employment."

"Is he a newbie, then?"

"Eh, he transferred in from some smaller insurance defense firm. He's completely incompetent yet walks around with all the arrogance of a seasoned attorney. And all the misogyny of one too."

Felicity rolls her eyes from her uncomfortable perch. *Why are men such assholes?* She wonders. She knows she is lucky, securing a spot working for one of the few female partners in her department. She doesn't have to worry about getting hit on or suggestive comments when she's working late. The trade-off, though, is that the female partners don't routinely put their female associates up for partner. The consensus is that the partnership pie is cut into slices and very few of those slices are reserved for women. The pie is mostly reserved for men. The ogling, sexist, misogynistic men. The kind these two women at the sink work for.

"Yesterday, he asked me to come to his office at 10 pm to work on a brief. When I got there, I kid you not, he was dressed only in *his* briefs. He still had his shirt on and his suspenders, but he was pacing in his office in his fucking boxers."

"You've got to be kidding me."

"Swear to God."

"What did you do?"

"I ignored it. I went through the other side's case with him, told him all the problems with their argument and the precedent cases they'd ignored, and he said, 'Good job, kid.'"

Laughter.

"Fucking guy. I'm at least five years older than him. But he'll make partner long before me. And on the way out the door he patted my ass and said, I like to treat all my co-workers the same. I'd do the same to any male associate who was in the proverbial dugout with me. So I promise not to treat you any differently, kid.' And then he winked at me like we were pals."

"Oh, gross. He's even worse than the last guy."

"You're not kidding. If I didn't have plans for myself—if I didn't need this opportunity—I'd sue his ass."

"Right? They're so lucky. We're just not *those* people. But one of these days, one of *those* people is going to walk into his dugout and man is he going to be sorry."

"Amen, sister."

Felicity waits until she hears the door click behind them and the soft strain of their voices heading away from the bathroom down the hall. She lets herself out of the stall quietly, washes her face clean of tears and regret, and reapplies some translucent powder. Then she deletes all the bad news emails from her phone. And when she leaves the bathroom, there is a little noticeable spring in her step. A renewed optimism. Felicity has a plan finally to make money and get out of debt. And this one, she is excited about. This one, she really feels, is fool-proof.

CHAPTER 14
Ava

Ava tried to distract herself from the bizarre Riversedge Law Club meeting with Nola by diving into her freelance writing work. She was flitting about from assignment to assignment trying to figure out something that might stick. The writing brought her joy, but little pay. Still, she hadn't given up hope that she'd find a way to merge her creative spirit and her analytical talent. Those late-night conversations with Jason haunted her—inspiring her to succeed in spite of the guilt they brought up as well.

Ava had agreed to write an article for a New York based legal journal about a Belgian scientist working in New York who'd applied for a record number of patents in the previous year. While she knew nothing about the science he was working on, Ava told herself that she'd be able to use her legal training to tell a compelling story about Dr. Zell.

Heart cells are constantly rebuilding on the fly.

This means that the heart does not beat the same way every time.

Pressed between a thin young woman and heavy-set older man on the subway headed downtown, Ava highlighted these words in a small notebook before tucking it back into her bag. After she'd been assigned by the legal journal editor to cover Dr. Zell's groundbreaking work, building artificial hearts at his lab at New York Hospital, she'd dialed into Dr. Zell's publicly available lecture yesterday and scribbled notes furiously trying to understand the foreign science behind the story she was meant to write. Most of what he said was lost on her, but these two lines made their way into her notebook, and she kept reading and re-reading them on the subway.

There was something comforting about this stranger's assertion that heart cells could indeed rebuild themselves. Ava's own heart felt damaged and she couldn't pinpoint the exact moment of rupture other than that hungover morning she rejected Jason McKoy's profession of love.

Had she broken her own heart irreparably by leaving Jason McKoy because of her ambition? Ava asked herself not for the first time.

No, that wasn't right. Ava shook her head, correcting her own sentimental thoughts. A broken heart would have hurt. A broken heart implied she might have felt *something.* A broken heart would have created piercing, jagged shards in her ribcage that might have reminded her she was still alive. She had none of that. All she had felt since she left Jason's rot-smelling apartment that morning, was a vacuum—a pervasive numbness that had started in her chest and now seemed to have taken her over entirely.

Roan had plugged the hole in her heart, but, of course, he'd created new fissures with his absences and his refusal to commit. She'd left the law to regain some control over her destiny—and inject some hope into her own story. But in truth, since her goodbye party at Rogers Hawk, Ava had been spending her suddenly very empty days writing stories about pets who look like their owners and trending TikTok memes created by bored teens.

Until now.

This assignment about Dr. Zell's artificial heart research breakthrough and record-breaking patent applications seemed like just the right story, if done correctly, that could justify to both herself, and Roan that leaving Rogers Hawk had been worth it somehow.

Maybe Jason would even read the story and be impressed. Ava let the thought in despite her misgivings. She couldn't keep Jason out of her mind. Couldn't even try.

Ava walked up the street, past a cannabis storefront and colorful coffee shop, until she arrived at New York Children's Hospital. She turned into the circular driveway that led to the lobby. She noticed a squad of valets swarming around the cars and vans as she walked up, as if the attendees of a big, celebratory event were arriving. For a moment, Ava thought a dignitary was arriving at the hospital. But as she got closer, she saw something else.

Children wrapped in blankets were contorted in wheelchairs, their parents hurriedly checking their coverings in the cold, short walk from the cars to the automatic doorways. It was early spring when the morning was still brisk and relentless. Other parents carried babies with oversized, brightly patterned head dressings. More children stumbled forward, in and out of the lobby, with walkers. Some had nasal tubes ... some were bald, pale, and visibly weak. Ava's eyes darted from the children surrounding her to the faces of the parents covered in horror and fear that she assumed only the parent of a sick child could know. Some of the parents had a thread of strained hope across their faces. Others showed a brave smile and cheerful tone as they encouraged their child or thanked the valets.

Ava walked into the lobby and headed for the security desk, where she traded her name and driver's license for a visitor's badge and directions to the elevator bank which, according to the detailed instructions she'd received via email, led to Dr. Zell's lab.

In the elevator, alone, Ava exhaled loudly, releasing the breath she'd held as she walked past the frail children and their parents. Ava crossed her arms tightly across her chest. An icy feeling—so cold it actually burned—worked its way through her whole body landing under her ribs with a jolt as she thought about the collection of emotions she'd just experienced on the faces of the families of the sick children. She certainly wasn't numb anymore. She suddenly felt as though she was wearing all of that visible, palpable terror, exhaustion, sadness, and desperation instead of a coat. Years of regretting her own childhood, of anger at having it robbed by her feuding parents, seemed to dissolve on the elevator ride. What these children were facing was obviously much worse than a pillaged trust fund. Ava's face was wet with tears by the time the elevator doors opened on Dr. Zell's floor, and she wiped at her cheeks roughly with the cuffs of her jacket trying to shed the emotions that had just overwhelmed her. In their place, she felt the sharp new pain of guilt that she could actually escape the emotional overload when the families below her could not.

The elevator doors closed behind her and she stood, trying to compose herself, when suddenly a white-haired man came barreling out of a door across from the elevator, and headed toward her. She recognized him as Dr. Zell right away, but was startled that he knew her, too, as he greeted her enthusiastically, "Miss Ava Simone!"

Ava nodded, then shook her head. "Call me Ava, please. Just Ava."

Dr. Zell smirked and walked past her, tapping the down button next to the elevator she'd emerged from. "Well, Just Ava. Pleased to meet you and thanks for coming. But if you don't mind, we have to walk and talk. I haven't had a decent cup of coffee all morning, and I need to fix that. Can I buy you a latte or something similar while we talk about hearts?"

Ava followed Dr. Zell back onto the elevator wordlessly, startled by the abrupt change in plans. But she was even more flustered when he said, "Ok, shoot. What do you want to ask me, Just Ava?" She reached into her bag and started rooting around for her notebook with the well-prepared, well-researched list of questions she'd planned to ask Dr. Zell while seated comfortably in his office, but Dr. Zell didn't wait for her to start the interview or find her notebook. Suddenly he was firing off statistics and formulas and researchers' names and scientific journal findings, and talking about how close his lab was to building the first four-chamber heart ever, and rattling off a list of recent patents that made the whole project possible. The patents of course were the reason her editor had sent her there in the first place, and Ava was trying hard to keep up with Dr. Zell's rapid-fire delivery.

As they reached the lobby, and walked back out to the driveway through the sea of patients Ava had only just recently escaped, Ava felt her legs grow heavier. She arrived on the curb alongside a young mother, not as pale as the child with her—but certainly *close*—just as she was helping the boy from a wheelchair into the back seat of a car the valet had just brought up. The young woman sounded almost robotic as she said, "All right, Ethan, let's get you *home.*" Ava watched the woman close the car door, and turn her glance away from the car where her sick son was sitting. For just a moment their eyes met, and as Ava smiled feebly, she saw how the mother's features re-arranged themselves again and again—in an instant—in a transformation from hope to brokenness to hope again.

Ava turned to see Dr. Zell at the end of the driveway that separated New York Children's Hospital from the city of Manhattan. She ran ahead to catch up with him, but even still, she struggled to keep up. She estimated he was about 30 years her senior, but with the stride of someone much younger. He was continuing to talk about ventricular chamber tissue engineering as if she'd been by his side without interruption.

"What does it mean?" Ava asked vaguely as she was trying to commit terms to memory like "rat myocytes" and "calcium propagation" so she could look them up later. But as she thought about the raw emotion she'd just walked through and witnessed, what she really wondered was: *what would all this science mean to them?*

She asked the question aloud then.

Dr. Zell stopped in front of a coffee shop and looked right at Ava for the first time since they'd met outside the elevator.

"It means that essentially two decades of work in this field are yielding the expected results. It means, Just Ava, that we were right."

Dr. Zell held the door open for Ava, but she brushed him off impatiently and put her arm on the door herself, as she continued on, "No. But, what does it mean for all of them? All those children that are in that lobby. Right now. Coming and going. Living and dying. I think we grownups often forget that while we are trying to make names for ourselves, and conquer the world and create a lasting legacy, there are actual children dying while waiting for us."

Inside the coffee shop, Dr. Zell regarded her quietly. She heard her voice grow louder. "What does it mean for them? That's the story I want to write. That's the story I want to tell. All this nonsense about rat cells and fake hearts. My God. It all just sounds like a lot of Frankenstein-science-fiction-make-believe. What are you doing for those kids? What are you doing for those broken-hearted parents? Is your heart going to help *fix them?*"

"Venti. Dark Roast. Black." Dr. Zell addressed the barista then turned to Ava, "I'm trying." Ava could tell she had hit a nerve. His jaw was clenched as he asked, "And you?"

"I'm trying, too. I'm trying to create something. To make an impact in the world. I'm trying to make my law degree and legal training make sense. I'm trying to be a better human than my parents were. I'm trying to make my choice to leave Jason McKoy and others just like him make sense as well."

Ava put her hand over mouth, in shock at the words that had tumbled out of her mouth seemingly without control.

Dr. Zell's jaw unclenched and he smiled and shook his head at her as if she was a child. "No, Just Ava, I meant—what will you have to drink?"

Another 13 minutes later, coffees in hand, they returned to Dr. Zell's office where Ava retrieved her notebook finally and asked her originally prepared questions, and with a softer tone, Dr. Zell delivered rather vanilla answers that connected the nuances of his team's work to the clinical challenges faced by the sick children in the lobby.

"Thank you. I think I have what I need now," Ava closed her notebook and said goodbye to Dr. Zell, thinking as she did, that he looked at her with a trace of disappointment. She winced as she remembered the Frankenstein comment blurted out in the middle of the coffee shop, and hurried to catch the train home so she could finish the story in time for her deadline.

Roan was out of town and sent her a quick text checking in. Ava couldn't remember where he was or who he was with, so she sent back a generic response.

Hope all is going well. Miss you!

Roan "liked" her comment instead of responding.

In her quiet apartment, with scribbled notes, Ava reflected on the day, and suddenly saw the interview with Dr. Zell through a fresh lens. She couldn't find a single quote that would inform why the artificial heart breakthrough was so important to the larger scientific community or even to the public. Instead her notebook was filled with quotes from Dr. Zell essentially bragging about his life's work.

As she stared at an empty document on her computer for hours, she alternated between frustration at the lack of content in the interview and resentment of Dr. Zell's dismissal of her.

Just Ava.

He had treated the so-called "interview" as nothing more than an effort to soothe a petulant child. As a publicity move, likely designed to get more grant funding.

This isn't what I want it to be, Ava thought as she tried to tame her pages of notes into a real story.

I can't be who you want me to be. Her own parting words to Jason McKoy rang through Ava's head as she typed words and deleted them. Typed again and deleted.

By the morning, after a frustrating all-nighter, her "big story" was exactly ten words long:

Dr. Zell claims he knows how to build a heart.

Under the guise of fact checking, Ava called his office and arranged to revisit Dr. Zell the next day. This meant, again, passing through the emotional cyclone of the hospital lobby. This time, she was prepared and not emotionally surprised by what she saw but nonetheless ... she felt it and wore it much like she had the first time.

When Ava arrived at Dr. Zell's office, she was surprised to see that he had prepared, not with heart models and images, but by remembering her beverage order, with hers and his coffees sitting on the conference table in his office.

She pulled her notebook out familiarly as she walked in, but Dr. Zell waved her off. "Can we just take a moment to relax before we get started? Yours is a skinny vanilla latte, right? Same order as my daughter, as a matter of fact."

Ava noticed then the family pictures on the wall of Dr. Zell's office. She sat down, plopped her bag to the side and sipped her drink, trying to discern her next move.

Dr. Zell reclined in his chair, legs crossed, taking one long pull as he looked at her. Ava was a bit uncomfortable as she realized she was being considered. She hadn't been looked at like that in a long time. Not since Jason—she quickly dismissed the thought.

"So Ava, you're doing freelance writing. I understand you've left the law behind ... but what's your real plan?"

She noticed that he'd dropped the "Just Ava," replacing with "Ava," and while she had told him he could use her first name, it suddenly felt oddly intimate. She looked away from Dr. Zell's gaze and studied the family pictures instead. It was hard to reconcile the intensity of this man with the casual pictures on the wall behind him, filled with laughing characters in cartoonish poses and various outdoor settings that hardly resembled hospitals or science labs.

"You have a beautiful family," Ava heard herself saying.

"Thank you. Married 23 years, if you can believe it. Wait, no that's not right. It's actually been 24."

Ava kept her gaze trained on the photos. Dr. Zell was a devoted researcher but also a father, and someone's husband. He was a brilliant man creating artificial hearts with enviable precision, but he also couldn't remember his own wedding anniversary without counting on his hands.

All of those things can be true, Ava.

Ava squirmed in her seat uncomfortably at the memory of Jason's words over late-night coffee and dream spilling.

"Really, Ava. Tell me. What is it you want to be?" Dr. Zell brought her back to the present.

"I want to be a writer," she replied, nervously.

"Nah, that's what you want to *do*. I am asking you what you want to *be*." He was so cool, so quick to dismiss her facade that she knew what would come next was unavoidable.

Ava thought of Jason, knowing exactly who he was, and what he wanted to be, while she was sitting in a hospital office flustered by a question that should have been so simple to answer. In response to Dr. Zell, she shuddered and then sobbed, holding her skinny vanilla latte with two hands, her head bowed, shoulders heaving.

Dr. Zell's response to her sudden emotional deflation was blunt.

"Ava, you came in here last time hell bent on making me the character you wanted me to be. You were forceful about it. I knew you'd be back because I knew you hadn't been able to make me fit into the little part of the world you wanted me to. I have seen it before—not just journalists—but young people, interns, new residents. I mentor a lot of high achievers. There are two classes: the ones who are trying to force the world to be a certain way and the ones who are trying to build themselves to be in the world in a certain way. The latter are the ones who succeed and they're happy because, frankly, they have a lot less to do. The world is immovable, Ava. You aren't going to get it to be the way you want it. So you have to build yourself for the world. Just like my heart cells have to build and rebuild themselves to keep on pumping."

And with that, he stood abruptly, leaving his steaming coffee cup and Ava behind as he walked out of the room.

Ava slipped her jacket back on and wiped her tear-stained face on the cuffs much like she'd done the first time she met Dr. Zell on her first fateful trip to the New York Children's Hospital. She would have felt like she was stuck in a loop, if this time she didn't feel so—different.

The heart does not beat the same way every time. Dr. Zell had said so himself.

Ava was soon on her way back uptown, after hailing a cab outside the hospital, trying to figure out how she could write a story with so many useless pages of notes from not one, but two meetings with Dr. Zell. She stared out the window at the city moving in full motion just beyond the glass—parents and children and workers and joggers and homeless and lovers— convinced that the story was right there, eluding her.

She pressed her face close to the window with a whispered plea to the universe.

What is it you want me to be?

The cab stopped at a red light, under the shade of a tall sky-scraper, and the glass window pane darkened and transformed into a mirror ... startling Ava with her own reflection.

CHAPTER 15
Sara

I dreamt of my grandmother last night.

You would think that would comfort me or anger me or make me feel some emotion at all. But it didn't. In my dream, I just wanted to wake up. My mind was racing and I was trying to sort it all out, and I knew, even asleep, that I couldn't sort it out with Agnes there. And so I wanted to be where she wasn't. I wanted to be awake.

Part of the reason (maybe a big part, of course) that my mind was racing that way was because of Archie. While Agnes was talking about her day which seemed to involve an inordinate amount of time playing with her cat, Esme, in the sun, I was thinking about Archie and trying not to mention to Agnes that I was, in fact, thinking about *Archie*. I kept trying to make my thoughts boring again and focus on what she was saying, but it became harder and harder to do, the longer I stayed asleep and the longer she talked about her cat.

It's funny that Esme would be the one intruding on my thoughts and dreams since I've been spending so much time with my grandmother's journal recently, and there is not one mention of Esme in there. Esme exists only in my own memories these days. But she was real, of course.

Esme was a black and white scruffy mutt of a cat that my grandmother found and rescued. The story went that the cat showed up one morning while my grandmother was sitting outside in her yard, humming and painting. The cat appeared out of nowhere, curling around Agnes's feet and then disappearing into the nearby woods. This went on for days and then one day the cat stayed curled around her feet, and that was that. Now the cat was Esme and Esme was Agnes's. She died about a year before Agnes did, and at Agne's funeral I had the strange thought that Esme was the lucky one, dying before her. She didn't have to grieve her the way I did

In my dream last night, I remembered all of that—the way Esme used to curl up at my grandmother's feet and in her lap when she was trying to paint. Sometimes I would watch Agnes paint and I'd daydream about curling up in her lap just like Esme.

A bunch of other thoughts bopped around my brain like popcorn. Because, in my dream, Agnes was there and because she was talking about Esme. But also because Archie was standing behind Agnes silently, with his finger up over his mouth through the whole dream. She couldn't see him, but I could. He was pale and sickly. I wondered if he was dying. In my dream I couldn't tell if that thought made me sad or relieved.

And so I was really, frantically trying not to accidentally say anything out loud, and certainly not say anything about Archie. I didn't want Agnes to turn around and see Archie. Or worse, turn around and see that he wasn't there at all.

CHAPTER 16
Holly

Oh man, I really wish I didn't have to go there. But, ok.

Here's what you should know. On the day we finally closed on 724 Easy Street, we were all ecstatic. Listen, it was a big number. Even though we got the sellers to slice and negotiate, it was a big number for us. And all the units weren't even finished yet. It took months from that pact at Archie's hospital bed to actually seal the deal. Summer had come and gone. We'd scratched and clawed to get to a number we could live with and even still, we were having trouble liquidating to get the cash needed to make the sale. But we were still so excited to finally close the deal.

What was that? Oh, Roan. Roan was the lead.

Yeah, Roan took the lead on the negotiations and we sort of let him run the show. You know? Archie was trying to keep some distance to avoid the appearance of a conflict of interest. Or so we thought. And no one else stepped up. Roan did and we were grateful so that was that.

But as we got closer and closer to the closing date, we were still having trouble figuring out how to make the math work. Felicity had recently written a pretty large check into the LLC account. Like really big. And she hadn't even put her place on the market like the rest of us, so that was a little confusing and concerning until the check cleared, but it did clear. So that check of Felicity's went a long way toward getting us to the finish line, but we were still short.

Yes, I know now how she got the money. We all know now. But that's not really the point, is it?

The point is—things were getting a little tense. Because we were still short on cash. And we were all starting to say out loud that maybe this just wasn't going to work. Maybe we'd been a little too ambitious.

Maybe Easy Street wasn't so easy after all.

But then.

Well, then Sara appeared. It was Sara that brought us over the finish line.

What we were told was that she was a contact of Archie's. And that she wanted in. And that she insisted on taking the top unit.

And frankly, that's the one unit none of us had been in because it was allegedly unsafe even to walk through given its complete state of deconstruction. So you know we figured she was taking on the lion's share of the renovations, and she could have it.

We let Sara in sight unseen.

What do I mean by that? Well, we never asked to meet her before closing. And we never asked to see the top unit either. Archie arranged for her signature on everything and brought her cashier check and signed documents to the closing.

Yes, I understand that these were crucial mistakes now. But on closing day, when we suddenly had enough money to make the sale, no one was asking the right questions. We were just patting ourselves on the back and congratulating ourselves on what we considered to be the best deal of our lives.

We were officially residents of Easy Street.

We figured that's all that mattered.

Well, yes, we know that *now*. But as I said, and I'm really trying to make this very clear here. Under oath. We didn't know any of that *then*.

CHAPTER 17

Ava

"Since we can't move into Easy Street for another couple months or so, and I'll be traveling most of that time, you're free to stay here. Honestly, Ava, it's wonderful that both our places sold so quickly. We can work out all the logistics in the meantime. I cut a deal with the new owners of my place for a month-to-month lease. I can stay here for a pretty modest rent while the renovations start on our unit at Easy Street. I'm told our unit should be ready by Christmas."

Roan was packing as he made the announcement. Ava was sitting on his bed watching him. She knew her expression was startled but she didn't care. "You're leaving for the Fall? With Tully?"

"We'll be in the Hamptons for most of September. Working, Ava. Stop being so dramatic, would you? We're staying with Tully's Writer Friend and I'll be revising her estate plan."

"Oh, Lord. That sounds like a blast."

"Ava, don't." Roan scolded, and Ava tried to backpedal her disgust, but it was almost impossible. She'd met Tully's Writer Friend. Last winter, she'd actually been invited by Roan to a Book Festival in the Hamptons. Tully had the flu and couldn't go along, but she insisted that Roan still attend in her stead. Tully's Writer Friend was being honored at the fancy black tie kickoff event of the Hamptons Book Festival.

Roan invited Ava to be his date for the weekend and she

thought maybe they'd turned the corner. That he'd stop pretending to be something other than Ava's boyfriend.

As she packed a bag for the weekend, Ava imagined a getaway filled with lobster rolls and gray goose cosmos at lush bars overlooking the water. She imagined a cozy bed and breakfast with a stoked fire and espresso martinis loaded with cacao and coffee beans. She packed oversized sweaters and sexy lingerie and one long black dress for the kickoff gala with a deep v neckline and a glittery overlay that would reflect the lights of the room should they decide to dance at the ball.

Oh let there be dancing, Ava thought as she zipped up her weekend bag.

Spoiler alert. There was no dancing.

They stayed with the Writer Friend in her stately clapboard Hamptons home and in fact, it was not anything like Ava had imagined or hoped. Instead, it was the longest three days of Ava's life. Writer Friend had one claim to fame. She'd hit the *New York Times* bestseller list with her debut novel, a thick hardcover book that purported to be a parable about race relations in New England in the 2000s that had always struck Ava as incredibly tone deaf.

"Her success is enviable. It would never be possible for a white woman to publish such a book today," Roan said out loud with no sense of irony on the Hampton Jitney bus that took them door to door: from Rogers Hawk after work on Friday evening to Writer Friend's summer home over an hour away.

Writer Friend had not written a thing since that hypocritical tome. At least nothing that was published or out for human consumption. On the bus, Roan jabbed Ava in the ribs with his elbow while she looked out the window. "Tully's Writer Friend says we should come directly to the house for drinks and dinner. She says we shouldn't bother going out tonight since we're getting in so late and have to get a good night's sleep before the event tomorrow. She's having her cook throw something together."

"How nice," Ava sighed as she fixed her gaze outside the bus window. It was at that moment, she resolved, on the spot, she'd never refer to the woman as anything other than Writer Friend. She would have loved to just get away for the weekend with Roan for real. Without it being a networking event, or worse. As she watched the city disappear and the leafless trees en route to the Hamptons replace the lights and buzz of New York City, Ava felt lost and started to drift off to sleep.

Roan interrupted her slumber. "She's excited to meet you," he claimed without basis. And then, "She's curious about you."

Ava rolled her eyes, still facing out the window so he couldn't see.

In Writer Friend's home, there was very little hospitality. There was a cold aloof, "Oh, hello there," at the threshold when Ava said "Thank you so much for having us." It was almost as if Writer Friend didn't know she was coming along. Ava was instantly dubious about Roan's claim that Writer Friend was curious about Ava. Unless "curious" was a euphemism for disdain.

Writer Friend took their jackets just inside the door, and made a not-so-subtle show of looking inside Ava's jacket for the label. It clearly didn't pass muster as her scorn was pretty evident. Ava thought it was ironic that Writer Friend was so disdainful of frugal living. Particularly since Writer Friend was living off her second husband's alimony checks. As she surveyed the glamorous Hamptons dwelling, Ava knew royalty payments alone—from a book that had been a modest success five years earlier—couldn't possibly have sustained the way Writer Friend was living.

The night got progressively worse.

Ava was the third wheel immediately, offered a chair in an awkward corner of the living room while Roan and Writer Friend sat across from each other, leaning into each other, laughing and talking without including her. From her invisible perch, Ava thought about the fact that Roan never had too many complimentary things to say about Writer Friend, but, as they sat down for "drinks" in her spacious living room, you would never know that he had previously described her as "vapid, tedious and decidedly lackluster." Of course "drinks" remained in quotes in Ava's head, because, as it turned out, there were no drinks. There was just a can of diet coke in front of Writer Friend and a halfhearted offer after they'd been sitting for 5-10 minutes. "You guys want something to drink while Bea finishes cooking? Or you're good?"

Roan answered for them. "Oh no. We're good. Don't worry about us. Just thrilled to see you. So happy to catch up a bit. How's writing going?"

Ava was not, in fact, good. She was parched from the long bus ride from the city where she had worked all day while Writer Friend had clearly, well, *not* worked all day, and she would have loved a drink. Ava thought—crazily—about leaning over and taking a sip out of Writer Friend's diet coke can, and afterward, she couldn't be sure exactly what had stopped her. Ava cleared her throat unwittingly, and Roan and Writer Friend both paused in their conversation to look at her. As if they'd forgotten she existed until just then.

Roan pointed to her then like she was a new toy. "Ava's a rising star at the firm. She works mostly on labor disputes. But she has secret dreams of writing a novel."

Writer Friend took notice of her for the first time since she arrived. "Really? How wonderful."

Ava smiled. And then, there was that moment, when she actually felt bad for doubting Roan. After all, here he was—doing his best to show her off. She swelled with pride under the gaze of Writer Friend. "Yes, I've been working on something for about a year now in my spare time at the firm, which you know, is in short supply."

Roan clucked and interrupted her then, looking at Writer Friend apologetically. "Well, you know, who knows if she'll ever finish it, but still—"

Ava felt like someone had punched her in the gut. Suddenly she didn't want to be part of the conversation in the room. She didn't even want to be in the room at all.

She leaned back in the chair, deflated, and looked down, humiliated. Roan took her in and jumped back in, "But still, you know ..."

Writer Friend parroted, "Oh yes, still, you know ..."

But Ava didn't know. Still.

After that, the drinkless visit over "drinks" felt interminable, and Ava watched Writer Friend banter back and forth inanely with Roan, and without her. Ava was happy to be on the outside by that point. She felt sad and rejected and didn't actually trust herself to say a thing.

Later, after a similarly uncomfortable dinner, when they retired to the bedroom down the hall, Ava watched Roan hug Writer Friend good night and she heard her whisper "Next time, come alone, so we can catch up for real."

Ava realized with a jolt—incredulously for the first time— that Writer Friend was something more to him than just Tully's friend. Most likely she was an ex-girlfriend or at least an ex-lover.

Ava was incensed at the deception, but mostly startled at the thought that Writer Friend was the kind of woman Roan could ever have been interested in. A few months later when she took her sabbatical, and picked up her novel in progress again, Writer Friend's disdain flitted in and out of Ava's spiteful brain, right alongside Jason McKoy.

I can't be who you want me to be.

But still.

The memory from the winter before distracted Ava as she watched Roan pack to go spend half his fall with Tully and his former lover. Ava was outraged that she couldn't be more different from Writer Friend, if she tried. Outraged that she'd lost all sight of who she was as she was trying relentlessly to be someone who Roan Knight could love.

But didn't.

Ava knew she was wrong to love him, but knew she still loved Roan Knight in spite of all of it.

All of those things can be true, Ava.

But still.

When Roan left her, with his packed bag, Ava acted on an idea that had been brewing ever since that lunch with Nola Dyer in which she'd told Ava about the pending lawsuit. Nola had made an outlandish proposal to Ava at the time, which she summarily dismissed. But after Roan left, Ava texted Nola and told her she was finally remembering a few things that might be important to the pending lawsuit against Rogers Hawk.

Meet me at the Club. Tomorrow. Noon. Nola's response was quick and decisive.

While Roan was off gallivanting with Tully and Writer Friend, Ava had already decided she'd take matters into her own hands.

She thought about Dr. Zell's words.

The world is immovable. You aren't going to get it to be the way you want it. So you have to build yourself for the world. Just like my heart cells have to build and rebuild themselves to keep on pumping.

Now that she'd left the law behind, she could be something new. Something all her own. Roan and Writer Friend and Jason McKoy, and even her parents, be damned. Ava's heart felt like it was rebuilding itself one cell at a time. It was time for a new chapter, and she wanted to prove to everyone that she wasn't an invisible character in the corner of a room eyeballing a can of diet coke.

She wanted that harsh goodbye to Jason McKoy to be worth it. Finally.

I am not my self-destructive parents. And I am not a vapid tedious woman pretending to be a writer, Ava thought, *No, I am the main character in my own story, and it's time I start acting like it.*

CHAPTER 18
Holly

Well, Daniel and I moved into our unit first. We were doing the least amount of renovations on ours. We took the second-floor unit, the one Archie had shown us that first night and thankfully, it was pretty much complete and turnkey by the time of closing. Let me tell you, we paid a hefty premium for the already renovated unit because we had less time to spend renovating. Our business required a working kitchen and a place to live.

Pronto.

Ironically, since Daniel and I weren't overpaid and overfed Rogers Hawk attorneys, we had less money to spend than any of the other Easy Street buyers, but we calculated that the money we'd be saving on renovations was in fact worth the extra money we put in at closing. I still had a little savings left from my Rogers Hawk days. Money that hadn't yet been invested in the business. Daniel had a much smaller savings, and we used some of the new profits from the catering business. It took a lot of convincing by me to get Daniel to agree to use those, but eventually that's the only way we could afford our increased share.

So, yeah, for a little while, that warm Autumn, we were the only ones at Easy Street, and we were running the catering business out of our unit.

And we liked being the only ones in the building. We pretended it was all ours. This grand building overlooking the river was our new Riversedge mansion. Furniture was sparse in those early days. We'd eat dinner on the floor by the windows at night and watch the boats. We'd drink wine in the middle of the day while we came up with new recipes and we'd play our music loudly. We felt like teenagers in our parents' home while they were away. We kept pinching ourselves because we couldn't believe this beautiful, perfect place was ours.

What was that? You want to know what happened to pierce that little bubble we were living in?

Well, for one thing, we got this fabulous job—catering a big dinner for a celebrity VIP's charity event in her Manhattan home. We signed a confidentiality agreement so I'm not sure I can tell you who she is but let's just say—it was a huge opportunity. We were literally GAGA over it. Get it?

I know, wink, wink. She had heard about us from the friend of a friend. A smaller but still fabulous dinner we'd done for some Manhattan socialites had gone so well. And we have this niche spot in the market, you know? Clean living. Clean cooking. But so delicious you barely know how good you're eating.

This. *This* is the point of vulnerability for me. The reason I was impatient with Daniel many times when I really shouldn't have been. Before we bought the Easy Street building, I'd recently been diagnosed with an autoimmune disorder. I felt like I was treating my body better than ever before and it was *attacking* me. The diagnosis had shaken my confidence. I'd told no one, only Daniel, and he suggested putting the business on hold while I figured out my new normal. But I told him, absolutely not. I was mad at him for even suggesting such a thing out loud.

Um, no. I didn't tell any of the others about my diagnosis when we first bought the building. I mean, it was personal. And it didn't matter. I didn't think so, anyway. Still don't.

So, yeah, we—Daniel and I—went into the new space with all cylinders firing. With all our savings sunk into the building, I needed to figure out a way to be healthy and keep my business alive. This new celebrity VIP job felt like all the validation I needed to keep going.

Oh, of course there's a *but*. When we were doing all the paperwork with her people, she wanted our licenses, the certifications for our new kitchen. Which we hadn't bothered to really finalize at that point.

Do I need to plead the fifth amendment here or something? You're not going to use this to get me fined for all those jobs we did before the new certifications came or anything, right?

Right. That's small fish compared to what you're actually after. I get it.

Any who.

We started the process of getting that kitchen certified for commercial use. Inspectors and paperwork and maybe a little bribing here and there to try to get the process moving more quickly.

Kidding. Definitely no bribing. Please don't write that in the transcript, Miss.

Ok, no, of course. You have to write it all down. I just need to be a little more careful, don't I, about kidding on the record? I used to be a lawyer, remember? I used to be sitting on that very side of the table in plenty of depositions, not unlike this one. I've told you that, already, right?

Yes, yes, of course, back on track. Honestly, I think it's all the medicine I'm taking these days. The cleaner I try to be the more my body betrays me. My mind. It's foggy most of the time. That's why I settled and why I'm talking to you now—

Of course not. No, we shouldn't talk about that here. Back to the kitchen inspections.

So one of the inspectors said we were going to have to replace a piece of the flooring that looked warped near the stove. She said it was a fire hazard, and I said, well, it's been like that since we moved in, and she said, that wasn't a reason not to fix it.

She was a little snarky if you ask me. Which I'm not sure you did.

But anyway, that's when it happened. We hired one of the contractors who was working on Ava and Roan's unit upstairs to come replace the kitchen floors for us, and the minute he pulled up the warped floorboard, he said, "oh, there's a bunch of these silver pools under here, too."

And I said—what do you mean silver pools? And what do you mean *too*?

I leaned in over his shoulder, and looked and sure enough—scattered around the kitchen were all these little circular pools of silvery, shiny liquid. He pushed a paint brush into one and it moved and swirled like a watercolor then back into its original circular shape.

No, I had no idea what it was. I asked him. And he said, "Well it's probably the same stuff that's upstairs under their floorboards. It looks like mercury, but I don't know what that would be doing here. You guys didn't break a bunch of old thermometers did you?"

And yeah, I didn't know what to say to that. I didn't know what it would mean if it *was* mercury. I knew mercury was dangerous and we shouldn't touch it. So I just told him to do what I thought was the most prudent thing. I said, "Seal it up with the new floorboards. Don't let any of it get out." And he said, "Yeah, that's what I was told to do by my boss on the upstairs unit as well."

I didn't know anything about mercury vapors back then. I didn't know anything about how my immune compromised body would react to living in an apartment with mercury lurking under the floorboards. Yeah, now, sure. But back then, I just trusted the contractor, and his boss. We passed inspection after the new floorboards were put in, so I trusted the inspector, too.

What else do I remember from that time?

Oh, well, there *was* one more thing. After we got the kitchen floors finished and the kitchen certification process done, we got a call from Archie one night while we were celebrating our new celebrity VIP dinner gig. It was going to cover our mortgage payments for the next 6 months, and Daniel and I were so relieved, and drunk, we were dancing around the apartment with our music turned up loudly.

Archie said Sara had asked us not to play our music so loudly at night.

Why does that call stand out in my mind? Well, that was the first time we realized someone was actually living above us.

And we still hadn't even met Sara at that point.

CHAPTER 19
Felicity

Pickles. She turns everything around with pickles.

After that conversation overheard in the bathroom stall, Felicity goes to Sheila Bauer, the partner she works for and tells her as politely as she can, that she doesn't want to work for her anymore.

"Sheila, I feel like I'm at a crossroad in my career. I love working for you. But I also would like to work alongside you eventually. You are my inspiration in so many ways."

Sheila nods sadly. For a moment, Felicity worries that Sheila might offer to take her under her wing indefinitely, and put Felicity's name up for partner herself. That would ruin everything. It's unlikely, but it would still ruin everything. The partnership track is long and grueling. It's not an answer for Felicity's financial situation. She needs to cash out *fast*.

Sheila does nothing surprising. She simply wishes Felicity well and releases her to go hunt down work for a male partner who has more influence, clients, and credibility with the partnership committee. There is exactly one female on the partnership committee and it's not Sheila Bauer. The female partners are still one step above tokens, many more steps beneath voting members of the firm.

Sheila does interesting labor work, argues cases on appeal monthly, and spearheads the p*ro bono committee* at the firm which logs hours that each attorney at the firm does for free for marginalized groups, low income populations and heartwarming causes. The work she does wins awards and publicity for the firm, but brings in far fewer actual dollars than her colleagues down the hall. For this reason, she will always be considered less than them by the firm management, and her mentees will have rewarding work only in the internal sense.

It's been unspoken between Sheila and Felicity that a spot on Sheila's team, while impactful, will do little to advance Felicity's career. Felicity writes winning brief after winning brief, and has changed the life of wrongly incarcerated prisoners and wronged low income tenants. Yet, the partnership committee doesn't even know her name. If any of them passed her in the hall, they'd likely assume she's the secretary to someone important. Or maybe a girlfriend. One floor below, Roan woos elderly women with little to no actual legal work for 6-figure bonuses. Archie slaves for Lou, a partner with a petulant teenager's disposition, for a similar reward. Felicity wants to stay on the path she's on. But she can't afford it.

So she pretends to like pickles.

In the attorney lounge, she overhears one of the loudest and most notorious partners, Kevin Dunham, bragging about his homemade pickles. "I promise you—I could put my pickles up against anything you're eating and win hands down."

"I'll take that bet." Felicity pipes up from the coffee machine in the corner. She watches Kevin turn around and notice her for the first time. He'd been so busy selling pickles to his male comrades, he didn't even seem to notice there was anyone else in the room.

"You will, will you?"

"Absolutely. My grandfather was a second-generation farmer in Illinois. His pickles were part of my childhood. Some of my best memories, actually. We lost him a few years ago. I'd love to take a little walk down memory lane, and taste test your pickles."

Kevin cocks his head to the side and takes her in. Felicity

thinks for sure he is going to see through her and realize that every single word she's just said was one calculated lie after another. But, like Sheila, Kevin does absolutely nothing surprising.

He says, "Deal. Come to my office at noon tomorrow."

Felicity stirs her coffee and walks out of the lounge, stepping past him more closely than necessary. "Deal."

"I'm on the 23rd Floor—Room 919."

"I know where you are. See you then."

Felicity closes the door behind her. She hears the laughter and back slapping behind her in the attorney lounge which has suddenly become something akin to a teenage boys' locker room. She squashes down the disgust, mostly at herself, and readies herself for the next day. Everything she wants depends upon her readiness.

The next day, Felicity arrives in Kevin's 23rd floor office a few moments before noon. He's prepared for her arrival. Several jars of pickles are lined up on a granite counter in his office that also houses an espresso machine and a small bar. For a moment the opulence of Kevin's office threatens to distract Felicity from the task at hand. Alongside the counter is a round table with five leather seats flanking it. The table is covered with neat piles of briefs and papers and also a tray with a crystal-cut water pitcher and matching glasses.

Sheila's office is so small, there is barely room for her desk and one chair. She and Felicity rarely meet in her office as there is no work space. They barter for conference room space and sometimes leave the office for the diner next door when they can't find any other empty rooms to work out of. Kevin Dunham has more than enough room. Too much room actually.

Felicity shakes off her anger and focuses again on the pickles. The counter is lined with glass jars that have had the labels removed. She surveys them quickly, trying to guess which one might contain deli pickles and which ones are more likely home-made.

"Ok! Are you ready?" Kevin looks like a child. His eyes are wide and glassy with excitement and pride. Felicity is jealous of his naiveté for only a moment until she remembers all the allegations against him. He's no child. He's a predator. He is performing every bit as much as Felicity.

"I'm ready for my taste test." Felicity takes a step toward the counter. But Kevin puts his hand up.

"Oh no. Not so fast. This is a blind taste test." He steps toward her with a silk tie and fastens it tightly around her head and eyes, as if there's a kinky proposal and not sour cucumbers at issue between them.

With her eyes covered, Felicity feels a stab of regret and wonders if she'll be able to actually go through with her plan. But in the darkness she sees her bank balance, her mounting credit card debt and a file of "declined" messages in her inbox that have spurred her into action.

"Ok. I'm ready." Felicity puts her tongue out and waits.

Kevin puts one pickle slice after another on her tongue and Felicity makes a grand show of savoring each one. The salt and garlic cuts her tongue and makes it impossible to tell the differ-ence between any of them.

"They're all very different," she lies with feeling.

"Yes, but which is your favorite? Don't answer yet!"

Felicity starts to assume that they are all homemade. She tells herself there's no wrong answer. It takes her only a moment to realize her mis-step.

"Number 3. That's my favorite." Felicity makes the pro-nouncement boldly, with certainty. She takes the blindfold off in time to see the look on his face.

Kevin is red. Enraged.

Number 3 was the spiciest, with the most layers. The best tasting by far, but Felicity bites back all those responses and instead watches Kevin's face contort, trying to figure out the best way to fix what she did.

"I'm kidding. Obviously. Number 3 was store bought and the rest are tied for number 1. How could I possibly choose?"

Kevin looks at her levelly and then bursts out in laughter. "Oh wow, you got me there for a minute, farmer girl. You really did. Number 3 was the only one I didn't make and I'm over here, thinking, you actually picked that one? The hell?"

Felicity laughs along with him.

"I'm just glad you took the whole thing seriously," he continues. "I've been working on my pickle recipes for an entire year. Some of my partners think it's easy, but I can tell—you—you get it, kid."

"Oh, I do. Like I said. My grandfather. God rest his soul. I shouldn't say this out loud. But, your pickles are even better than any of his."

Kevin lights up then, and Felicity relaxes. Her misstep is long forgotten.

"So listen, Miss—"

"Huck. Felicity Huck."

"Right. So you're an actual attorney in this department, right? Not just some secretary or paralegal breaking into the attorney lounge."

Felicity sighs in spite of herself. "No, I'm an actual attorney, Kevin."

"Good. Because I have a case that just came in and I'm looking for a new associate to help work up the file with me. Do you have time to join the team?"

"I do, actually. A matter I was just working on for the last year was resolved. Successfully, I should add. So I have time to bill on a new case."

"Great, great. Come back here at 5 pm. We'll get started."

Felicity nods and thanks him and leaves the office. Now she'll go spend an afternoon billing on nonsense until a 5 pm meeting with Kevin Dunham. While most people are ending the day, Kevin will expect her to start her day at happy hour. He doesn't know a thing about her—her resume, her credentials, her research style. Up until 10 minutes ago, he didn't even know her name.

But he wants her to work on his new case, because she complimented his pickles.

Felicity heads to her office, closes the door and sobs with her head on her desk. Everything is going according to plan, which is both reassuring and frightening. She thinks about calling her mother in New Jersey to check in, but she knows that won't accomplish much. Without meaning to, her mother's questions will make her feel guilty and sad.

Is Manhattan everything you want it to be these days?

Are you working on anything exciting sweetheart?

Do you know how very proud I am of you?

Felicity doesn't call home. She just moves papers on her desk and waits for the witching hour to arrive. When she returns to Kevin's office, the counter is cleared of all the pickle jars, and instead two glasses of wine are poured.

"So," he smirks, as he hands her a glass. "Felicity Huck of the nice ass and good taste. You ready to get to work here?"

CHAPTER 20
Ava

Ava sat in front of her computer screen with the blinking icon in front of her. Nola had told her it was on its way. A signed letter from a litany of female associates detailing all of the complaints about the male partners and associates at Rogers Hawk.

Yes, Roan will be included in it, Nola warned her.

"Although, I should tell you, all of the names have been temporarily changed and coded for purposes of investigation. No one's name will be revealed until the lawsuit is actually filed."

The document that arrived in Ava's inbox was titled ILL-BRINGTHEDONUTSTOMORROW as if renaming the document would protect its confidentiality somehow. Ava laughed at the absurdity. She stopped laughing as soon as she opened the document.

> *We, the undersigned, are writing to report a pattern of unprofessional and at times, illegal, conduct by the male partners of the law firm, Rogers & Hawk.*
>
> *Efforts to bring these matters to the attention of the managing partners of Rogers & Hawk have been ignored and largely futile, as many of the offending male partners at issue are also managing partners. We the undersigned feel there is no choice but to air our complaints in a public forum. We are prepared to testify about all of the matters herein under oath. We are prepared to exercise any and all legal rights and remedies avail-*

able to us. The allegations against the employees of the firm include, but are not limited to:

[Partner #1: T.T.]

o This partner has engaged in a pattern of neglect and harassment toward the female associates working on matters managed by him. More than one associate reports the partner missing critical deadlines despite repeated reminders from the associates, subjecting the firm to malpractice liability. On one occasion, a female associate reports that Partner #1 cursed at her when she showed up at a client dinner to remind him that the appeal deadline was approaching at midnight that same evening, for a case they were working on. His review of the brief papers was still pending. This took place a week after she'd first given him the papers. "You have some goddamn nerve," Partner #1 said to her when she came to the dinner, and he told her to wait in his office until he returned. When he did return, at 2 am, he was intoxicated and told the female associate that he would not report quote "your malpractice of letting the appeal deadline pass" if she slept with him.

[Partner #2: K.D.]

o This partner has committed persistent and pervasive harassment based on gender and parental status, including inappropriate comments, micro aggressions, and discrimination against women and parents in the firm, including associates, paralegals, secretaries, and other support staff. On one occasion, a female associate reports that Partner #2 told her she should "consider giving up her kids for adoption" because a young associate had no hope for work life balance at this firm. And quote "nor should they."

Ava continued scrolling through the document with a sickening feeling in her gut. She knew exactly who the document was referencing—to a person. Nothing contained in the document was false. And worse, none of it was a secret. This was how the men behaved at Rogers Hawk. Unapologetically. Unabashedly.

She'd spotted it quickly when she first arrived at the firm. Walking down those plush hallways, swallowing down the disgust at every turn. The culture was sexist, old-fashioned, and misogynistic. But she'd secured something not every female associate had. She had Roan Knight. He was well thought of at the firm, and while Ava wouldn't have been comfortable actually calling herself his girlfriend while she was working at Rogers Hawk, it was seemingly understood that she belonged to Roan and mostly the male attorneys kept to themselves where Ava was concerned. They didn't hit on her overtly or keep her after hours. She kept her head down and worked long hours, but it wasn't harassment that drove her out the door into a sabbatical.

No, it was her desire to prove Roan Knight wrong. Ava wanted to prove that she wasn't just some needy girlfriend, jealous of his intellectually empty but lucrative career. She wanted to write. And she wanted to write something that wasn't a legal brief and wasn't some pretentious novel misappropriating another culture or lifestyle. She wanted to write something that would put Writer Friend and Tully Cross in their rightful place—on the periphery of Roan Knight's life.

Of course, Jason McKoy was also in her head more often than she liked to admit these days. She wanted to write for Jason, too. Not to spite him, or prove him wrong. Jason had never been anything but supportive of her back then. Ava wanted to make him proud, even though he'd probably never read a word she wrote outside Rogers Hawk.

Ava scanned the document nodding and wincing, wondering if Nola was wrong and maybe there were no real allegations against Roan in the document. Hope was lost as Ava neared the end of the document and spotted a paragraph titled:

[Partner #18 R.K.]
This Partner engages in a pattern of predatory behavior

toward clients and female associates alike. Demanding sexual and/or monetary favors. On one occasion, a female client reports that Partner #18 insisted they get adjoining hotel rooms while traveling together on a business trip as he was concerned about her safety. She had confided in him that she had just been through a hostile divorce and her ex-husband had threatened her. The client thought the request for adjoining rooms was innocent and indeed well intentioned until Partner #18 showed up in her hotel room at 3 am, intoxicated and nude from the waist down, demanding sexual favors which she declined and instead called hotel security to come escort him from her room.

Ava looked away from the screen, the words swimming due to tears streaming down her face. How could Roan behave this way? How could she be so wrong about him? And who was this client? Who reported him? She turned back to the screen forcing herself to keep reading and gasped as she saw the next section. It was the only thing that could have made her madder than the section about the Partner RK.

[Paralegal #1 J.M.]

This paralegal has engaged in a repeated pattern of harassment and sexual discrimination, refusing to work for any male associates, insisting on working only with new female associates and leveraging his long time tenure with the firm, and connection to many senior influential partners, and even up and coming senior associates named herein, to entice female associates to trade advancement opportunities at the firm for sexual favors. One associate reports that she overheard JM telling a male colleague that he'd once fallen in love with a female lawyer who broke his heart. Another reported that when she asked JM why he treats female associates he works with like commodities, JM told her "Sorry babe. I can't be who you want me to be."

It was the veiled reference to Jason McKoy and to their relationship that sent Ava over the edge. Worse than reading what she already suspected to be true about Roan Knight, the thought that Jason felt betrayed by her and channeled that betrayal into a career of manipulation made Ava guilty, angry and frustrated. Ava headed to the bathroom to be sick. And later, with a warm washcloth on her forehead and trembling hands, she texted Nola.

Ok. I read the document. How can I help?

CHAPTER 21
Sara

Saturday mornings are quiet at Easy Street.

Holly and Daniel have most of their catering gigs on the weekends and they leave early, with equipment and trays clattering in the early morning hours. I'm always up already. It's not the noise that wakes me. It's not even the noise that bothers me. It's the loud silence that follows after they leave, that I hate.

There's still ongoing construction in the other units and so no one else has moved in, but there are no construction workers in the building on Saturday mornings. On Saturdays, I have the place largely to myself. I loved that fact until I didn't.

One day I was standing at the windows looking down at the river, when I noticed a bunch of paddle boarders lying on their boards in the river, floating and rocking, moving into awkward positions of child's poses to downward dog to crocodile and back to child's pose again. I didn't intend to join them but suddenly I was walking down the back steps of the building onto Easy Street and down to the nearby pier. There was a sign announcing that the next stand-up paddleboard yoga class would start in 30 minutes. It was a warm autumn morning, and as I stood by the river, I realized I could not be sure how many more of these classes they would hold, and how many I'd want to join—before next summer. And next summer could be too late. I knew that even then.

"Can I join?" I asked the woman standing there with a clipboard near the sign. She held up a flyer with a QR code and tapped it with a long fingernail. "Go online. Sign the waiver. There are still two spots left."

"I only need one," I nodded as I logged onto my phone earnestly.

"Yes, I see that," she laughed. And I laughed too just to make sure she liked me and let me into the class.

Thirty minutes later I was stretching and bending and following the instructions of our perky SUP yoga instructor because suddenly I wanted nothing other than to float on the river and what was it she said again? Oh yes, "connect with my body and the water and the sky above me."

On the water, on that paddleboard, I could see Easy Street looming above me. And I can't lie, it looked different from that vantage point. It looked ominous. It was harder to forget what had happened there to Agnes when I looked at Easy Street from the water, towering over me, with its blood-stained floors and underground secrets. From inside Easy Street, I'd started to feel cocooned. In a sanctuary of sorts. I felt close to my grandmother from that unit up there in the sky. But from the water, and that paddleboard, looking up at 724 Easy Street, well, it looked like death and destruction. I kept up with those stand-up paddleboard classes for the next few weeks until it turned too cold to be on the water anymore. And it was on that board, staring up at 724 Easy Street, that I started to hatch a plan.

To destroy everything.

CHAPTER 22

Ava

"Good riddance."

"Holly!"

"I'm sorry, Ava. But I am compelled to remind you that Roan Knight? He's kind of an asshole."

It had been a week since Ava called Roan in the Hamptons and told him that when he came back she'd be gone.

"Don't be ridiculous, Ava," was his first response. "Are you really that jealous of Tully Cross? We're moving into Easy Street in just a few months. You and I. Have you forgotten?"

Ava didn't mention that she knew about the pending lawsuit. Nola told her that the named defendants already know about the suit. The court approved Nola's motion to file the initial pleadings under seal to protect the identities of the women making the claims. Hence there had been no publicity to date. No big *New York Times* front page story just yet. But the order was only for 30 days to give the parties a chance to resolve the claims before escalating everything.

Nola had warned Ava. "You and I both know, Ava, that this is not going away in 30 days. You're going to have to pick a side. And soon."

Ava picked herself. And now she was camped out on the sofa in Holly and Daniel's Easy Street unit while renovations continued upstairs on a unit she was no longer sure what to do with. She and Roan had the good sense to sign a contract outlining their ownership rights in the unit. They'd both put up half of the down payment but the contract gave each of them the right of first refusal to buy out the other one's interest in the unit. Either party could also force a sale if the other was unable or unwilling to buy out the interest. Should it come to that.

Ava was wondering if it had indeed come to that.

According to Nola, the firm had advised each of the defendants to hire their own counsel to supplement the defense the firm was putting together on their behalf. This was going to be expensive for everyone. Ava suspected that Roan would need to mortgage his share of the unit to get out of this thing alive, and she wasn't about to agree to that.

Ava hadn't told Holly and Daniel what she knew about the lawsuit yet. All she had admitted so far was that she and Roan were breaking up.

Holly looked at her sadly when she said that, as if there wasn't really much to break, and then, "God, really. He's such an asshole."

Ava looked over at Daniel, thinking maybe she could form some sort of alliance with him simply because he was a man and Holly was bashing another man, but Daniel met Ava's pleading glance over his coffee and shrugged. "She's right, Ava."

Come to think of it, Ava thought. Daniel never really did like the attorneys Holly used to work with. Ava wasn't sure he even liked *her* before she took her sabbatical.

With a laugh, that turned to a cry, and then a snort, Ava conceded that Holly and Daniel were both right. "I know. But he was my asshole." She wiped her nose on the sleeve of her tee shirt while holding out her plate to Holly for seconds and Holly heaped another large helping of macaroni and cheeseless cheese onto Ava's plate.

Ava had been nursing her wounds for the last week or so since she'd read the document Nola sent her. She was still raw and bruised and sad. But she was also hungry. Ava interrupted her grieving to lean back in her chair and sigh loudly with her mouth full.

"Holly, are you really telling me this is gluten free?"

"Indeed, Girlfriend. And dairy free and animal free and ..."

"Ok, ok, shut up please. I want to enjoy it. Stop trying to give me reasons to hate it."

"Alexa, Play Breakup Playlist," Holly commanded

The Bluetooth speaker came to life with Kelly Clarkson's *Happier Than Ever.*

Ava smiled, "Oh that's a good one."

"Yep, just added that one for you."

Ava continued spooning the delicious food into her mouth and glanced over her shoulder out the window toward the river below. The river was a large part of the draw of this town and a big part of the value of the building, she knew. With the promise of outdoor activity and Zen reflection, the river lured attorneys from their fluorescent-lit offices in Manhattan to set up home bases in Riversedge. Of course, it wasn't lawyers who ended up enjoying the river. They were too busy working, too busy billing countless hours to afford the lifestyle they couldn't even enjoy. The river? It was mostly filled with tourists. People who believed the hype about Riversedge from the outside looking in.

Or lawyers who'd taken a sabbatical. Lawyers who knew the truth about what really went on inside those hallowed law firm halls.

"God, it's absolutely gorgeous. Do you guys love being here?"

Ava turned back to the happy couple doing their cooking dance in the loft's state of the art kitchen.

"We do. I mean look at this view," Daniel pointed at Holly as he said it and she laughed and leaned over to wipe something from his cheek and then kissed the spot instead. "Very funny, you cornball you."

Ava thought of something then.

"Hey. How are you feeling, Holly?" Ava knew Holly had had a lot of ups and downs since her autoimmune diagnosis. She'd only just started talking about it recently, as her symptoms seemed to have become noticeable for the first time since she and Daniel moved into Easy Street ahead of the group. Rashes and fatigue and mild tremors were pretty apparent to everyone. Holly admitted to Ava that she'd hoped to keep it a secret for longer given the sensitivity of the diagnosis and the infancy of the business. But her body had other plans.

Holly's face clouded a bit at Ava's question. "Eh. Good days and bad. I'm looking into some experimental treatments and really trying to approach the whole thing holistically. I'm still just so embarrassed to be in ill health when my whole business hinges on the promise of health and well being for our clients."

"Holly. Come on. No one will think any less of you because of your diagnosis," Ava reassured.

"Exactly what I keep saying. Especially if you keep cooking like this," Daniel smiled across the kitchen at Holly.

Ava grinned warmly, watching the two banter and joke, grateful that the mood had been restored. She left her seat and walked over to the window staring below at the busy river. Boaters and kayakers and paddle boarders littered the scene below like colorful confetti. Ava wiped a tear away as she watched the happy sight below while avoiding the happiness behind her. She was reluctant to admit, she was just a little jealous of Holly finding a nearly instantaneous commitment from Daniel that had eluded Ava for the entire two years she'd been with Roan.

Holly and Daniel had met a little more than a year ago and started a business and bought a place together and there was no denying they were a sure thing.

After all, Daniel wasn't about to be named in any high-profile sexual harassment claim.

Even as Roan and Ava had decided to purchase the Easy Street unit together, it was more transactional than romantic, as they signed a notarized agreement detailing the terms of the partnership. A partnership that was now, for all intents and purposes, over.

Ava shook off the sadness and dread and decided to try something else out on Holly and Daniel. Something likely more shocking than the fact that Ava and Roan were breaking up.

"So I have some other big news. I got a job."

"Really? Is it a legal job?" Holly looked up from a cutting board with something that looked like genuine surprise.

"It's not. I meant it when I said I wanted to take a real break from the law. I'm going to be writing an actual book."

Ava was disappointed at the confused expression on Holly's face. "You are?" she asked.

"Well, I've always wanted to write a great book."

"That's your job? I mean, doesn't it take a while to write a book? And then, don't you have to find an agent, and sell the rights? All that stuff?"

Ava sighed. She hadn't counted on all this skepticism from Holly, although she couldn't deny it was completely warranted. That was exactly what *would* be required if she was going about this from scratch. But she wasn't.

At her most recent meeting with Nola, Nola had told her exactly how she could help the cause. It was kind of brilliant, actually. A creative, out-of-the-box idea actually. It was no wonder Nola was so respected in the Manhattan and Riversedge legal communities. And so feared.

"Well, here's the thing. I'm going to be a ghostwriter. It's a great way to get my foot in the door of the publishing world, which apparently, is almost as hard a nut to crack as the Riversedge Law community."

"Really?" It was Daniel who responded with the most interest to the news.

"So are you ghostwriting for some big celebrity or something?"

"Not exactly. It's the story of a woman who wants to tell her story about how she was sexually harassed by her own lawyer. She's actually going to be filing a lawsuit making some pretty outrageous accusations. She has a book deal already but the publisher is insisting she get a ghostwriter because she can't seem to string two sentences together. Plus she's trying to preserve her anonymity given the pending lawsuit, so we're going out under a pen name. Nola Dyer re-negotiated the whole deal to include me. I'm getting a modest advance and the book deal is already inked."

Holly looked at Ava with her brows knitted. The ghost of lawyers past came out as a string of warnings suddenly. "Ava, what are you up to? How can you work on a memoir while there's a pending lawsuit and still preserve everyone's anonymity? Seems like a pretty difficult line to dance, no? And how can you be sure it's a true story if it's not yours? You're at risk for defamation claims just working on the memoir. Are you making everyone sign the appropriate waivers?"

"Oh, that's the thing. We're not writing a memoir. We're writing a scathing novel. Only it's based on all real events. No one can sue us for defamation as the book will be shelved as fiction. Just because it's fiction of course doesn't mean it's not true."

"Hunh." Daniel looked a little confused. Holly looked less so. As she scooped more dinner onto Ava's plate she said, "Just you be careful, Ava. I don't want to see you get out of one bad situation—Roan Knight—and smack dab into another one."

Ava nodded. She knew exactly what Holly was experiencing right now because Ava had felt the same feelings sitting across from Nola Dyer listening to the terms of the agreement. Nola had actually brought the ghostwriting contract to lunch and slid it across the table over round two of crab cakes and sauvignon blanc.

When will I meet with your client to discuss the book?

You won't. Nola replied. *She demands complete and utter anonymity. I'll provide you with her sworn statements and her redacted deposition testimony and you can take it from there.*

But how will I handle it if I have questions?

You'll make up the answers.

Make up the answers? But—

Ava, this is a novel you're writing. The farther you are from the source of the story, the better for all concerned. The key is that a press release will issue about a debut novel by an unknown author with this exact premise and it will come out at the same time news about the pending lawsuit against Rogers Hawk hits the New York Times.

While the wheels of justice are turning oh so slowly in the Manhattan courts, the court of public opinion will be racing to judgments of its own. There will be pressure on the firm to act reasonably. To settle. To commit an act of speedy justice.

So, I really do have creative license to write what I want?

Absolutely. You'll have the book pitch that was accepted by the acquisitions editor and the early drafts written by my client. Be forewarned. They are garbage.

You'll sign this agreement including its Non-disclosure clause. You will receive the entire advance up front, and a generous share of the royalties when and if the book is published.

If?

Purely a technicality, of course. The nature of this publishing business is even less predictable than the law. I need to say "if" but the reality is you get the advance no matter what. It's guaranteed payment despite what happens to the book. Even if you don't finish it.

Well, of course I'll finish it.

No, no, of course you will. So what do you say, Ava? Are you ready to sign? Time is of the essence here.

Will your client know it's me? That I'm the ghostwriter?

Indeed, she asked for you, specifically.

Ava knows exactly what Holly is feeling and why she's so skeptical. Ava is as well. But this feels like a sure-fire way to get her foot in the publishing door, and the advance will pay the next few months' mortgage while she figures out what to do next. Professionally *and* personally.

"All right. New subject. Tell me again that this is all healthy—are you sure?" Ava changed the subject and then ate the rest of her dairy free dinner in silence as Holly and Daniel continued to insist that their food was completely healthy despite how good it tasted. When Ava finished, she looked down at her empty plate, and then back again at Holly and Daniel, and all she could think was, *It's still really hard for me to tell the difference between what is good for me and what is absolutely not.*

CHAPTER 23

Holly

Well, at first I didn't really believe Archie about the asylum, to be honest.

Ok, let me back up. It took about two months to get all the inspections we needed for the commercial kitchen license, and those inspectors kept asking for access to the basement fuse boxes, but apparently, Archie was the only one with the keys, and he was being really difficult trying to coordinate with them.

Until one day, I went to his office at Rogers Hawk, and I said, "Archie, this is my life we're talking about. My livelihood. If I can't make money, I can't keep paying my share of the mortgage and you're making it almost impossible for me here. Something's got to give."

I remember he was sort of hemming and hawing and telling me that he'd coordinate with the contractors himself, but I pressed him. I said, "Archie, cut the—you know. Can I swear on the record? For accuracy's sake? Yes? Ok, I said, Archie, cut the bullshit."

And he said, "Holly, I want this all to go smoothly, but there's something you should know. Something everyone should know about the building."

It was all very cloak and dagger and he asked to schedule a meeting with all of us at Easy Street that very night. He sent out a group text, and everyone responded except Sara who never responded to group texts, and Roan who was apparently traveling or doing who knows what. It was right before he and Ava broke up—the first time—so I don't remember exactly where he was. I just remember that he wasn't at that group meeting. We gathered in my unit. I made appetizers. Lobster crostinis with fresh lobster meat and silken tofu substituted for the much less healthy cream cheese that a lot of people make them with. I'm telling you, when you spice the tofu, no one can tell the difference except your arteries. And since Roan wasn't there, I could serve seafood which was a pleasure. A real, literal chef's kiss moment, you know?

Sure. Sure. Stick to the facts. So it was me and Daniel, Felicity and Archie, Ava and ... that's it. No Roan. No Sara, obviously. And that's when Archie told us that the reason he was wary about letting anyone have a key to the basement area was that there was some very sensitive history for the building he had just recently learned.

"Is it about the mercury?" I blurted out. And everyone just looked at me, like I was nuts.

"What are you talking about?" Ava said.

And I said, "Well the contractors told us they found it in your unit, too. Under the floorboards. When they were doing the renovations. But they sealed it up in both of our places so we should be fine. But I'm just wondering how it got there? Was there anything in the history of the building that explains that, Archie? Broken thermometers or medical equipment or something?"

And listen, Archie looked at me for what felt like a long time. It was like he was sizing me up or something. Trying to puzzle something about what I'd just said. Everyone else was looking at me like I was crazy. So, I confess, I got embarrassed and just sort of glossed over it. I said, "Well, who knows what it was, right? I'm just telling you what the contractors told me."

So that was the end of that discussion. But I told them. That night I told them about the mercury, so no one can really say they didn't know. Not after that night.

No, I know. That's not why we're here.

Anyway, Archie deftly changed the topic. He said, "So, the thing everyone should know about this building is that I've learned that there is an underground tunnel leading away from an area in the basement. There used to be—well, apparently—an asylum next door, and this building was some kind of annex or something for patients and staff. They used to transport them via the underground tunnel. Secretly. Back and forth.

"What the heck, Archie? When were you going to tell us that bit of critical information?" That was Daniel. And this time I wasn't annoyed at him challenging Archie. I was finally getting fed up with Archie's withholding of his due diligence information myself.

I chimed in. "You've known there is an underground tunnel since you did the due diligence and you didn't bother to mention it?"

"No, I only just learned about it."

"How?"

"From Sara, actually. Her grandmother was a patient there. And here, apparently. Sara is doing some historical research on psychiatric patient treatment modalities from the 1950s and 1960s and I've promised her that we won't close off that tunnel just yet. Which is why I've kept that whole area securely locked and limited the number of people who have access to the basement area."

"Archie, we all own the building together. You can't keep things like that from us." It was Felicity who looked the most confused. She looked to be the most betrayed by the secret. The rest of us were just trying to keep up.

"No, I know. I only just found out about Agnes' history at the asylum recently, and honestly, work's been so nuts, and the renovations have been so time-consuming that I haven't been able to summon us all together like this and dole out new information. I'm sorry. It turns out that Sara is primarily interested in the building for research purposes. She's going to finish the renovations in her unit, finish her research and then sell her unit. To someone we all approve. She's signed a contract to that effect as part of her joinder to the LLC—just like the rest of us." "Something feels really off here, Archie." Daniel again that time. And I looked at him gratefully, while Archie continued on.

"Look, Sara's contribution helped bring us over the finish line to buying this place. She sold her mother's floral shop in Riversedge to come up with the cash. She's signed a contract to front her own money to finish the renovations for the top floor, and the prior sellers wouldn't budge without that final contribution. With her renovations, Roan has told me the insurance adjuster is prepared to appraise at over $5 million. Five-fold what we paid for the whole building. So, believe me, whatever Sara's motivations were for wanting in on this deal, it's all for the best. We can seal up the tunnel as soon as she finishes her research. I hope you all understand. I didn't mean to make things difficult for you, Holly and Daniel." He turned and looked me right in the eye as he made his apology and I accepted quickly.

What can I say?

Back then, I still really thought Archie meant what he said.

CHAPTER 24
Felicity

Felicity is, in a word, *confused* by the group meeting. Archie's disclosure about the underground tunnel seems to come out of nowhere. And truth be told, Felicity is getting a little annoyed about how much time Archie is spending with Sara, the mysterious co-owner of Easy Street. He is working such long hours lately, and heading across the river, checking in with Sara incessantly, spending almost no time with Felicity who is still living in Manhattan, waiting for the renovations to finish on their own Easy Street unit.

Because, Felicity? Well, she has time on her hands these days. And a lot less stress—financial and otherwise.

After one week of working for Kevin Dunham, Felicity had gone to HR to report his bad behavior. It was impressive, even for Kevin. Felicity had thought it would take a month or two to amass a list long enough to approach HR, but no. Only one week in, Felicity had a stack of offenses, most of them—unfortunately for Kevin—backed by recorded audio evidence. She played the audio for the HR director, one Monday morning. When the audio finished, the HR director looked pretty unsurprised, and even more tired.

She sighed and then said, "You want a quiet transfer, I take it? You want us to arrange for you to move departments?"

Felicity was disgusted by how casual the HR director was about the evidence, and how quickly and easily the formulaic solution rolled off her tongue.

"No. I do not want a quiet transfer. Thanks for the offer. I want to keep working on interesting cases available to me in this department. Only I want to do so after I sue Kevin Dunham and the firm in a very public lawsuit."

"Oh, Felicity. Not you too." Now Felicity's disgust morphed into realization. Someone *had* actually pressed forward with a lawsuit. Or at least had threatened to. Good for them. She'd need to act fast before Rogers & Hawk was enmeshed in litigation and any resolution for Felicity would come at the high price of delay.

"I'd be happy to settle my claims—quickly—for a reasonable sum," Felicity responded.

"What do you want?"

Felicity wrote a number down on a pad of paper and slid it across the polished desk, like she was bidding on a new car. A modest amount. Enough to pay off her mounting debt, match Archie's half of the Easy Street down payment and buy herself a new Louis Vuitton bag as well.

The HR director nodded with resignation. "Ok. Anything else?"

"Yes," Felicity had said. "I want Sheila Bauer to be added to the Partnership Committee."

So now Felicity is working with Sheila again, and is working reasonable hours at Rogers Hawk. She has some found time on her hands, and no boyfriend to spend it with. She's still got her condo. Now that she's no longer saddled with debt, it's easier to afford, and there's no real reason to sell it while their Easy Street unit is still being renovated.

Archie's bombshell revelation about the underground tunnel to an insane asylum strikes her as a little fantastical and she isn't even sure she should give it another thought. She rolls her eyes during the meeting a few times. But he dropped that name in the middle of the meeting in Holly's apartment—*Agnes*—so familiarly. As if they should all know who she is. Felicity doesn't.

She googles Agnes and Easy Street, and the cached entries are topped by one odd one.

Showing results for Agnes & East Street instead.

Felicity clicks on the top story, reading with stunned sadness. It's a story about a woman named Agnes Carson who was accused of killing her husband, Jasper Carson. Jasper, it seems. allowed psychiatrists to study his wife's brain after a particularly gruesome bout of postpartum depression. Essentially, he sold her brain to science. While she was still alive.

And then, in a plot twist no one expected, Jasper Carson ended up missing, presumed dead, with his blood streaked across the floorboards of a building at 724 East Street with some hair fibers of his frail wife mixed in with the blood. Only after Agnes was acquitted of his murder and took over ownership of the building he'd bought before he died, did she have the name of the entire street changed. To Easy Street.

Felicity scours the article and reads the quotes of the local residents recorded after the trial ended. She looks at the grainy photos of Agnes Carson and tries to make out the color of her eyes despite the black and whiteness of the pictures. There's something familiar in her face that Felicity can't quite read but it stirs her as she scrolls through the archived piece. She googles the Riversedge Asylum and determines that it was a real place.

A place of actual business until shortly after the trial when it shut down and became the subject of a lawsuit. Felicity logs onto the Riversedge court database with her Rogers Hawk credentials, and searches for legal pleadings relating to the lawsuit against the Riversedge Asylum. Much of it is redacted, and even some of it still under seal, but it seems that Agnes Carson sued the holding company that owned the Riversedge Asylum, and a Stipulation of Settlement and Dismissal was entered in the case a few years after Agnes's acquittal.

Something about the holding company's name tugs at Felicity's memory.

Riversedge Medical Solutions, LLC.

She keeps searching through the legal databases and chain of title for Easy Street and that's when she finds it. Riversedge Medical Solutions, LLC transferred ownership of Easy Street ten years earlier to a Miami-based developer.

Felicity remembers that first night she'd set foot in Easy Street. The night Archie surprised everyone by picking up the tab and bringing them into the building late at night.

He had told them, *So the building was bought by a Miami-based developer ten years ago in a short sale. The previous owner was some obscure LLC, apparently a holding company, but I can't seem to find out too much about them, other than the fact that they were in dire financial straits by the time they had to dump the property. At least one of their subsidiary companies was a medical center that went belly up after a lawsuit was filed against them. Apparently they settled the lawsuit in terms that are under seal but it must have been a big enough hit that they couldn't hold onto this property and they dumped it in the short sale. The property had been mortgaged and re-mortgaged several times over, but the bank approved the sale and the LLC sold it for less than they still owed. As far as I can tell the holding company dissolved after that.*

Felicity is confused as she sorts through the legal documents. Agnes Carson owned 724 East Street at some point because she actually petitioned to have name of the street it sat on changed.

But ten years ago, the holding company that had settled with Agnes must have owned the building or the bank would never have allowed the transfer of property to go through. How could that be? Could it be that part of the terms of her settlement with the Riversedge Asylum after their grotesque treatment of her was that they'd have to buy the building from her?

Maybe because Agnes knew exactly how saddled that building was with environmental and biochemical pollutants given the illegal medical procedures carried out there daily, she didn't want the building, but also wanted to be paid handsomely for it. Instead of selling the building on the market—a transaction that might have proven quite complicated given its history—Agnes made the building sale a condition of her lawsuit settlement.

Genius, Felicity thinks.

And yet, now, Felicity realizes, Agnes's granddaughter, Sara, has helped a group of current and former lawyers buy back the money pit decades after Agnes worked so hard to get rid of it.

As she reads and re-reads the article, Felicity's heart sinks realizing that the building they all own is home to more than mercury pools and secrets. It may very well be a burial ground as well.

Why on earth would Sara want this building back? Felicity wonders as she reads.

And what dark plans might she have for it now that she does?

CHAPTER 25

Ava

Roan was intrigued by the idea of Ava's ghostwriting contract and asked to review the terms for her. *As a favor*, he said. Ava was disappointed in herself by just how pleased she was that Roan was impressed.

They were still broken up—the first time—when he sent her a text.

Congratulations on the book deal.

Ava was staying with Holly and Daniel and she wasn't sure how he knew, but she was well aware that news traveled fast with the group.

She agreed to meet Roan for brunch at the Riversedge Law Club—ostensibly to discuss the logistics of proceeding with the Easy Street unit rather than her ghostwriting contract. Ava was pretty sure she wanted to buy out Roan's interest. The time she'd spent in Holly and Daniel's unit had been magical. The view from the building alone was worth the financial investment. She'd been checking on the status of the renovations daily and she was convinced the duplex she and Roan had bought together—located just above Holly and Daniel's, was going to be even more spacious—and more beautiful. Ava wanted to stay on Easy Street.

Ava had even ordered a few pieces of furniture for the unit that had arrived and were stored under tarps in a corner of the loft during the last stage of renovations: a bed, a sofa, and a writing desk.

She and Roan hadn't discussed the pending lawsuit. It seemed clear from his positive interest in the book that he didn't know what she was actually writing about. But Ava knew from her conversations with Nola that the legal costs for Rogers Hawk and the individually named defendants were going to be substantial. The order keeping the case filing under seal had been extended another 90 days while the parties all continued to bargain and work on a settlement. Nola did not anticipate a successful settlement at this early stage of things and had told Ava she was buckling in for a long road.

Roan was successful, and he had a comfortable savings, but Ava suspected that carrying the legal fees alongside the building costs was going to be uncomfortable for Roan. She didn't want to share her life or the unit with him any longer. If the allegations in the pleadings that she read were true, she wanted nothing to do with Roan Knight at all.

Ava felt empowered by Nola's request that she craft a story that would help vindicate all the women who had been wronged by male Rogers Hawk attorneys.

So Ava brought her confidence to that lunch meeting with Roan. She came to the Riversedge Law Club, armed with a proposal to pay Roan a monthly fee for the next two years to purchase his interest in the unit, while assuming the full mortgage immediately. She greeted the concierge with a reciprocal plastic smile. She declined an escort into the dining room.

"No," Ava said. " I know where I'm going." She pretended it was true.

Inside the Club, the meeting and all of Ava's good intentions went awry almost from hello.

First of all, Roan looked good. Too good. Being named in one of the biggest lawsuits in New York City by one of the most feared litigators hadn't dimmed his charisma one bit. In fact, he looked toned and tan and relaxed, Ava noted with surprise.

He hugged Ava on the floor of the Club dining room and she let him. As they took their seats she looked around quickly for any familiar faces but saw none. Just a blur of suits and Bloody Marys.

"Ava, you look good. Sabbatical life is treating you well."

Ava blushed and smiled. "Thanks, Roan. You do, too. Listen— let's get right to business."

She slid some papers across the table at Roan outlining her proposal but he turned them face down and reached across the table for her hand. Ava looked at her hand in his as if it didn't belong to her. The traitorous limb had settled greedily into Roan's.

The thing was, Roan had never brought Ava to the Club for anything other than a group business lunch. He'd never brought her there for a one-on-one meeting. And he'd certainly never entertained any public display of affection, showing her off for the Riversedge Law Community with any sign that she was his, and he was hers. The whole moment was unnerving, and strangely, satisfying.

There was something nagging at her brain. A warning. An admonition.

He's using you. He needs to play the role of dutiful boyfriend and solid human to survive this lawsuit.

Ava sat back in her chair, pulling her hand out of Roan's and looked around at the room again. Through the blur, her eyes locked then on a familiar face across the room, sitting at a full table with senior Rogers Hawk partners and some younger female associates Ava didn't recognize. Jason McKoy was sipping a tall Bloody Mary and smiling at Ava.

Ava startled at the sight of him and turned her head quickly back to Roan. She leaned forward and put her hand back in his. With the other hand, she retrieved the proposal papers from the table and slid them back in her bag.

"Roan, I know about the lawsuit, and honestly, I think I can help. That's what this book project is all about."

"Oh? What do you mean?"

Ava ignored the fact that Roan didn't look the least bit surprised that she knew about the lawsuit or surprised that her book was related to the whole sordid affair either.

"I'm ghostwriting a novel that is going to be a scathing commentary on the culture of a fictional law firm that will very closely resemble Rogers Hawk. I'm working with one of the plaintiffs in the actual lawsuit. While Nola litigates the case in the courtroom, we are going to put the culture of Rogers Hawk on trial in the court of public opinion."

"Funny. Sort of biting the hand that fed you don't you think, Ava? Maybe that's not the best use of your talents. And time." Roan's expression was tense.

"Well, I hate to remind you, but they're not feeding me anymore. The generous advance I was paid on this book does."

"Is it?"

"Is it, what?"

"Generous? Is the advance actually generous? Let me take a look at the ghostwriting contract, and I'll happily give you some free legal advice."

Ava shrugged off the suggestion. "Absolutely not. I've signed a non-disclosure agreement. I can't let you look at it."

"Sounds like you've already violated that NDA just by letting everyone know you're writing the novel." Roan's smirk was infuriating.

"I have not told everyone. I've told no one!"

"Interesting. And yet, I know all about it. I wonder how many others in the room know about your defamation suit masquerading as a novel."

Ava tasted bile in the back of her throat. As much as she hated to admit it, Roan was right. She'd already violated her NDA just by telling Holly and Daniel about the book deal. Unfortunately one of them must have mentioned it casually to Roan and now, well, who could say now many people Roan had actually disclosed the fact to. She was losing control of everything. The luncheon. Her buy back proposal. Her writing contract.

Ava's litigator brain spun out of control. It felt like a roulette wheel spinning recklessly in her head with a small ball of panic jumping in and out of slots until finally the wheel slowed, and an answer emerged. It was a gamble. A risk. But she tried it anyway.

"Listen, Roan. I know you're named in the Rogers Hawk lawsuit. And I know it's all bullshit. I can make that clear in this book. This project can benefit both of us."

Roan's face relaxed.

"Hunh. I was just telling Tully's Writer Friend that you are finally getting the accolades you deserve. A new book deal—a generous advance. She was very impressed with you. She said the current state of publishing has not been very generous with new authors, and the fact that there is so much trust placed in you bodes well for your future. She says she can't wait to read it. I told her this is likely not the book she'd want to read of yours. I'm hoping you're going to parlay this into something much more interesting. More substantial."

Ava smirked with realization. Now she knew what he was up to. Roan had been sent here by his colleagues to talk her out of the book. Or at least talk her out of writing what she'd been contracted to write about.

It was a ploy—all of it—meant to get Ava to write a book that neither Roan nor anyone at Rogers Hawk believed would ever see the light of day. Nola seemed to understand that possibility as well.

You will receive the entire advance up front, and generous share of the royalties when and if the book is published.

If?

Purely a technicality, of course. The nature of this publishing business is even less predictable than the law. I need to say "if" but the reality is you get the advance no matter what. It's guaranteed payment despite what happens to the book. Even if you don't finish it.

All she knew was that Roan was trying to manipulate her, and intimidate her. All his old tactics. Probably the same ones he'd used on every other female client in his wake.

The server came and placed two Bloody Marys in front of Ava and Roan and asked if they were ready.

"Sure are. Two eggs benedicts. I'll have one with crabmeat." Ava responded for both of them.

"Great," Roan laughed. "Guess you're trying to kill me with shellfish. Just bacon on mine, thanks."

Two can play at this game, Roan Knight.

"I'm writing this book, Roan. But I'll protect you in it. And in return, you protect me from the Rogers Hawk patriarchy. Tell them there's nothing to fear here. Just a lot of drivel from a no-name author. Keep them out of my hair. I'm telling you, Roan. Rogers Hawk is not going to come out of any of this unscathed—but if you do, you can still have a legal career in this city. Let's work together here."

There was a pause long enough to make Ava question her confidence. And then.

"Sure, Ava. After all, it's us, baby, right?" Roan said with a nod and a smile.

The two of them lifted their drinks in the air and toasted. Ava looked over at Jason and caught his eye again.

I can't be who you want me to be.

Ava took a generous gulp of her drink and let the warm quick buzz rush through her.

Roan and I are both on the same page, Ava thought. *He's not pretending to be anything other than what he is. And neither am I. That's why we work. Roan Knight is nothing like Jason McKoy. That will all be made clear in this book.*

After all, just because it's fiction doesn't mean it's not true.

CHAPTER 26

Felicity

"Felicity. Don't take this the wrong way. But I can tell you're distracted by something."

Sheila and Felicity are working out of a conference room next door to Sheila's new office. It's not that they can't fit in there anymore. Sheila's new office is enormous. A wall has been knocked down to expand two offices into one. It's the renovations that keep the women out for now. But only temporarily. When the construction is done, they plan to work on a new glass-topped conference table that has been ordered for the space.

Since Felicity's quick settlement, all hell has broken loose at the firm. Felicity is well aware there is a pending lawsuit still under seal against the firm. Nola Dyer has contacted her at least a dozen times to enlist her help, but Felicity has told her the same thing over and over again. She's not interested. She signed a waiver when she got her generous settlement check. She's not bringing any more claims against Rogers Hawk. She and Sheila are going to make a name for themselves that has nothing to do with suing the men they are smarter than and more talented than.

The best revenge is doing well, Felicity's mother always told her when she was young, bullied mercilessly by the pert, pony-tailed classmates whose resumes included field hockey all-team accolades and bedding football captains and very little actual studying. Felicity's lean resume included valedictorian status, a medical leave of absence from high school, and not much else, but her mother always swore she'd come out on top. Felicity is determined to finally prove her mother right.

Still, Sheila's correct. Felicity *has* been distracted. The story about Agnes Carson has kept her up at night. She can't stop thinking about the woman whose husband sold her brain. It's not the murder—alleged or no—that keeps Felicity up at night. It's not the sealed settlement and the clever resolution that seemed to involve the holding company taking ownership of a building with demons and pollutants and biohazards in its every floorboard.

No, it's the scary written accounts of Agnes's postpartum depression in that one cached article of the murder trial that has Felicity reeling.

All these years later, Felicity feels the tug of depression threaten to unravel her, just under her skin. She barely survived it the last time. All told, it was brief. It lasted maybe a month or two, but it was consuming. And Felicity couldn't tell a soul besides her mother, because Marilyn Huck was the only one who knew the cause.

Something is wrong with me. Felicity would show up at her mother's bedside in the dark of night at all hours. *I'm not going to survive the night.*

Her mother, Marilyn, sat up with her. Night after night. They talked and laughed and played board games. It was almost summertime. Felicity was on an extended medical leave, and finishing up her junior year virtually. Felicity couldn't imagine actually going back to school at that time. Her mother told her eventually she'd be ready and sure enough, gradually it subsided. The wiring in her brain shifted and settled and by the end of summer, she and her mother were sleeping in separate rooms again and Felicity was starting to look forward to school again. To fresh starts and new beginnings.

Felicity didn't have a name for it at the time. She just thought she was crazy and experiencing something unique.

But reading Agnes's story has helped her realize.

The depression she suffered that spring wasn't unique or imagined. It was chemical. And Felicity is distracted by the thought of this poor woman, named Agnes Carson, without a mother to stay up with her night after night during that difficult time.

"What do you need, Felicity?" Sheila asks gently, with meaning.

"One day. Just one day. Let me have the day tomorrow. I'll drive to the beach. Put my toes in the water. I will come back recharged. I promise. I just need one mental health day, Sheila."

"Of course, Felicity. That sounds like a great idea. Get out of here. I'll see you on Thursday."

Felicity doesn't even tell Archie where she's going. Every day, he comes home to the Manhattan condo after she's asleep and leaves again before she wakes. She pulls the car out of the Manhattan parking garage where it sits most of the year for a ridiculously high rental fee just in case someone needs a ride out of the New York area, which no one ever does.

Except today.

Felicity heads south to a place she used to go as a child and a teenager. A place she and her single mother used to travel together from their suburban New Jersey neighborhood, long before Felicity was a New York lawyer. Long before she was the co-owner of an apartment on Easy Street.

When she parks the car at a lot near the boardwalk, and steps out, the air is warm and familiar, and Felicity starts to regret this trip almost before it begins. In fact, as she walks to the boardwalk, she notices all the closed-for-the season signs and realizes this might be an even quicker trip than she hoped. She hasn't given much thought to the fact that the boardwalk is closed most of the year. She hasn't given much thought to this place at all since that summer.

Felicity shields her eyes and squints when she sees it.

Open.

There is one and only one window with a blinking open sign. Next to the closed ice cream shops and hermit crab shops. Sandwiched between the non-moving ferris wheel and the closed-for-the-season summer boutique, Felicity sees a single beckoning, blinking sign.

She walks toward it and then through it as if hypnotized. On the other side of the door, a dark-haired woman sits behind a table covered in a velvet tapestry of moons and stars. The woman puts down a vape cartridge and looks levelly at Felicity as she walks in. Her eyes are piercing although her expression is almost bored—but as she stares at Felicity, something else emerges.

Is it recognition, Felicity wonders?

Felicity measures the distance between herself and the woman in ounces of courage and worries that the distance is too long, as she walks to the tapestry-covered table anyway while the woman addresses her. "You've been here before, yes?"

Felicity nods. "A long time ago. When I was a -"

Felicity stops before she says "child." That summer she was only 16, but she was not a child. She can't believe the tarot reader is still there. She would have assumed that the boardwalk tarot readers turn over faster than fast food line chefs. She's not sure she would have come back to this spot if she'd known that this place was still here. Still open. Still changing people's lives.

The woman, who Felicity knows is named Raven, because Felicity had asked her all those years ago, starts turning over cards as Felicity sits down. "Full deck or half deck?"

Felicity looks over at the wall where prices are printed in large block letters.

Full deck read for $60. Cash.

The prices have changed, even if very little else has.

Felicity pulls out her wallet and counts out three bills. "Full, please."

Raven doesn't stop turning cards to take the money. She just brushes the bills off to the side. "You have made a very big transition. A very brave transition. Is this correct?"

Felicity looks down at the cards, with eyes stinging. *Which transition is Raven talking about*, she wonders. *The settlement with Rogers Hawk? Buying the Easy Street unit? Which one?*

Maybe she's not even talking about a recent transition? Maybe she's talking about that decision made all those years ago after a summer spent right here in this place?

Felicity doesn't know, but she wants Raven to keep going so she nods. She keeps nodding as Raven points to cards and narrates to Felicity.

"There was someone. Who cared only about himself."

Felicity looks up briefly, suddenly, but when she catches Raven's eyes, she shivers and looks back down at the card Raven is pointing to—the King of Swords.

"You trusted him. And then he left. But he gave you a gift. A great gift. And you are finding your own way now. And so is she. All is well."

Felicity looks up at Raven now with confidence. She knows exactly who she's talking about. She nods tearfully.

Raven turns over more cards. "You have more chapters to write. You are finding your voice. Don't be silenced now."

Felicity's eyes pool over then with tears, seen and heard. She thanks Raven and turns to walk out quickly. Not unlike the first time she had her cards read. When she was 16. At that time, Raven told her that summer would change her life.

Raven was right when she was 16, and her words feel equally right now.

Just before Felicity walks out the door, Raven calls out to her. "One more thing. You should know before you go back."

"What's that?"

"You think there are two. But there's only one."

CHAPTER 27
Sara

The underground corridor below Easy Street is cold and dank. Exactly what you'd expect it to look and feel like. Only worse. My grandmother's journal does not even do it justice. Every morning and evening these days I go down to the basement and travel back and forth, underground and on foot, picturing Agnes' journey. Reliving it as a memorial to her pain, of sorts.

According to the notes and what I've pieced together by researching the legal papers that I've been able to get my hands on despite the sealing order, there was a private hospital across the street from what was then 724 East Street. The hospital, which was owned by a holding company—Riversedge Medical Solutions LLC—and which appeared to be a for-profit enterprise, was engaged in some rather unorthodox medical treatments for its wealthy psychiatric patients, shock treatments among them.

According to my grandmother's notes, scribbled in the margins of her recipes and weather clippings, she had been a guinea pig for the hospital. A beta tester of the newest procedures and protocols and equipment that were not sanctioned by any professional board or true medical professional.

As Agnes was struggling with postpartum depression, my grandfather, Jasper, who had been a contractor, working at the hospital, saw an opportunity. He authorized the hospital to conduct whatever tests necessary on her. But rather than pay them, he'd accepted large checks from the hospital for the use of his wife's brain—and his silence. When some staffers at the hospital got wind of the experimental treatments and threatened to expose the questionable medical practices, Jasper Carson coordinated the creation of an underground tunnel from the hospital to 724 East Street, an investment property he'd just recently purchased to renovate, with his budding wealth. The former welder's son had married into high society and he intended to use that investment, at a high cost to everyone involved.

Later, after the trial, the Riversedge Asylum had been razed, too expensive for anyone to maintain, a crumbling eyesore until the holding company detonated it two decades ago.

724 East Street—now 724 Easy Street—is the only structure that exists on the small half street once owned by Jasper and then Agnes before she sold it in a blood-letting deal with Riversedge Medical Solutions. No one knew what to do with that building. And so it sat. Until now.

But I know exactly what to do with this building.

In the corridor below 724 Easy Street, I put my hands along the walls and close my eyes. I picture my grandmother on a gurney being wheeled out of the hospital that was really a residential facility as described by Agnes, rather than a place of legitimate treatments. Riversedge Asylum was a home for psychiatric patients transported from wealthy neighborhoods all over New York where their families wanted little to do with their treatment, or, what they perceived as the embarrassing nature of their various conditions.

Relatives of dignitaries and politicians and other of New York elite were all brought here to be hidden, rather than treated. Among these patients was one Agnes Carson, placed by her husband with her wealthy family's consent because she had dared violate one of the most revered tenets of her socialite family. She failed to embrace motherhood with a zeal and unfettered enthusiasm. Instead, Agnes was riddled with fears and insecurities, and yes, depression, at her new status following the birth of her only child, my mother, Delilah.

I close my eyes and hear the ghostly echoes of the hospital traveling through space and time. I can make out the patient's yells, the staff's loud retorts. It's as if I was there, even though of course I wasn't. No matter. I can feel Agnes's pain as if it is my own.

How dare they treat you like that, Agnes! I whisper in the darkness.

They had treated her like a bowl of moldy leftovers perched on a refrigerator shelf. Standing back, shaking their heads, declaring Agnes' shelf life over, and tossing her out on garbage day.

In her journal she describes the shock of quiet when arriving underground to 724 East Street. Even though she hated the trip, she relished the peace, short-lived though it was.

I close my eyes and try to picture quiet, but Holly and Daniel are so damn loud I can hear them even now, through the vents and grates and pipes of this old building. Their voices travel and disrupt my morning as they do so often these days. Soon all the units will be complete and the whole building will be filled with noise and people and I won't have even a moment's peace to myself.

I already hate that time in the future.

It's so frustrating that I couldn't afford to just buy the building myself and enjoy its majesty all to myself before destroying it. But I couldn't, so I had to let all these hangers-on come aboard as well, and it's just so damn unfortunate.

These are the thoughts plaguing me as I start the ascent to my top floor duplex. I climb the steps as quietly as I can because I don't want Holly and Daniel to come out and surprise me or spot me. I just want peace which is getting harder and harder to find these days. My breath comes fast and hard as I climb the steps. I try to summon my SUP yoga breathing techniques to regain equilibrium, but by the time I reach the top floor, I am out of breath. Inside, I stand by the window gasping, sucking in air rapidly, bent over, trying to settle myself.

My grandmother's journal is splayed open on a coffee table next to a small sofa in the living room of the loft. The loft is barely furnished, but I don't anticipate buying any more pieces. *This is enough*, I think, as I look around the space.

I sit on the floor by the coffee table and flip the pages of the journal back and forth. I notice something new—still—every time I look at this book.

Today, the something new is acutely painful. I read my grandmother's writings about my mother and how she watched for symptoms of postpartum depression herself.

Her pregnancy was fairly uneventful. I watched her closely. But after her son was born, I watched her mood grow a bit gloomy. I was worried.

A son? I read the line again and again. I turn the page, but there's nothing more to read. Just another Yeats poem excerpted. My grandmother's ramblings are almost impossible to decipher, which is why I must have missed this short statement sandwiched between other clippings.

After her son was born ...

What is she talking about? What son? A brother?

And then I remember.

I hate this moment of recollection disrupting my memories of my grandmother. Disrupting my peace. My calm. I wonder if it was like this for her, each time the effects of the shock treatment wore off. When she'd be abruptly summoned back to the world around her.

Like the end of a yoga class, when all focus inside turns again outside.

Namaste.

I close the leather-bound book, and I look down at my grandmother's scrawled writing and then I throw the book across the room with violent anger at the reminder. That goddamn daily reminder—that this book wasn't given to me at all.

It wasn't meant for me at all.

The name on the post-it note still taped with aging, browning tape all these years later, does *not* read Sara.

It reads ***Archie.***

PART II

CHAPTER 28
Ava

After the Bloody Mary toast at the Riversedge Law Club, Ava moved back into Roan's Manhattan condo to wait out the last few months of the Easy Street renovations.

Holly's expression was all disappointment as she hugged Ava goodbye.

"Aw, come on. I thought you'd be thrilled to get rid of your deadbeat houseguest," Ava joked.

"No way. I'm losing a roommate and a beta food tester." Holly winked. "Listen, you know how I feel about him. I think I made that clear. He's an asshole, and if it comes out in the sexual harassment lawsuit that he did terrible things, I mean, I'm really going to have a hard time having him live upstairs—"

"One step at a time, girlfriend," Ava interrupted Holly. News of the lawsuit had broken recently, and Ava had confided more of the details to her. Of the lawsuit and the book deal. Now, Ava worried that she'd told Holly way too much.

"The lawsuit is filled with nonsense. You and I both know Roan is a lot of things, but he isn't *that guy*. Nola Dyer is taking advantage of a moment in time to help some women make accusations they never even mentioned to anyone before."

"Ava, stop. You can't honestly believe that it's *all* nonsense."

"No, of course not. We all know there was plenty of bad behavior at Rogers Hawk when we were there, but Roan? He's not sleeping around. He's just, you know, charming."

Holly laughed, "Don't I know it." Ava startled, and Holly seemed equally surprised at her own words. She recovered quickly. "Listen. I just don't want you to get hurt. And this book you're working on that Nola Dyer negotiated the advance on? It just feels like there are so many conflicts and red flags, but, you're a big girl, and I trust you'll do what's best for you ultimately. I can't wait for you to move back to Easy Street. How long do you think until the unit is ready upstairs?"

Ava shrugged. "They say 4 weeks, so I figure 8. Roan set up a writing space in his condo, so I'm going to push ahead and really try to get some work done. By the time we move in, I want to be focusing on decorating and getting ready for a grand book launch ... where no one will really know I'm the author." Both women laughed and hugged some more and then Ava headed outside to her Uber on the curb.

But as she left, she couldn't stop wondering what Holly had meant when she agreed that Roan Knight was charming.

A few weeks later, Roan delivered the news to Ava that the unit renovations were finished ahead of schedule. With a yelp.

Well specifically, the *yelp* came from a small French bulldog that leapt out of his arms as he arrived home after dark. Ava was sitting in her writing nook, toiling over a chapter about the fictional firm's one paralegal named in the sexual harassment lawsuit. She was working hard to craft the right tone between villain and archenemy when Roan came in loudly and enthusiastically, crashing the door open with one leg, his arms burdened with a furry bundle.

"Good news! Move in date is a week from tomorrow!"

The bulldog ran right to Ava like he'd been trained to do so, reaching up to her lap with his front legs and waving his bum back and forth with delight as he danced on his hind legs and slobbered all over Ava.

"Oh my goodness, who are you?" Ava laughed as she picked up the slobbering dog and let him lick her clean.

"That. Is Ruby," Roan announced dramatically.

"Well, hello Ruby. And who do you belong to? Are we dog-sitting for the week?"

It wasn't unheard of for Roan to bring home a creature every now and then. He often did favors for his wealthy clients who were traveling with last-minute notice and no suitable dog sitter in town. Ava had gotten to know most of them over the years. A white French poodle named Snowflake who preferred eating toilet paper to actual food. A tan labradoodle named Cocoa who could only eat a special diet of raw meat and chicken heads. An English bulldog named Mac who had to wear diapers in the house.

"Ruby belongs to us."

"To us? Really, Roan?" Ava tried to catch up to Roan's exuberance. It wasn't hard. She'd tried to talk Roan into getting a dog many times over the last two years, but his responses were always the same.

We work too many long hours, Ava.

We travel too much.

Too much work.

Too much mess.

"What made you change your mind?"

"Well, one of my clients needed to re-home this puppy because she just moved into a no-pets-allowed building, and she was simply devastated at the idea of strangers taking Ruby. She insists that you and I are not strangers, even though she doesn't know you and has only met me twice."

Ava laughed and nuzzled the bulldog to her chin.

"Well, welcome, Ruby. How would you like to help me write my next chapter? Maybe I'll add a puppy named Ruby to the mix?"

CHAPTER 29
Holly

Well, yes, as we know now, the mercury was only one of the various hidden surprises—environmental and otherwise—at Easy Street.

Within a few months of moving in, I was in terrible health. I'd been diagnosed with an autoimmune disorder before moving into Easy Street, but living there seemed to exacerbate things almost beyond control. I was taking cocktails of anti-inflammatory drugs and pain relievers every night. I was eating the most stripped-down diet I could muster. No dairy. No meat. No sugar. No preservatives. No matter. My body was still betraying me every chance it got. I was covered in rashes most days and suffering from almost weekly migraines that were debilitating.

Of course I know now that the building itself was trying to kill me, but at the time—well, I was so discouraged about my health, I couldn't think straight.

Every day was a new finding. For example, it was about a week before Roan and Ava moved in that I found the black mold in the back of my pantry. I'm not sure why I hadn't noticed it before. I guess the fresh paint sort of disguised it but I was rooting around looking for some new boxes of spices I'd stashed back there when all of a sudden, I saw the black splotches along the back wall crawling upward to the ceiling and beyond.

I was still standing there staring at it in disbelief, when I heard some loud banging above me. I marched upstairs and found the contractors cleaning up paint supplies in Ava and Roan's unit. Tarps and brushes and buckets were gathered in a corner of the room. I demanded to see the pantry in the unit. It was situated literally on top of mine, and when I looked inside, all I saw was shiny white paint. I showed them pictures of the inside of my pantry and they just nodded.

"Yep, that's what this one looked like too until an hour ago."

"Well, that's mold," I said. "You can't just paint over it and make it go away. I mean, look at my pantry. It's growing right over the new paint now."

I tapped my phone and the lead construction guy just shrugged at me. He said "Ma'am, I don't know what to tell you. But we were given a budget, and treating the mold with anything other than some cheap primer and paint? It ain't in the budget."

I was astonished. I said, "I didn't tell you to paint over it. No one even told me about the mold."

But the contractor—I think his name was, Joey, said, "Ma'am, listen. We were given a budget for each unit and we were told very clearly not to go over that budget."

So that pretty much put an end to that discussion.

Well, yes. It's true that we did each of us come up with a budget for renovations. We put the money in escrow at closing so that we could each count on the renovations getting done. At closing, Daniel and I had very little money left for renovations, so we put the smallest amount in. But, I mean, Ava and Roan put in several hundred thousand dollars. Same for Archie and Felicity. Surely, there was enough money left over for treating black mold? I texted the group and asked for a group meeting to discuss the escrow accounts. No one responded for hours, and when a response came, it was just one line:

Everything is covered. No need for a meeting. We're on budget and ahead of schedule.

That didn't relieve me so I dug up some of the closing paperwork and called the bank myself. To check on the balance of the escrow account.

And that's when I found out.

Well, that it was empty. And that it had been emptied out soon after closing.

Excuse me?

Oh Roan. Roan was the only one who had signing powers on the escrow account. Roan was the one who texted me to say everything was covered. We agreed to give the power of attorney to him when we drew up everything that night in Archie's hospital room. I mean, we were still a little drunk and emotional that night. We might have signed anything at that time. After all, no one knew what Roan was capable of back then.

I mean, I should have known. Because of my history with him.

No, I mean *mine*. Not just Ava.

Well, I guess I have to admit this—being under oath and all, but Roan and me? We were an "us" before he and Ava were. Back when I was still a newbie Rogers Hawk associate. Before I met Daniel, of course.

I swore Roan to secrecy when he started seeing Ava, even though I knew he couldn't ever keep that big mouth of his shut. She and I were friends, and I didn't want it to be uncomfortable. After I left the firm, I figured the past was the past. But as I watched Roan start to really manipulate Ava, well I started trying to warn her. And then I *really* didn't want her to know about us, because I didn't want her to just assume I was some jealous ex-girlfriend, or something.

I wasn't. Believe me, I wasn't. I was just looking out for Ava. But no matter how many times I tried to warn Ava about him, she didn't listen. Not until it was too late.

Because Roan Knight was trouble. And I wouldn't put anything past him when it came to Easy Street. Or anything else for that matter. But that doesn't mean the rest of us should be punished for his sins, of course.

CHAPTER 30
Ava

On move-in day, the drive from Manhattan over the bridge to Riversedge was 3.5 miles and 45 minutes long. Traffic was crazy that day. Ava decided to use the time though, alone with Roan, before they arrived on Easy Street, to signal a fresh start. They were about to move in together. Into *their* place. Even though they'd been staying in the same space for months while they waited for the renovations to finish. Even though they'd broken up and gotten back together since the closing. Still, this day felt like a brand-new start. Ava wanted to mark it as such.

Roan asked her how the writing was going and Ava noted warmly that he seemed genuinely interested. They danced around the topic of the lawsuit.

"It's going well. I'm really enjoying the whole process. Developing characters and inner conflict. It's so different from brief writing. By the way, how is work going, Roan? You don't talk about it as much lately. You know, since everything happened?"

"Well, obviously, I'm not supposed to talk about it. But that's not why. I don't want to burden you or worry you. We're lawyers, Ava. We're used to lawsuits. You know that. On one hand, it means absolutely nothing except an exchange of phone calls between insurance carriers and attorneys. On the other hand—"

Roan hesitated for a long while.

"On the other hand—what?"

"Well, you know, it's horrible to be defamed in any way. I've worked my ass off for that place, for those clients. To have anyone say such disgusting things about me is—you know ... frustrating. I'm glad you're setting the record straight. In your own way. I'm really glad about the book project. The lawyers that the firm hired to handle this lawsuit—well they're giving me a lot of pause, you know. They are not really inspiring all that much confidence. I guess that's the downside of the best law firm in the country hiring another firm. You're not really getting the *best*."

Traffic opened up then suddenly, and Ava looked out the window as the cars became bridge rails and in no time, they were over the bridge and Manhattan was behind them.

Ava had texted the group to let them know they were moving in that day. She got a vague response from Holly that she and Daniel wouldn't be there because they had a catering gig. Her response seemed a little curt, but Ava told herself Holly was still mad at Roan for being named in the lawsuit. She'd get over it when he was vindicated. And he *would* be vindicated. One way or the other.

Felicity and Archie both said they were working and Sara didn't respond. No surprise there. They included Sara in all the co-owner group texts even though she never responded. She kept to herself mostly. Holly said she'd still never even seen the woman.

"Walk Ruby with me," Ava pleaded to Roan as soon as they unpacked the car at Easy Street. The sound of her voice registered as a whine in her own ears, her nervousness and insecurity taking audible form. It was a big day. She stood in the middle of the loft, staring out the windows across the river and suddenly wanted only to ... get out of there.

"I can't. Too much to do," Roan said from the couch, where he lay, doing, as far as Ava could tell, nothing.

The connection and intimacy that had been brewing on the

car ride seemed a distant memory suddenly. She wondered if she'd imagined it altogether? Ava tried to swallow her own nervousness and put herself in his shoes. What must it be like to be facing down this lawsuit when he was sure he was innocent? Ava walked Ruby alone, browsing the neighborhood with fresh eyes as she did so. She'd grown up only a mile or two from the Easy Street building, but the building was in a formerly industrial area of town and so it was completely unfamiliar to her. There was a deli less than a block away and a bakery that was swathed in pink stripes two blocks away. Ava met other people walking their dogs and introduced herself and Ruby. When she returned to Easy Street, she shielded her eyes and tilted her head up to the sky. The windows were opaque from the street and hard to see through. Still, she could swear she could make out a woman standing with her back to the window at the top floor unit. Her long dark hair was visible in the silhouette.

Sara.

Well, now, I can tell Holly that I've actually seen the woman. And on my first day, no less.

Ava chuckled to herself and brought Ruby back inside. She bumped into Archie in the stairwell.

"Archie!"

"There you are! I left the office early to try to give you a hero's welcome to the building. Did you and Roan finish moving in? Have I arrived just in time for you to be finished?"

"Indeed," Ava laughed and threw her arms around him.

"Thank you, Archie. For this opportunity. It's more than I could have hoped for, as a little girl growing up in a tiny split level in this very town."

"Oh, Ava I'm thrilled. Can't wait for us all to be together. Felicity and I should be in by next week. Construction just finished today. Which reminds me. Now that the construction is all done, I'm having all the locks changed tomorrow."

"Oh! That was a good idea. I wouldn't have thought of that."

"Well, you can't be too careful. I do follow the police blotter in town. Very little crime, of course, in Riversedge, but some burglaries here and there. An open car, an unlocked basement door. You know how it is. They can be attractive to someone looking for extra cash for booze or dope. I'll bring you a new key tomorrow, but in the meantime, make sure to remember to lock all the doors, including this one." Archie pointed to the building's front door that Ava had specifically left unlocked when she went out with Ruby. The one they had all entered that first night, drunk on expensed wine and Archie's dreams.

"Of course. Thanks for the reminder, Archie."

"No doorman, Ava. We're not in Manhattan anymore." Archie smirked and headed out the front door. Ava heard the lock turn after he left and feared he'd actually locked her *in*.

She tried the lock a few times from her side, back and forth, reassuring herself that in fact, she was free to leave Easy Street any time she'd like.

Although why would we want to? Ava murmured contentedly to Ruby.

Upstairs, with Roan dozing on the couch, Ava opened her laptop at the writing desk with Ruby nestled in her lap. While she wrote, their first afternoon in the new digs flew by and Ava resisted the fear that they were settling into Easy Street as strangers rather than lovers.

At dinnertime, Roan was awake, but scrolling through TikTok videos and instagram reels loudly from the sofa. Ava was unsure how to proceed. Should she offer to cook something? They had brought a few groceries with them from Manhattan but she wasn't anxious to cook alone on their first night. Roan looked pretty locked into his place on the new sofa.

Begin as you mean to go, her mother often said. And Ava did not mean to cook for Roan every night. But they hadn't addressed the division of labor in their new home.

In Manhattan they ate out nearly every night, mostly expensed to the firm. But Roan hadn't even gone into the office today. He'd taken a vacation day to help with the move, and then proceeded to sleep the day away. Ava wasn't sure where they'd even secure takeout in this neighborhood. The deli? The pink bakery?

When she tried to bring up dinner, Roan shushed her so he could hear his phone sing to him.

Ava thought about heading downstairs to Holly and Daniel to see what they were eating, but as far as she knew, they were still at their catering gig. She was humiliated that she and Roan could barely navigate their very first day of living together.

At around 7 pm, Ava could no longer contain her rumbling stomach. According to her phone, there was a local pub a few streets over that she'd missed on her walk.

"Check this out, Roan. There's an adorable gastropub not three blocks from here. Let's go try it. Who knows? It might just be our new favorite place."

"Ha. I'm not so sure about that. I miss Manhattan already." Roan looked longingly out the window wall across the river.

"Roan! This isn't a temporary holding pattern. We live here now. We have to make the—"

"What? Make the best of it?"

Ava stared at him. They had come here willingly, hadn't they? She had talked him into it, yes, but hadn't he been willing? That day in his office, after their noon rendezvous, he had gotten excited about the prospect of investing in Easy Street. He'd been enthusiastic throughout the renovation phase, checking in with contractors and the bank regularly. This had been a project for both of them, right?

But that was all before the lawsuit. Before Nola Dyer summoned Ava out of her sabbatical to write a book about it. Before.

Before.

"Roan. I don't want to fight with you. We live here now. Us. Let's go." They locked up Ruby in his crate and headed out into the night.

At the pub named Mollys—no apostrophe—Roan sneered at the old-fashioned decorations on the wall and made fun of the heavy-set waitress behind her back. To the waitress's face of course, he was charming. Ava grew frustrated waiting for her gluten free burger and fries to arrive. The waitress acted like Ava was the first one to order such a thing in quite a while, even though it was listed on the menu.

"This town. Jesus." Roan said under his breath while they waited for their food.

"Roan. Come on. I grew up here. It's not so bad."

"I know, I know, Ava. But, come on. You escaped. Made it all the way to Manhattan. And now you've come back home."

Ava felt her impatience growing. Why was Roan acting like Manhattan was a time zone away instead of three miles back over the bridge? Why was he being so patronizing? She was excited to return to Riversedge victorious. Thrilled to remedy the legacy her feuding parents had left her. With everything going on at Rogers Hawk, she would have thought he'd be happy for the respite from Manhattan.

When the burgers arrived, Ava dove in. Headfirst.

"So Roan, why do you think you've been named in the lawsuit at all? Why is Nola Dyer out to get you?"

Roan looked startled at her frank question. Ava was surprised at herself, truth be told.

He bit into his burger and with a half full mouth, said, "Well, I wouldn't say Nola Dyer is out to get me. I think she's a very savvy, probably unscrupulous lawyer, who is doing her best to pad her suit with as many incriminating facts as she can possibly muster. It doesn't make it true. She just hasn't done her homework."

Ava nodded in silence, chewing the rubbery burger. There was no chance this was going to be their new favorite place.

"I mean, the thing is, Ava—there was one night I'm not proud of that I think has made its way into the narrative of this lawsuit."

"Oh?" Ava looked at him coolly. She'd never told him she'd previewed the plaintiff's complaint. She never asked him about the accusation that he'd shown up in one of his client's rooms drunk and naked. From the waist down.

"It was Tully's Writer Friend."

Ava felt punched in the gut.

"She'd just been divorced and she said she was nervous about her ex-husband. We were on a trip to Napa to check on a winery she had an ownership interest in and to finalize her estate plans in the process. The ex? He'd been harassing her. He didn't believe she was on a business trip to Napa. And he was having her tracked."

"Wow." Ava didn't know which part of the story was believable. Possibly none of it. She let Roan plod on.

"Anyway, I told her I'd get us adjoining rooms so she could have a little extra security on the trip. Some peace of mind. I told her to lock the door from her side and told her to come get me if she needed anything. Unfortunately, I took a sleeping pill with a glass of cab before bed, and fell asleep nude like I always do, forgetting that she might in fact need me. When she heard a noise and called out to me, I went barreling into her room, half-asleep, drugged on Ambien and wine and well, nude. I don't remember much about the night. It was a big misunderstanding from my vantage point. I was just as embarrassed about the whole thing the next morning as she was. But according to my lawyer, this is enough to keep me in the case and survive summary judgment at this early stage."

Ava reviewed everything Roan was telling her and tried to make sense of it. True to her word, Nola had only provided Ava with redacted statements and written interviews of the plaintiff's story. The one who was including Roan in the lawsuit. It never occurred to Ava that it was Writer Friend. She loved Roan, or so Ava thought. It seemed that there was no honor among thieves after all.

Ava thought about the fact that she'd been brought in because the plaintiff couldn't write. Was that part true, or not?

She remembered Nola's words at the Law Club luncheon

when Ava had signed the ghostwriting contract.

Will your client know it's me? That I'm the ghostwriter?

Indeed, she asked for you, specifically.

Sitting there at Mollys, Ava wasn't sure what to make of Roan's confession. Was she being had? By Writer Friend? By Nola? By Roan? All of the above?

Ava waded in tentatively.

"I'm sorry Roan. This is a very difficult situation for you, I'm sure." Ava felt a flood of emotions. Roan was describing what she'd read in the complaint, and it didn't make her feel any better, hearing it described in quite this way.

Her appetite gone, Ava picked at her burger and started eavesdropping on the tables around them.

The couple at the table next to them was talking loudly about a rash of recent break ins. "Be careful," they warned, turning and looking right at Ava. "Lock your doors at night. We didn't use to think that was necessary in this town but lately it is. The police think the break ins are drug related. Non-violent crimes. But still, lock your doors because you never know."

"You never know," Ava nodded.

Back at home that night, Roan collapsed loudly into their new bed in the new loft, with his phone in hand, scrolling through his instagram feed. "We didn't even see anyone we knew tonight," he said with disdain.

"Well, isn't that the point?" Ava asked him. "We came here to get away from New York City. To get a fresh start. In this beautiful place. You should be happy." Ava waved her hand at the window to the river below.

"Oh, sure, thrilled," Roan said as he scrolled through his social media channels. He didn't look thrilled at all.

"I have to walk the dog one last time before bed," Ava announced loudly. Roan nodded at her over his phone dismissively.

"Do you—do you want to come with me?" Ava spoke slowly trying to avoid any hint of sadness that was overtaking her.

Roan shook his head distractedly. She wasn't even sure he heard her.

Ava stood next to him, dog leash in hand, wondering where they were in this phase of their relationship where they now lived together. Was she supposed to be strong and confident? Was she allowed to ask for things? Was she supposed to be completely self-sufficient? Would it be more attractive to be honest with him and say she wanted him to come or should she pretend it was just fine that he was ignoring her? In the end, she walked out the door with Ruby and without Roan.

On the way out the door, a scruffy, unshowered man greeted her. He tried to hold the door open for her as she came out. Ava closed the door behind her loudly, locking it. The dog barked loudly and jumped up, but the stranger calmed the dog with a biscuit. Ava realized with a start that he had been expecting her. And the dog.

On the curb sat a beat-up clunker still running, albeit sputtering and smoking. Ava stood frozen outside the building taking in the details.

"Can I use your phone?" the scruffy man asked. "My car is giving me trouble. I need to call AAA."

"I'm sorry, no. I left my phone inside," she lied.

"Oh, no problem, I'll come back inside with you."

"Um. Listen, I don't know you and I'm sure you're a very nice guy, but I'm really not comfortable letting you inside." Would it make the man more or less determined if he knew there was a man inside, Ava wondered. She tried it out.

"Besides, my boyfriend is in there. He's—" All the words felt foreign on her tongue. She was so uncomfortable, she wanted to just go back inside but she didn't want this stranger to follow her in. "He's showering. So I can't even knock and have him come out here with the phone. Sorry, I can't help you right now."

"I'm sure he won't mind." The scruffy man reached behind her and rapped loudly on the door. Her phone buzzed quietly in her pocket. She refused to answer it. Refused to acknowledge to this guy that she had a phone after all. She walked away quickly pulling the dog around the corner keeping one eye on the scruffy man who was still banging on the door. Her phone rang again and this time she answered with a whisper.

"Hello?"

"Is that you banging on the door downstairs? What's with the racket?"

"I think I've found the town thief," Ava replied. "He's trying to get in, but I wouldn't let him. I'm waiting for him to leave. He's standing right outside the building on the curb next to a clunker of a car. I'm around the corner sort of out of earshot."

"Ok wait there. Wait right there."

Ava exhaled. She stood around the corner. Waiting for her boyfriend unapologetically. The discomfort of the dinnertime confession washed away and she leaned into the safe feeling of waiting for Roan to come rescue her.

A few moments passed. Ava was still waiting around the corner from the building under the only streetlight she could find. The night was so quiet her breathing hurt her ears. Eventually Ava peeked back around the corner and saw no one. No scruffy man, and no Roan either. The beat-up car was no longer idling on the curb. The most frightening images raced through her mind. The thief must have snuck into the building unobserved. Roan had found him as he was racing out to protect her. The thief had stabbed him—no he'd threatened to run out and stab her so Roan had protested and then succumbed to his injuries right there in the vestibule of the newly renovated industrial building while the assailant got away unnoticed with anything valuable he could carry.

Ava bit her lip and ran for the door tugging the dog away from a patch of grass. Like a heroine in a horror movie, she raced inside, bolted it quickly, and leaned back against the door, sucking air with her heart pounding.

She crept up the stairs wondering what the crime scene

would look like, fearing what she'd see.

It was worse than expected.

Roan was laying in bed right where she'd left him. Scrolling through his instagram feed. Laughing and talking to his phone as if it were a lover.

"Oh absolutely gorgeous. I will be liking that, thank you very much." He tapped his phone and laughed and scrolled while Ava stood frozen in the doorway.

"What are you doing?" She asked.

He turned to her. Surprised almost. Did he expect her never to return?

"What are you doing?" she asked again. "Why didn't you come for me?"

"Come for you? Where?"

"I really can't believe you." She sighed loudly.

Ava passed him and went into the bathroom, where she sat on the closed toilet seat, with the water running and tears streaming down her face. The dog followed her in and sat silently at her feet watching her cry. She'd expected a crime scene. But this was even more gruesome than she'd expected.

When she left the bathroom, Roan was snoring loudly. Ava thought about the story she'd been writing. The one Writer Friend had set her up to write. The one no one believed she could finish. She sat down and deleted the last few chapters.

It was time to write the truth.

CHAPTER 31
Holly

It was the week Felicity and Archie moved in, if I remember correctly.

Daniel and I had been working catering jobs every night that week, starting early in the morning and going late into the night. We had a lot of balls in the air, but we were essentially starting over. We'd sunk all our money into Easy Street and we couldn't turn down any work. My health wasn't the greatest and there was a pall of gloom over us from that fact as well. I wanted to keep working as long as I could muster the energy.

One day, we reported for work at this brownstone in Manhattan for a fundraising luncheon. I was trying out a brand-new menu with watermelon gazpacho and the most amazing little tofu bean sprout sandwiches that were all vegan and sugar-free.

Um, I can't remember exactly what the fundraiser was for. Is that important?

Ok, anyway, I was in the kitchen plating the sandwiches when this gentleman comes in and sort of politely introduces himself and thanks us for putting together such a nice event for his wife.

"Everything looks wonderful. My compliments to the chef!" he exclaimed. He was so nice, I remember, that I didn't even recognize him at first. But then suddenly, I looked at him in his stiffly pressed button-down shirt and gold dragon cufflinks and realized it was him. It was Lou. The most feared and often hated partner at Rogers Hawk. The one who'd first given Archie the assignment of looking into Easy Street for due diligence.

"Lou Arroz. So nice to see you," I said, taking a chance that he might remember me without further explanation. He didn't. He just looked at me with confusion in his eyes. So I had to go on.

"I'm sorry to startle you. I used to work at Rogers Hawk before I left to become a clean fuel ambassador for myself. I'm her. I'm the chef you were just complimenting. Holly Riddle."

Recognition slowly replaced his confusion, and he reached his hand out to clasp mine.

"Holly Riddle. Wow. So great to see you. What have you been up to?"

"Working. Paying the bills at Easy Street, I guess."

"Easy Street? What do you mean?"

I got nervous then. Because I remembered then that there was likely some conflict of interest that led to Archie getting that sweet deal on the building. But I also realized we couldn't all hide forever. We lived there now. On Easy Street.

I said as much and then I said, "And to think—I have you to thank for all of it."

He said, "I'm not following you. What are you talking about?"

I remember I sort of chose my words carefully from that point on. I went in slowly.

"Well, after the Rogers Hawk client decided not to bid on Easy Street, we did. A few of us formed an LLC and we bought the place. We renovated it top down, and now we live there."

"The property in Riversedge? That old industrial building?"

"Right," I said. I remember I was getting very nervous at this point. And then Lou just leaned his head back and started laughing. Like the kind of laughter where you literally can't get your breath back. And I was worried he was going to stop breathing altogether.

But he didn't. He settled finally and he looked me dead in

the eye, and he said, "There was no firm client interested in that property. Archie was the only one interested in the property for God knows what reason. In fact, Archie tried to talk me into going in on that property with him—investor to investor. I took one look at the due diligence report and told him hell no. That place is a money pit, with more environmental hazards than the Exxon Valdez. Only a band of idiots would buy that place."

Yeah. Then I remembered what Archie had said that first night he took us into the building. It was very lawyerly of him, frankly. Giving us the idea that Easy Street was a plum assignment without actually saying so. Remember? It's right there on the record from my testimony earlier today. He said:

Lou and I have been looking at this file since Monday. A developer wants to buy it and Lou and I are doing a quick search on prior owners to see if there are any red flags that should keep them from buying the place.

Yeah. So, Easy Street might have been on the market, but according to Lou, Archie wasn't working for them. Apparently Archie was working on his own. Right from the beginning.

So, anyway, I had two thoughts after Lou's little monologue.

First: *Ah, there's the old Lou.*

And second: *What in the hell did Archie get us into?*

CHAPTER 32
Felicity

Felicity and Archie arrive at Easy Street with a little bit of fanfare. Holly and Daniel agree to make dinner for the whole building, and Roan and Ava RSVP yes. Sara doesn't respond to the group text invitation.

Felicity takes a half day to help the movers unpack their things and Archie shows up late in the day after most of the hard work is done.

They've never lived together before, and Felicity wonders if there's some sort of ceremony that should accompany the event; but instead, they simply head upstairs to Holly and Daniel's unit with a bottle of wine tucked under each of Archie's arms, for a move-in day toast and dinner.

When they arrive, there's a giant pot on the stove simmering and the whole place smells delicious. Warm and spicy with a hint of nutmeg. Also, Holly's a little drunk, which Felicity thinks is odd, as Holly is rarely drunk. But Holly's an adorable drunk so Felicity leans into it. She pours a generous serving of chardonnay for all six of them, and then looks around.

"Is Sara joining us?"

Silence and then everyone looks at Archie, as he's the only one who ever actually hears from Sara. He shakes his head. "No, I told you. She's not very social."

"Are we ever going to meet this woman?" Felicity asks.

Ava pipes in then. "I saw her."

All eyes turn to her, and Felicity can't help but notice that Archie's expression actually seems angry.

"What do you mean?" he asks.

"I saw her. The first day we moved in. I was walking Ruby, and I looked up and I could make out the silhouette of a woman in the top floor window. Her long dark hair. Not much else. But I saw her." Ava shrugs like she's proud of herself.

Archie shakes his head and changes the topic.

"So, how have you guys all been enjoying this place? The views, right?"

Holly hiccups and Felicity giggles at her, calling her out, "Holly, are you drunk already? Dipping into the cooking wine, maybe? But by the way, these quiches are divine. Don't remind me that they're actually eggless. I'm suspending disbelief and pretending this is all very, very, bad for me. Your food is just way too delicious to be good for us."

"Well, I guess we're all suspending disbelief, aren't we?" Holly's tone is pretty accusatory, and Felicity cocks her head wondering what's coming next.

"What do you mean, Holly?"

"I mean. Now that we're all here, I think it's about time we had a little come-to-Jesus moment. I'm done with the surprises and the secrets. We've got mercury under the floorboards, underground tunnels, and black mold covered up by shoddy paint jobs."

"Holly!" Felicity looks at her like she's a child acting up at the dinner table.

"No. It's time we all start talking frankly here, Felicity. We are not just friends anymore. We're business partners. We all sunk a lot of money in this place, and frankly, my share is worth a hell of a lot more than all of yours because I can't replace it with some ridiculous Rogers Hawk salary anymore. I dropped all of my savings into this place—every last dime—and I don't have any reliable income other than the catering business, and if we get shut down here, I'm going to lose everything. *We are* going to lose everything."

Holly points to Daniel then, and he looks like he is not in on the news that they are about to lose everything, Felicity notes with some trepidation.

"Holly?" Daniel looks concerned and tentative.

"And I'm breaking out in hives every other day from the goddamn toxins in this building. They are everywhere! I want some answers and I want them now."

Roan rolls his eyes now. "Geez. I thought we were getting a free dinner. Didn't know it was going to be an inquisition."

"Oh, please, Roan. You have absolutely no reason to talk back right now. If it wasn't bad enough that you're named in the Rogers Hawk lawsuit—"

"Holly!" Ava nearly spits out her wine at Holly's revelation. The lawsuit is a don't ask, don't tell subject among the group. An implicit understanding has evolved that no one will bring it up or discuss it, but Holly seems to be breaking all rules tonight.

"No, no. I'm not going to get into all that. But I *am* going to ask if that's the reason you drained the escrow account just after closing?"

"What in the hell, Holly?" Roan leans into Holly with the accusation. No one in the room could miss the electric tension between Roan and Holly then. Felicity notes that it is almost, sexual? But that doesn't make sense, does it?

Roan points a finger directly in Holly's face. "I paid the contractors with those funds. Maybe you're missing the part where these units were renovated top to bottom?"

"Not mine," Holly reminds him.

"Correct. And therefore you put the least amount of money into escrow. What exactly are you trying to do here, Holly? The units were paid in full. Everything came in exactly on budget and ahead of schedule. You all asked me to have the unenviable job of keeping track of all of the expenses and payments. What are you pissed about?"

"Exactly on budget? Isn't that a little convenient, Roan?

According to the contractors, they were told to cut corners at every turn. They painted over black mold, for heaven's sake. Including in your unit, Ava!" Holly points a wooden spoon at a wide-eyed Ava who appears as shocked as everyone else in the room.

Holly reaches over and pours herself another glass of wine. Felicity watches as Daniel leans over and whispers, "Um, you good?" But Holly waves him off like a fly on cheesecloth.

"And *you*, Archie. Let's talk about what you did here."

"Me?" Archie looks nervous.

Felicity feels a warmth spreading along her neck that does not feel comfortable.

"I ran into your buddy a few days ago. Lou Arroz. Turns out he didn't assign this place as a due diligence case. Oh no. He says you tried to get him to invest in the property and he ran away screaming after he saw the due diligence report. Why didn't you tell us that, Archie? Why did you make us believe this was a bargain instead of a money pit, Archie?"

Felicity watches Archie's expression turn from confusion to a smirk.

What exactly is he enjoying about all this? Felicity asks herself as she waits for him to respond. But the wait is over quickly, as she sees him point to the pot behind Holly which is boiling over, sputtering and splashing its liquid contents all over her brand new, just paid for Viking gas stove. And he says, "Holly, I think dinner is ready, don't you?"

CHAPTER 33

Ava

Ava and Roan returned to their floor upstairs a little shell shocked.

Holly's performance over appetizers was temporarily interrupted once dinner was served. Kale and tofu soup served with large slices of gluten free crusty bread. It was absolutely delicious. Also helpful were the four more bottles of chardonnay poured. It was hard to know who drank more. Holly or Archie. But the alcohol loosened both of their tongues.

Archie made a small speech at dinner about the fact that yes, he had gone to Lou first to invest in the property. That the group had misunderstood him when he explained Lou's involvement that first night. It wasn't an assignment from Lou. He'd never said it was one and he couldn't help everyone's rush to judgment.

No, the building started as an investment opportunity that he brought to Lou, as an attorney, not a subordinate. No one could remember now exactly what was said, and it wasn't like there was some recording of the evening. Archie said that his plan was always to come to this group as well, and he hoped Lou would purchase the top unit, but when Lou refused for baseless reasons, it became necessary to bring in Sara. Archie said he was grateful for Sara's enthusiasm to join in the venture, even though she brought with her some dark history about the building.

"No, scratch that," Archie said. "She's been an asset because of, not in *spite* of the knowledge she brings about 724 Easy Street."

Everyone just dove into dinner at that point. The wine was flowing. Tempers were soothed. Friendships were remembered. Daniel tapped Holly's arm a few times at dinner as if to say—*it's all ok. It's all worked out. We're here now. No need to turn the tables upside down.*

And Holly seemed to have a lighter expression over dinner. Greeted with accolades and praise for her meal, she settled into a calmer mood. No more talk about Roan pillaging the escrow account or Archie's back-alley deal. Or underground tunnels to an asylum. Or money pit toxins.

When they arrived back in their apartment, Ava wasn't sure whether to bring up the events of the night or not.

"Well that was wild," Roan offered. But Ava knew better than to take the bait. Roan had been so prickly since they first moved in. She couldn't let go of the first night's events when Roan had revealed his inappropriate night with Writer Friend and then left Ava outside. In danger.

Since that night, Ava had been channeling all her angst into the manuscript. Nola was asking for Ava to send pages to the publisher by week's end. From the beginning it was Ava's job to craft a story even though she didn't really know whose story she was writing. Nola said it was better that way. Plausible deniability for the book's contents.

But now that she knew it was partly Writer Friend's story, Ava was inspired anew. She threw herself into the writing in order to both hold up her end of the bargain and avoid the tension with Roan. She sunk into the manuscript each night. While Roan drifted off to sleep, Ava tapped the keyboard.

Tonight was no exception. The story was taking shape. A story about a place where no one could be trusted. Where the women were preyed upon by the men and then took full advantage of the men in return. Where the facades rarely matched the insides.

A place where the truth was buried far beneath the surface. A fictional place, but still based in large part on the law firm she'd just left behind.

Ava had traded one place for another with its own secrets and sadness.

Rogers Hawk was not unlike Easy Street, Ava was starting to understand.

CHAPTER 34
Felicity

Felicity wanders around the Easy Street apartment restlessly. Archie has been late every night this week and the uneasiness of being left alone with her dark thoughts is eating at her. At night, when she is alone, she thinks about Raven, the tarot reader, and her weird warning.

"You think there's two of them. But there's only one."

What was she talking about?

Felicity knows damn well there was only one.

She was 16 that summer. Her mother told her they'd be taking a summer vacation. A real summer vacation. "Not in September, but in the summertime. In June, actually. I finally managed to get some time off in June."

Felicity's mother was a single mom and a real estate agent whose busiest season came every summer. They rarely got away during Felicity's school vacation, but this year, her mother seemed to notice something different in Felicity. Something that required a little attention. She meant well, Felicity would always note later. Even if she didn't really hone in on Felicity the way she needed that summer, her mother certainly meant well.

They were on a two-week June vacation that would change Felicity's life forever.

Marilyn and Felicity Huck arrived at a beach motel walking distance from the boardwalk, just after school let out. The heat of the boardwalk and the newness of the season burned Felicity on all sides. They'd walk the boardwalk each day and then eat cheesesteaks and pizzas in the room. Her mother was exhausted each night, and busy with work. She wasn't able to unplug the same way she could in September. She logged into her computer every morning and every evening. Work-related phone calls came in incessantly. Marilyn didn't seem to be on vacation at all, but they made the best of it every afternoon as they headed to the beach and boardwalk. After dinner each night, Marilyn gave Felicity money to walk down the boardwalk for ice cream.

Felicity met him on the fourth night of the trip. He was sunburnt and barefoot. He was from there, which seemed to her to be as unreal as the feelings he stirred in her when he shared an ice cream cone with her and later held her hand and the next night leaned in to kiss her on the sand under the boardwalk near the ice cream stand.

Her mother was increasingly distracted by work as the week went on, and Felicity was equally distracted by the boy who met her outside the boardwalk ice cream stand every night that week. On the tenth night, they went inside the palm reader's shop. They traded wrinkled $5 bills for fortunes that included promises and love and assurances that what they felt was true.

On the last night, Felicity clung to him and cried, convinced that what she felt was as real as anything she'd ever felt. *Remember what the palm reader said,* he growled as he convinced her to press on. *This is everything. This will change your life. This is love.*

Yes, she cried into the night. *Yes.*

When she got home, it only took a month to realize that the phone number he gave her wasn't real, nor his name. Nor any other promise he made. Save one. To change her life.

Forever.

Her mother helped her hide the pregnancy during the winter. "Erratic weight gain, she's trying to get it under control." This was the story everyone heard and believed. Felicity gave birth during an early March snowstorm, and then stayed home for the rest of the school year under the guise of the medical excuse. In truth, she was dying from a broken heart with no one to tell.

"Now you'll never have to think about that boy, again," her mother said as they drove home from the hospital that day. The baby was handed off to a family who promised to love and protect her. Felicity was proud of her body for what it had done. She soothed her heart by remembering how happy her baby looked in another grateful woman's arms.

And while it was true that she really didn't think about the boy again, she thought about that baby every damn day of her life. Since reading about Agnes Carson, Felicity had come to realize that the summer of depression was actually hormonal and chemical. She'd suffered from postpartum depression, and while her mother hadn't been perfect, she'd been attentive, careful with Felicity. She'd done the best she could. So had Felicity.

But there had been only one baby. She was certain of that. She was there. *What on earth was Raven referring to?* Felicity wonders.

There's a low simmering current of angst coursing through her as she walks around their Unit at Easy Street, waiting for Archie to get home. She's been home for hours. She and Sheila settled a big case recently and Sheila told her to take a few days off. Felicity is grateful for the promise of respite but she's not sure she can stand being alone for the next few days. She's already decided she probably won't take Sheila up on her offer.

Felicity paces for a while and then she calls Archie, but he doesn't pick up. A moment later, he texts her back.

Sorry, honey. Got stuck in a meeting. In an Uber on the way home. Want me to pick up any takeout?

No thanks, Felicity texts back. She doesn't have much of an appetite. There's no room for anything in her gut besides confusion and nervousness these days.

The move across the river was supposed to be a good one, she knows. She's had a fresh start. No more financial stress and no more working like a maniac around the clock. Felicity knows she should be happy. She wants to be happy. But something is gnawing at her. Ever since they bought this place together—the place that was supposed to help Felicity and Archie take their relationship to the next level ... Archie hasn't been around.

He's been working like crazy, sure. But there's more to it than that. He's been distracted. Spending so much time with *her*.

With Sara.

Felicity stops pacing and decides to do something she didn't expect. She walks up the back steps of Easy Street to the top unit of the building.

Sara's unit.

Felicity is not sure what to do next. She stands at the heavy door for only a few moments before she hears the unmistakable sound of Archie's voice—low and teasing—on the other side getting louder as he must be heading toward the door. "Oh shoot. Where are my shoes?" Felicity runs back down the steps two at a time, nearly breaking her neck to get back to the apartment before Archie. When she arrives, breathless, back on the first floor, she wonders how she's allowed things to get to this point.

Where she is the one feeling guilty catching Archie cheating on her.

When Archie opens the door a few moments later, he is flushed and red-cheeked and Felicity doesn't know whether she's willing to confront him or not. She watches Archie come in and start his evening rituals. His keys go on a hook by the door. His pocket change drops in a small dish on a reclaimed oak table next to the door. He lays his wallet parallel to the dish. Everything has its place for Archie.

Even his mistress apparently.

"Why did you bring Sara into this deal, Archie?" Felicity blurts out.

"Excuse me?" Archie looks startled. It's not a good look for him, and Felicity is tempted to say "never mind," and drop the subject into the abyss.

Archie's face grows paler and paler and Felicity is worried about him. But she also worried about their future. She tells him that she heard him upstairs in Sara's apartment when he was supposed to be in an Uber. She tells him that she now realizes he bought Sara into this deal because she is Archie's mistress and now he has both Sara and Felicity under one roof. Felicity is emotional. Tears are streaming down her face as she stands in front of him.

This must be so much easier on you, Archie. So more convenient now?

Archie is not repentant or defensive or angry. Instead, he takes Felicity's hands and guides her to the enormous u-shaped sofa in the middle of their unit. He tells her it's time. That he trusts her implicitly, and that it's time for him to explain it all.

It's a sad story that Archie tells. About his childhood. Times and events he has never opened up to Felicity about before. Archie's mother had a parade of boyfriends who were incredibly abusive—each one worse than the last. His mother was more interested in finding husbands than stepfathers. And she didn't pay any attention to how much trauma the men in her life were causing Archie. Archie's time with his gentle grandmother was some of the only tranquility he had in his life.

"But what does any of this have to do with Sara?" Felicity is impatient. Archie stops suddenly and Felicity feels that they are on the cusp of some admission. Some truth. But then it just ... stops.

"I needed Sara in on this deal. We all did. You know that, Felicity. She's not my mistress. I'm going to bed now."

Felicity has more questions than answers at this point, and she debates going up to Sara's unit and rapping on the door loudly and incessantly until she lets her in. But in the end, she can't bring herself to do so. Felicity lays down next to Archie, and sends out a fervent prayer to the universe that it's all *for* something after all. That it all hasn't been in vain.

CHAPTER 35
Holly

Well, personally, I'm not surprised that Felicity started to unravel.

What do you mean objection? Isn't that what we're here to figure out? What happened at Easy Street?

No, I get it. You want just the facts from me. Nothing more. But that's the thing. It is a fact.

I was there. Right there.

No! Not when *it* happened.

Right, right. Ok, um, let's see. We were in Archie and Felicity's unit one night. They'd only just moved in a few weeks before. I hadn't seen much of them and I was feeling a little bad about their welcome to the building dinner party. Why? Well because, I'd gotten kind of drunk and accused Archie of dragging us into the money pit idea of his without full disclosure.

But, you know, I softened when I thought about it. Truly. When I sobered up. Daniel and I talked about it at length. And he was right. No one could claim they didn't know about the environmental risks of taking on such a project. None of us. Not even Daniel and me.

We each had our reasons for wanting that building. We each had wounds we wanted that building to soothe over for us, right?

Me? I wanted a luxury space to grow my brand-new catering business. I wanted validation that I was on the right track—

leaving the law to fuel people's health with food and nurturing. Even though my own body was betraying me—well, actually, *because* my own body was betraying me with the still recent diagnosis, it was important for me to feel like it was all worth it. Leaving the law and the security of that Rogers Hawk position. Leaving behind the 401k match and the health benefits—I really wanted to believe it was all worth it.

Daniel? He wanted validation, too. He left a family business behind to join me—a well known pizzeria on the Upper West Side of Manhattan that he watched his father devote his life to. And also die in. Daniel didn't want the same fate for himself. He took a big risk starting the catering company with me. And going in on the Easy Street loft as well. But Daniel wanted to grow the business with me. Because he loves me. I know that now. That's one thing I know for certain since all this happened. And let's not forget, Daniel was the skeptic from the beginning. No one can argue that he went into this project with open arms. He was appropriately cautious even from the beginning.

But Daniel was the level-headed one. He kept us all honest every step of the way, and I'd be remiss if I didn't mention that here.

And Ava and Roan? Well, I think we know now that Roan did this for the money. While we were all scraping together money to make payments, Roan was collecting that money and transferring it to his own account to pay off his mounting legal bills. Roan knew that lawsuit was on the horizon long before any of us did. And while he was stealing from us—Ava was trying to prove something to herself. She was the Riversedge native among us. Returning home. Local girl does good, and all that stuff.

Felicity and Archie? Well, their motives were a little murkier, weren't they?

I think we know now that their motives for buying Easy Street truly erupted from trauma—for each of them.

Hurt people hurt people. Isn't that what they say? I don't

know. Just *they*.

At any rate, soon after they moved in, we were in Archie and Felicity's loft, and it was clear to me Felicity was a little, let's say off. She was prickly. She was snapping at everything Archie said and, I mean, Archie's a showboater, as I've said, but it's hard to snap at him. Everyone has always just loved Archie. He seemed to have his shit together. It was annoying for those of us who didn't. But that was *before* we found out what was really going on.

I remember that one night, Felicity was asking about the underground tunnel. None of us had really pressed the issue since the revelation by Archie about the underground tunnel that needed to be sealed up. I think we were all figuring that sounded expensive and we were all sort of out of money by then.

But Felicity started drilling Archie that night.

What's going on with the tunnel, Archie?

Is Sara still doing her research, Archie?

When do you think she might be done?

Oh, and when do you think Sara might actually show her face to the rest of us?

You know, that kind of thing. Sort of the Spanish inquisition-type stuff. And as I remember it, Archie was just kind of patting her hand and patting her head and telling her to relax. It was all under control according to Archie.

Listen, I didn't know what that meant either, but I *was* interested in going down there.

To the basement.

Felicity insisted on going down to the basement. Down to the locked area.

"I want to see it, Archie," she said.

"What do you mean? See what?" Archie asked.

"Take us down," she insisted. "We own the space as much as you do. I want to see it."

"I don't think that's a good idea, Felicity. I don't even know how safe it is down there. You got a hard hat?" He laughed then, but I got the feeling that it was more of a "leave it alone, Felicity" than a "this is genuinely funny, Felicity" kind of laugh. You know what I mean?

And things kind of escalated from there. She was snapping at him. And he was trying to quiet her, and then all of a sudden out of nowhere, Felicity slammed her fists down on the coffee table and said, "I am so sick of this place. This whole damn building. If I had to go back in time I wouldn't have let you talk me into this ridiculous idea of yours. I wouldn't have sold myself for bricks and a view. I'd have nothing to do with this at all. If only I *could* go back in time. I'd do so many things differently."

What was that? *When* did that conversation happen? Well, it must have been about a week or so before the fire. Yes. About a week before Easy Street burned to the ground.

CHAPTER 36
Sara

It started when Lee left.

I mean, I guess it started when my grandmother killed my grandfather and I inherited a family history that made me question quite a few things and made me think long and hard about who I wanted to be. How I wanted to be defined.

But I prefer to blame it on Lee who never knew my grandmother and certainly had nothing to do with my grandfather's death.

When Lee left, I lost my confidence. I had just graduated from college and I was pretty direction-less. I had moved back home only temporarily, as I was certain Lee and I were going to move in together and go the distance. When that proved false, I tried drowning my grief in booze but it didn't take long to realize that wasn't going to work. As the pendulum of my emotions and motivation swung in the other direction, I started signing up for classes at the local gym. I found out that they had a trial period. All the classes you wanted to take in two weeks for a $10 pass. I bought that pass and got my full money's worth. Cycling in the morning and hot yoga in the afternoon. I helped myself to the complimentary water bottles in the lobby, and even stuffed a gym towel or two in my bag in the locker room. I was spending more time in the gym than I was at home. By design, of course, trying to outrun Lee. Determined to outrun my grief and loneliness.

I was just coming out of the locker room when a good-looking man in a too tight polo with a giant swoosh mark and a name tag that read "Ben" greeted me with a clipboard. "I've seen you here a lot this week. I would love to talk to you about a membership if you have a few minutes?"

I wasn't sure how to feel about the attention. It felt more accusatory than welcoming and I was immediately on the defensive. "I bought the trial pass. It says right on it: all-you-can-gym. For $10." I held up my gym bag where the pass was clipped for dramatic effect. Ben seemed unfazed. "Oh yes, of course. But we always hope that clients who—like you—take full advantage of all the opportunities afforded by the all you can gym pass will love it so much, they'll want to join on the spot. You've enjoyed yourself haven't you?"

"Oh, I—well, yeah, I have." I glanced back down at my bag wondering if Ben could see the outline of the gym hair dryer that I managed to smuggle into my bag just moments earlier.

Ben put his arm around my shoulders and guided me toward an office located just inside the entryway of the gym. For a few minutes, I considered screaming out that I was being kidnapped, but my tongue stuck in my mouth which was suddenly very, very dry.

In his office, Ben scrolled through a bunch of boring paperwork on his computer screen, twisting it at an angle for me to see. My ears were ringing, and I couldn't hear much of what he was saying until he pointed at the screen and said I could sign with my finger.

"But, what am I signing exactly?"

"The membership papers,' Ben sounded bored. And annoyed.

I squinted at the screen trying to find a number. I spotted only one. $327.

"Three hundred twenty-seven. Is that a year?"

Ben laughed. " A year? You're funny. That's the discounted rate per month, for the first four months. We usually only offer that for three months, but I'm willing to extend it for you."

"Oh, thanks—I—"

"I mean, you wouldn't believe how some people just come in here and really try to soak us with that $10 2-week pass. No intention of ever joining the gym. Just coming in here to practically steal gym towels and yoga mats."

"Really? I didn't—wow—that's incredible."

"Yeah, exactly, that's not you. Obviously. Someone like that I wouldn't even bother talking to. You? You look serious about your fitness. About your health goals. I could tell you were the real deal, so I already talked to my manager about extending the 4-month trial period. It won't go up to $427 until month seven."

Ben sat back smugly. He looked like he wanted thanks, so I obliged. I was incredibly uncomfortable and just wanted out of the office. I wanted out of the gym, really, but I couldn't exactly figure out how to leave. I was sweating even more than usual after a workout and I was wondering how much longer I could hide the gym hairdryer in my bag.

I knew I couldn't afford $327 a month. But I also knew I couldn't afford a petty theft charge.

"What's the—you know—cancellation policy? In case I decide in a month or two this isn't working for me?"

Ben looked at me like I'd just bitten the head off a small animal right in front of him. "Cancel? Why would you want to cancel? I mean, yeah, of course, there are all the usual cancellation policies spelled out right here in the contract. But I've never seen anyone actually use them. Are you going to suddenly wake up uninterested in your own well being tomorrow? Or next week? Of course not!"

Ben pointed again at the screen and practically lifted my finger to sign the yellow highlighted section on the screen. The screen flashed with a gold banner across it.

Registration Confirmed!

"Voila!" You're now a card-carrying member of Revolution.

Come on, I'll show you out. He grabbed my arm too roughly, and I bobbled my gym bag. It clunked against the side of his desk as I stood up and made a loud clanging sound.

There was a long pause, and Ben stared at the bag and at me—back and forth a few times—before breaking out in laughter. "Well those are some noisy gym shorts you've got there. Come on. Let's get you a bottle of water on your way out."

For three months I watched my bank account decrease with the $327 monthly gym membership I couldn't afford. In the third month, I could no longer afford both my rent and the gym. I went to Ben and asked for a copy of the contract. "What do you need it for?" Ben asked as he stared at me.

"I really need to look at that cancellation clause, I said.

Ben just shook his head. "I can't believe it. You're one of those after all." He didn't make a move to actually pull up my contract so I walked out of his office, sheepish, defeated and broke. The next day I asked a friend to pretend they were joining the gym and see if they could get an electronic copy of the contract to take home. My friend was a recent law grad, studying for the Bar Exam, and after throwing her weight around a bit, she left the gym with a copy of the contract Revolution was making every new member sign at the time.

She ended up helping me get out of the contract by threatening to bring a legal case against the gym and expose their less than ethical means of signing new members. She scheduled a bunch of depositions and filed a bunch of legal papers—all *pro bono*, free of charge. Ben and his too tight red polo looked smug at the deposition. Yes, I went. I wanted to prove something to Ben and myself. I wanted to prove that I wasn't intimidated by him. And that I hadn't been completely ruined by the breakup with Lee.

I actually called Lee to brag about the legal case.

Lee said, "Wow. You seem really busy since we broke up. Really motivated. You should go to law school or something."

So I did.

CHAPTER 37
Ava

"Ava, look at me."

She did, then, but not because Roan ordered her to. Instead she looked at him because she didn't appreciate what was certainly an ill-timed joke, and she wanted him to know it. When they had first started seeing each other, Roan said she could stop him in his tracks with just a look, and this was one of those times Ava wanted to use exactly that skill and with exactly that result.

Ava turned her attention begrudgingly away from Holly who was at the bar glamming it up for her newly engaged selfies, and also away from Daniel who was looking incredibly proud of himself—back to Roan who'd just announced to Ava that he wanted to take a "break" and maybe even move back to Manhattan for a while.

Ava gave Roan her sternest look, eyes pinched together, smile erased and put her hands on his shoulders, with the intention of shaking him a little. Maybe a lot. This was just a stupid prank, of course, and she wanted to get back to Holly. Holly had a perfectly fresh manicure, Ava noticed, so maybe she wasn't exactly in the same state of surprise as the rest of the group was? That's what Ava was discussing with Roan, when he interrupted her.

"I think I want that level of surprise," Ava told him. "The kind where you know it's about to happen, but you walk around your life in a constant state of anticipation until it does. Are you taking notes, Mr. Knight?" The gin and tonics made Ava bold. So did Easy Street and the writing. Now that she and Roan were living together, Ava was starting to futurize in spite of herself. *And why shouldn't I?* Ava would ask herself while she worked away on the manuscript of a novel that featured a fictionalized version of Rogers Hawk. Nola had provided audio tapes of another of her clients, a female associate at Rogers Hawk who claimed that she was sexually harassed by every male partner she'd been assigned to in her short tenure of Rogers Hawk before leaving to go work in-house at a social media consulting firm. The manuscript wasn't about Writer Friend anymore. And it wasn't about Roan either.

The story in the audio tapes was familiar to Ava. She knew that there were plenty of pigs at Rogers Hawk. She portrayed them as such in the novel. But she exonerated one, just one. A Harvard law grad who helped a roster of female clients with end-of-life issues. She wrote a narrative about him that was squeaky clean as she wrote an indictment about the rest—including the career paralegal who used women like pawns and then discarded them for the next challenge.

At night when Roan collapsed into bed with loud complaints about the commute out of Manhattan, the unavailability of good takeout in Riversedge, and the obscene cost of the loft renovations, Ava would take all of his negativity and weave a narrative that spun it, discarded it, and tossed it aside. In Ava's mind, she and Roan were pushing past the discomfort of the last few months and planning a future together. Of course, with Holly's engagement, it was clear that only one future was really solid these days—and that was Holly and Daniel.

At the bar where Daniel had just proposed dramatically and loudly over a cover band's rendition of "Don't Stop Believing," Ava batted her eyes at Roan coquettishly, like she knew he liked. But instead of acquiescing and saying something like "Well, of course, love, I can't wait to propose to you, and better yet, I can't wait to be married to you," Roan took Ava's hands in his, looked her in the eye—with a dead expression—and said, "Ava, there's no good time to say this, but I don't want to lie to you. I don't really see an engagement in our future any time soon. In fact, I've been thinking I need to take a break from things, to tell you the truth."

Ava swatted his hands and his words away like a pesky bug and turned to Holly who was teary but unstreaked.

Did she also have the foresight to put on waterproof mascara in addition to the fresh manicure? Ava wondered.

When Ava looked back at Roan—really looked at him, eyes pinched and warning—he startled her with his intensely returned gaze.

"You're not joking?" As the words came out, she instantly wanted to take them back. Her annoyance started to turn to something else—vaguely familiar. A cool jolt of loneliness took root at the base of her spine and she shivered as it traveled throughout her bloodstream up to her ears and down to her toes. Two decades after watching her parents torch their life and discard Ava in the process, she still couldn't shake the lonely sadness they'd infused into her childhood.

"Roan. Please tell me you're joking." Ava knew her words sounded desperate and she cleared her throat hoping to say them again with more authority. But Roan just looked at her sadly—in a way she had never seen him look at her—and in a way she hoped in an instant to never be looked at again. The strange mix of pity and apology and relief in his eyes was overwhelming. Ava stopped asking if he was joking. And she stopped thinking he might be.

Ava walked away from Roan and shook her whole body free of the last five minutes as she strode confidently to Holly, wrapping her in a tight hug. Holly smelled like cinnamon and aftershave and lilies. Ava wondered briefly if this was the smell of wives instead of girlfriends.

"I am so happy for you, Gorgeous. You deserve every good thing."

Holly smiled and hugged Ava and returned to her celebration with Daniel at the bar, leaving Ava alone with her thoughts as she stared down the bar at Roan. He waved her down to him, and she walked back to him far too quickly, hoping he'd come to senses after another beer.

"Listen, Ava. I gotta get out of here. I have a meeting over at the Law Club. A new client. I won't be at Easy Street tonight. Probably best for me not to stay there for the time being. We can have lunch at the club next week and work out the legalities. We'll need to sell the unit, but we can discuss a timeline that works for both of us."

Ava stared at him with her gut stinging from the punches that kept coming.

"Take care, Ava. We'll talk about the sale next week." were the last words he said to her that night after they broke up the second time.

"Over my dead body," were the last words she said in return. But Roan didn't hear them because he was already out the door and on his way to the Law Club to meet a new client. Which for Roan Knight most likely resembled a date.

As Ava returned to the bar and joined Holly in a celebratory shot, she realized she still held all the cards. She was still working on the manuscript that could burn Roan Knight's entire reputation. She could also make sure Roan couldn't touch the Easy Street unit. And she was suddenly quite interested in ensuring a plot twist.

CHAPTER 38
Sara

I find myself with a little more downtime lately. My grandmother's journal doesn't distract me as much lately. Maybe I've read and reread it too many times, although there is a part of me that still thinks there's something left. Something I haven't yet discovered. But my attention span for the whole thing is waning.

I wanted to be here in the space so badly. I thought it would bring me clarity and healing. Yet, being here in the building where it all happened is its own distraction. I've brought some of my grandmother's art here to the top floor of Easy Street. What little I have. Much of it she gave to that man, Tom. That's what my mother insisted on calling him until the day my grandmother died. "That man, Tom." It was clear to anyone that Tom was more than *that man*. It was clear too that he was more than Agnes's friend as well. That she loved him. Until her brain gave up knowing him and then she could no longer remember him or remember loving him. Even before my grandmother's early onset of dementia, I knew very little about Tom. Just that he took much of my grandmother's art before we moved her into the assisted living facility. My mother managed to salvage only a couple of pieces. And now those few pieces of art belong to me.

I surround myself with the art and with it, of course I'm surrounded by Agnes's history. It's like I'm immersed in her pain and most days I don't know if that wounds me even more or comforts me. Generally, the answer is both. Some days I want to destroy the building on Easy Street with all of its bad history and some days I want to preserve it forever. My emotions are on a constant pendulum ride, back and forth.

Since I can't seem to distract myself with the journal right now, I've become addicted to social media like some ne'er-do-well teenager. There's this TikTok reel I keep stumbling on that has 300,000 likes, and I understand why because it's hilarious. This woman filmed herself in five different angles with five different hair styles and five different outfits playing five different versions of herself. I can't stop laughing.

Out of the five personalities in the reel, "yellow" was the best one. It's the one I relate to most of all. I mean red was funny—but all that stuff about feminine energy went a little over my head. I guess red is supposed to symbolize blood or periods or something like that? And white was innocence of course. That pure state we're all in before someone comes along to break our heart. Boy, do I know how that feels. But yellow—that was the best. That's the one I liked the most.

That one was all about revenge.

CHAPTER 39
Holly

Well, we wanted to come forward at first.

Daniel and me. We called a meeting. I made vegan lasagne. Which is no small task. The trick is making the cheese out of a nut paste and really getting the consistency right—no, of course. This is not a cooking lesson. If I was, I would be charging you. Haha. Anyway, Daniel and I were very united by this point. We wanted to come forward about the building.

Remember, Daniel was skeptical about this project from the very beginning. I dragged him into this and he invested out of love and support for me, but the evidence was all starting to point in the direction of disaster. We'd made a mistake trusting Archie. And Roan. I could forgive myself for trusting Archie. After all, we all trusted Archie back then. But boy, was I angry at myself for trusting Roan again. After all I'd learned about him while dating him and working with him at Rogers Hawk, you'd think I'd know better.

But I like to believe the best in people. My diagnosis has taught me a lot of things, not the least of which is empathy, frankly.

So, we called a meeting in our unit—the vegan lasagne, et cetera, and everyone came. Wait, no. Not everyone. There was no Roan and no Sara, of course. Just Archie. And Felicity and Ava and Daniel and me.

And we laid it all on the line. We had pictures of the mold

and the mercury and I said, really, guys, I don't think we can stay quiet about all of this anymore. Daniel and I are trying to make a living here and we're getting married and starting our lives for real, and we don't have the Rogers Hawk parachute to pull anymore. We have a business and a reputation and it's been hard enough getting all the certifications we need. We cannot ignore this any longer. I think we have to contact someone. An environmental specialist. Someone who can take a look at this building and tell us what we need to do to get it up to code.

Believe me, Daniel and I weren't anxious to spend money on environmental remediation either, but we were certainly willing to do it for the sake of saving our investment. Saving our future.

Well, it was Archie who was adamant that we *not* do that.

He said if we brought someone in from the outside, then we'd all risk our investment.

They could shut us down, he said. They could turn this into a superfund site, and demolish the whole building. We'd all lose everything, he said. Then what?

Well, Daniel and I kept arguing, but our voices were drowned out by Archie. In the end, everyone else wanted to keep it quiet.

Who will ever find out? Felicity said. And she also asked, *Wasn't everything contained now?*

I told her I wasn't so sure since I was still having terrible migraines and rashes and other flare-ups from my autoimmune disorder. Felicity said, gently, that maybe that had nothing to do with the building at all. Which felt like the lawyer in her talking, frankly, rather than my friend.

Ava said Roan was in enough trouble over this building and we should all let the system play out the way it would over Roan's embezzlement. *We all stand to gain from Roan's trial,* she said. And I thought that was a kind of mercenary way to look at things, but I didn't disagree.

In case, I haven't made it clear, I neither like nor trust Roan.

In fact, I wouldn't be surprised if you told me Roan Knight stole everything from us and then burned the building down for the insurance money.

There. I said it.

I mean Roan is the one who arranged for us to get that incredible insurance policy from your client. That's what you're thinking, right? That one of us did something to start the fire? That's why you won't just pay us the proceeds of the policy and leave us all alone? That's why you're getting ready to take us all to trial and why you've dragged me into a deposition this entire goddamn day?

Well, I'm sick of sitting here on the hot seat all day while Roan Knight is on the lam. He's literally nowhere to be found. And I wouldn't be surprised if you told me he burned the building down. But I also know that you can't hold that against the rest of us even if it is true. You still have to pay us the policy limits and then go after Roan Knight for the money.

Because we didn't do anything wrong.

Remember, I used to be a lawyer. I know the rules here too.

CHAPTER 40
Ava

After Roan left, Ava was on fire. She wrote like a woman possessed. All day every day, sometimes going days without showering. Sometimes forgetting to sleep. To eat.

One morning, she got a call from an unknown number. Normally, she'd have screened such a call, ignored it. But her defenses were down. Perhaps she even missed Roan a bit. Morbidly, ridiculously. Afterward, she couldn't say why she'd answered it, but she did.

"I'm looking for Roan Knight."

"This isn't his number. It's—wait who is this?"

"I'm calling from the IRS Criminal Investigation Unit—and we are looking for Roan Knight."

"Have you tried his place of business? He works around the clock at Rogers Hawk."

"Yes. Of course, we've tried there. He hasn't been to work in three weeks. No one seems to know where he is. We're hoping you do. We're hoping you have some answers."

"I don't. I don't know anything about Roan Knight as it turns out. I'm sorry." Ava hung up the phone and texted Nola.

I need to see you.

"Listen, Ava. I've been down this road before. These men.

These lawyers. They think they can command whatever they want. They're arrogant and their arrogance betrays them. I worked for Barr Knoll, for heaven's sake."

"Yes, I always wondered. What really happened there?" Ava asks the question while looking around the Law Club dining room. As she's away from the law longer and longer, she knows fewer faces in the room. It's happened so quickly. She's not sure if that should relieve her or threaten her.

Nola shrugs at the question, but launches into a historical narrative at the same time. "Barr Knoll? He shot himself in the damn foot. Blew up the biggest case his self-created firm ever handled, all because he didn't believe that a woman could do a better job than him.

"He was pompous and ridiculous. At the time, I was just a paralegal and my boss, Carly Jenner, she knew that case inside and out. It was the biggest sexual discrimination case of the year. A-Tech had asked its female employees to take a 20% pay cut to work from home, while rewarding male employees with bonuses when they made the same decision. A-Tech saved substantially on overhead expenses when 75% of its workforce moved to a remote work model but the disparate treatment of their male and female employees had been nothing short of egregious.

"I worked on that case with Carly for months and it was locked up tight. I found a key witness and got her to agree to testify. But she was delicate. She had not-so-great things to say about Barr Knoll. Rightfully so, but still, she needed to be handled with kid gloves on the stand and Carly was prepared to do so. Carly told Barr not to question the key female witness himself. But he didn't listen to her. He got in the witness's face, blew the whole damn case up. Of course, that's only part of the story. What was going on, really going on, at Barr Knoll, surprised everyone when it came to light. But that's a story for another time.

"What I'm trying to say, Ava, is, I know this kind of man. No, don't shake your head at me. Roan Knight is not really any different than any other male attorney in this city just because you thought you loved him. You're not the first woman to be duped by Roan Knight, and you certainly won't be the last."

CHAPTER 41
Sara

I had a dream last night. The smell of smoke carefully masked something more sinister—a metallic, ugly odor coiling up from the ground and wrapping itself around my nose.

Someone is bleeding.

No, that wasn't quite right, I thought.

I'm bleeding.

Looking down the dark hallway, I saw a figure—a young woman, with a mane of long dark hair, eyes wide, as her head bobbed mercilessly on her small neck sitting up on a gurney that was wheeling itself back and forth underground. For a moment I thought her body couldn't possibly hold up the weight of her head. Her face glimmered with fear and horror. I reached for her, but she was too far away and my legs wouldn't work. I looked down at the river of blood pooling under me and cursed loudly. I felt nothing in my legs, but my chest hurt from the pounding of my heart and the mounting frustration of not being able to move.

Behind the woman I saw something that I first mistook for her shadow until I realized there could be no shadow because there was no light. Blurred lines came into sharp focus and the woman bent her head forward, making it easier to see behind her.

The evil was gliding up behind her, slowly, soundlessly, visible only to me as I lay bleeding. Helpless. I thought about yelling out to her, warning her, but just as quickly, I put that thought out of my mind. How could she defend herself? She was on a gurney. How could she get out of harm's way? She couldn't. As the shadow came suddenly into focus, I took one last look down at my broken, bleeding body, and hurled myself head first into the path between it and the gurney, determined to be the first thing she'd see when the smoke settled.

And the last thing that monster saw ever again.

CHAPTER 42
Felicity

Felicity takes a few days off at Sheila's insistence after all. She has dug up some old newspaper clippings at the Riversedge Library about Agnes Carson's murder trial. She makes copies at the library for 15 cents a page and brings them back to Easy Street where she studies them constantly.

She keeps coming back to the last day of the trial. The day of Agnes's acquittal. The expression captured by the newspaper photographer is hard to read. It's neither happy nor sad. It's just ... resigned.

Felicity wonders as she reads and re-reads the article what Agnes must have been feeling as she sat in the trial day after day waiting for others to decide her fate. Felicity wonders if she was worried about what would happen to her baby. If she was grateful or resentful that some other family might raise her new baby. Imagining Agnes' emotional roller coaster brings back memories of Felicity's own.

As a recent resident of Riversedge, she doesn't know anyone who might have been alive at the time of the trial to give her a first-hand account. Sure, Ava, and even Archie, were Riversedge natives, but the trial was long before all of their times.

Still, Archie *had* mentioned Agnes by name that night he told them all about the underground tunnel. Any time Felicity tries to talk to him about it, he waves her off dismissively. Archie definitely doesn't want to talk about Agnes Carson. That is clear—even if not much else is these days.

Too bad Ava doesn't have any family in the area anymore that I can ask, Felicity thinks as she reads the series of articles front to back one more time.

Her eye catches on the byline and suddenly an idea occurs to her for the first time since she's discovered the story of Agnes Carson.

Jay Finley. The reporter who covered the trial. I wonder if he's still alive?

A quick Google search reveals that he is. Or at least there's an octogenarian in Riversedge by the same name, who, according to his LinkedIn page started his career as a journalist for the now-defunct *Riversedge Chronicle.*

Of course, it's not the *Riversedge Chronicle* entry on his LinkedIn resume that catches Felicity's eye. Turns out Jay Finley discovered an interest in the law. He's a retired attorney still living in Riversedge. On a whim, Felicity decides to reach out to the email address listed in LinkedIn. She asks him if he's still in Riversedge, and if so, if he'd like to meet her. To discuss the secrets in the past of her new residence—namely 724 Easy Street.

Jay Finley responds within the hour and asks Felicity if she wants to meet him for dinner one night at the Riversedge Law Club. She's not sure how to interpret the speed of his response. Whether it means good things or bad things. But Felicity knows for certain she needs to hear what he has to say.

"Ms. Huck. What a pleasure to meet you."

Jay Finley is portly and red-faced. He doesn't look all that healthy upon first glance, but then again, he does look younger than his 80-odd years.

"Mr. Finley. I'm so grateful you responded. And that you were willing to meet."

"Of course. I read about the recent sale of the building, and I was interested in knowing more about the newest buyers. But ever since the trial, I've taken the position that if people want to know more, they'll reach out. No sense in me stirring old pots."

"Know more? What do you mean by that?"

The server arrives at their table side to interrupt them for their order and Mr. Finley takes his time. Felicity wonders if he thinks she'll forget her question. She doesn't.

"What did you mean, Mr. Finley? What more is there to know about Agnes Carson's trial?"

Jay Finley folds his hands in front of his face and leans on them, head to the side, appraising Felicity for what feels like a very long time, and then he suddenly becomes very talkative.

"Well, Agnes Carson's family paid the paper handsomely to let's just say—*edit*—my pieces on the trial. I always wondered if people realized that when they read my articles, they were really reading highly sanitized reports, but no one came to me. No one asked. Eventually, I realized that if I wanted to make a difference in the legal system, I'd need to become an insider myself."

"You went to law school because of the Agnes Carson trial, then?"

"No, I went to law school because of my son-of-a-bitch editor at the *Chronicle* who thought he could silence me. Pardon my language. I wanted to be my own boss. Decide which cases to take on. Decide how to tell those stories in court without an editor who was on the take—breathing down my back every time I was working."

"Ah, how did that work out?"

"Mostly, well. I had a wonderful career as a solo practitioner in Riversedge. Representing small business owners and home-buyers and handling real estate and estate planning issues. Just a lifetime of helping people navigate the law to carry out the business of life."

"That does sound nice. When I was in law school, they always made solo careers sound unappealing. Like something you should do if you don't get a big law firm job. I'll be honest with you. I see right through that sham now. I wish I'd gone to work for myself out of law school. Now it's too late."

Jay Finley leaned his head back and roared.

"My dear! You're a baby. You have all the time in the world left to pivot and make your career something you love. You still have plenty of time to do something meaningful with your law degree. Where do you work now?"

"Well, I work at Rogers Hawk, and unfortunately—I'm pretty tied into the paycheck right now. Especially after the purchase of the building. I've sunk everything into that building and even if I wanted to sell it—it would be impossible for us to sell it right now with everything we've been discovering."

Jay Finley nodded like nothing Felicity was telling him was a surprise. Or a secret.

"Tell me. What is it you think you have discovered in that building?"

"Oh the list is long. Is this confidential?"

"Sure. Need representation?" Finley winked at her.

"I might."

"Well, consider this an initial attorney consultation. Everything you tell me is privileged. And I can't take on the representation of anyone who has a competing interest with you after you tell me your story, so feel free to speak your mind freely." More winking.

Felicity knows he's only half serious. They both know that he's not taking on any new clients right now and she's not hiring Jay Finley to help her get out of the Easy Street sale. But she does want to know more about the history of the building. She has a feeling there are secrets buried in that building that go far beyond what Archie has already disclosed. Archie seems to have lied about so much. Which reminds her—

"The tunnel. Did you know anything about that?"

Jay is silent for a minute. And Felicity wonders, if that, too, is a lie. But no.

"I did. Every reference to the tunnel and the sanitarium it led to was edited out of my articles. I made multiple attempts to tell the truth, but every one was denied. And the interesting thing was that—as I told my editor—it didn't make sense for Agnes' family to squash that information. It was humanizing information. The fact that Agnes Carson was transported back and forth between Easy Street and the sanitarium to have her brain studied and manipulated and jolted in the name of science made her quite a sympathetic character in the story. But her family was worried it just created more evidence of motive. I was only allowed to write very general, very sparse information about her treatment at Riversedge Asylum."

"I hate to say it, but I think they were right. It certainly looked like Agnes had reason to kill Jasper."

"Well sure she did."

The server arrives with plates of penne glistening with olive oil and pesto and Jay points to her. "Salud."

As Felicity dips a piece of her bread into her pasta, Jay says "Yes. Agnes had every reason to kill Jasper. Only—she didn't."

Felicity looks up abruptly from her plate. "How can you be so sure? Did you hear pieces of exonerating evidence that were left out of the news reports?"

"No. I watched the same trial everyone else did. Agnes's eyes were filled with fire and that hair of hers was always a little wild. But she was frail. Small. And in the end, no one could believe that Agnes Carson dragged her welder husband across those floorboards."

"Was there evidence of anyone else?"

"Not a one. I mean all that talk about Jasper being in debt, but there was no real evidence. No real evidence that some loan shark wanted him dead was presented at trial. At first I couldn't understand why the defense didn't work harder to create reasonable doubt by pointing to someone else. Anyone else. But

EASY STREET

they didn't. And then—after the trial, well at that point, I eventually understood."

"What? You understood *what* exactly?"

There was a leather bag sitting at Jay's feet that Felicity hadn't noticed until just then. Not until he reached down and pulled a folder out of it.

"My editor did most of the editing of my pieces. But I did some editing of my own. I decided not to submit pictures taken of Agnes immediately following the verdict." Jay tapped his folder. "I'll show you these, but I won't give them to you. I haven't decided yet if I want them to go public or not. I've held onto this information for many decades now. I'll ask you to keep this information as confidential as the information you've asked me to keep confidential as well. Deal?"

Felicity nods expectantly. Almost breathless, waiting for the contents of the folder to be revealed.

Jay opens the folder and with one finger, spins a black and white photo around to face Felicity. In it she sees the profile of Agnes Carson, eyes closed, a smile on her face. She is standing at her counsel table, presumably just after the verdict. Her attorneys are shaking hands with each other next to her, almost ignoring her. Everyone in the courtroom has turned to the person next to them or in front of them. There appears to be a fair amount of chaos. The only person who appears to be paying attention to Agnes is a young man, leaning over the front row of the courtroom, his hand is clasped in hers and his profile is evident as well. Agnes's smile is reserved for him. He looks young, maybe 19 or 20. He also looks a little rough and unkempt. His shirt has visible holes in the elbows. He's large and sturdy. The hand he reaches out clasping around Agnes's hand engulfs it. Agnes has her other hand on her heart and is leaning into him as if in offering. As if in gratitude. She looks like she's thanking him. And he looks very much like someone who could have easily dragged an evil man across many a floorboard.

"Oh wow. You think it was him who killed Jasper?"

Jay closes the folder shut and pulls it back to them. "I think he was protecting Agnes. And in turn, she was protecting him. I did a little research at the time. He had been an orderly at the sanitarium. He'd quit before the trial and for some reason, no one named him on the witness list, or even seemed to question him. He was quite anonymous to everyone but Agnes. He sat behind her every day of that trial in silent and solemn support. I never saw her acknowledge him until that moment after the verdict was read. The courtroom was quite a scene and no one seemed to be paying attention to him. Or Agnes for that matter. No one other than me. I took these pictures, but I never offered them to my editor. As I mentioned, he was a son-of-a-bitch."

"What happened to him?"

"My editor?"

"No, that man." Felicity points to Finley's bag where he's already stashed the photos. She'd like to look at them again.

"Well, I didn't tell anyone what I'd seen. And I decided to let them live their lives in peace. Bonded with their own secrets and guilt. Whatever that meant. I figured if someone ever came to me—like the police or a relative of Jasper's—if anyone ever came to me, demanding some truth, I'd give it to them. I wouldn't stand in the way of justice. But no one ever did. No one ever reached out. Except you. From what I can tell, Agnes and he remained close friends. He looked after Agnes until she died. Even went to visit her quite frequently at the assisted living facility she died in. Although she didn't know him any longer by then, I'm told. All that experimentation on her brain took its toll and took her far too early."

Felicity nods quietly, taking in all of this new information.

"Anyway, now he lives quietly. A little lonely, if you ask me. Which I know you didn't."

"Interesting. Can you tell me his name?"

"I'll tell you his name if you promise to leave him in peace."

"He's still local?"

"He is. You have to promise or I can't tell you anymore."

"I promise. I won't bother him. It's just living in that building with its history and its secrets has made me curious, that's all."

Jay paused again and then nodded. "His name is Tom Clark. He's got a farm stand by the river. He's there most days until dusk, no matter the season or the weather. You can go meet him and satisfy your curiosity. He'll make small talk about the produce and art he sells there at the stand. But don't you bring up any topics he doesn't bring up first. You got me?"

Felicity nods. She has a very hard time not rushing through the rest of the meal. She wants to get down the river as soon as possible.

She picks him out in an instant.

From that grainy black and white photo of the young man he once was, yes, but also—because of the art. He's selling tomatoes and fruit and a variety of root vegetables but he's also got paintings on display that are so clearly the work of Agnes Carson, Felicity feels like she's entering sacred ground as she approaches him. She's googled Agnes Carson enough to know her art on sight. She's imagined Agnes's postpartum depression and her creative musings enough to recognize her legacy in oil.

Felicity wanders around the wooden farm stand which is sturdy and also appears custom adapted to showcase the art rather than the produce. "These are absolutely beautiful." Felicity says. She notices then a "Do Not Touch" sign near ones. She startles at a "Not For Sale" sign on another.

"They're not for sale?" She questions.

"Oh no. Not the art. Only the fruits and vegetables, miss. The art is for looking. Not buying."

Felicity shakes her head. She figured this orderly turned farmer was supporting himself on his late friend's art. But apparently not so.

"Between you and me?" He stage whispers.

Felicity is charmed. "Sure," she acquiesces.

"I don't even like to bring these beauties out in the world. But I don't like to be apart from them either. So I bring them down here with me to work each day."

Felicity gasps. "Oh, that's beautiful." She feigns ignorance. "Are you the painter?"

Tom Clark looks indignant. Angry at the question. Felicity half expects him to yell at her and banish her from his sight. But he softens in a minute. "No, Miss. I could never do this. A beautiful, beautiful soul made these paintings."

"Someone close to you, then?" Felicity treads lightly.

"The closest."

Felicity stands in front of one of the pieces. The silhouette of a woman with her head outlined in deep red, the top of her head capped with a tuft of hair that has been sliced open and hinged like a top of a pineapple. Dancing in the space created under the hinge are miniature men and women who are either wearing elaborate costumes. Or nude. There are musical notes painted softly in the background as if the entire story contained in oil is set to music. The piece is both beautiful and chaotic—a crescendo of hurt and healing.

Tom Clark arrives at Felicity's shoulder while she studies it. "The artist was like a wounded deer. Mistreated and abused by those she trusted the most. This was her self-portrait afterward."

"Afterward?"

"After I saved her."

Felicity looks at Tom Clark closely trying to see if there is, in his eyes, the kind of thing that could cause a man to kill. She sees it without too much effort. Yes, there it is. It's love.

"You loved her?"

"I did. I miss her every day."

Felicity picks out some fruit and Tom Clark weighs it and she trades some bills for the fruit. As she turns away, Tom Clark says, "Hold on."

He rounds the corner, and picks up a small painting. It's a view of the river from high above. Serene and tranquil. The city peeks out abstractly, blurry, on the other side, but the focal point is clearly the river.

"Oh, it's beautiful."

"You have it."

"But I couldn't!"

Tom looks at her and nods. "You can have it. I'm not ready to part with the rest of them yet, even though I'm not getting any younger. But that one, you can have. It was painted from the top floor of that building of yours."

"I'm sorry?"

"You live in the building on Easy Street. Used to be East Street. Back when she painted that one. She renamed the street to try to erase its history. Not a very big departure, I always used to say to her, but she said that was kind of the point. A nod to the past. A move forward into the future. She made that hospital buy it back from her. But not until she renamed the whole block. Put her own stamp on it before she moved on. You know what, though? I think she'd like knowing you guys were there now. That you got the building back. That you were fixing it up to make something beautiful out of something so ugly."

Felicity feels something creeping up her spine. Fear. This man is a murderer and she has come here ill-prepared for this meeting. She suddenly feels that she has made a mistake coming here.

He knows where I live. She thinks as she backs up slowly, the painting still clutched in her hands.

She is thinking about running away when Tom suddenly says—"These will all be left to her grandson. When I die. That's how the will read. She made it when she was still lucid so it's all set. You might as well start enjoying that one now. Soon they'll be lining all the walls of that unit you live in."

Felicity swallows hard. Fighting down nausea. "I'm not—I'm not following you."

"I'm just saying. When I die, Archie will inherit them all. Agnes Carson's grandson. Her only living relative."

After that last line, Felicity *does* run away.

CHAPTER 43

Sara

Sometimes when I head out to my paddleboard class, I see him. He doesn't look at me and the way he avoids looking at me tells me everything I need to know. He knows who I am. He's not ready to accept that I know who he is, too. I respect that. I respect his privacy.

Tom Clark is a pretty prominent figure in my grandmother's journal. I've read the passages about him over and over.

She described him as having thick black hair and dark cocoa-colored eyes and a scar over his left eyebrow that he apparently got from a dog bite as a young man. She met him during her earliest days at the Asylum. He was in charge of her transport back and forth in the tunnel. She didn't understand in those moments that Jasper had sold her. She still believed she was there to get well, to return eventually to her baby daughter, my mother.

But as the days and weeks went by with little improvement, she described the nights of panic and fear and tears as she was transported back and forth from the underground examination room under 724 East Street, where the secret laboratory experiments took place—back up to the Asylum's 7th floor that had become her new home.

I worried it would be the place I'd live forever. I worried it would be the place I died.

I confided that very fear to Tom one night.

Tom told me not to worry that he would look out for me. That he would make sure I was well taken care of. I believed him. From the very first moment I met Tom Clark I believed him.

They developed a friendship—my grandmother and Tom Clark and the friendship was spelled out in the pages of that journal. And then one night, Tom Clark came to my grandmother and shared some troubling conversations he'd overheard between the director of the hospital and her husband, Jasper.

He told me that he'd heard Jasper renegotiating the terms of an apparent arrangement. Tom told me that the best he could figure out was that Jasper was exasperated at the delays in the payments by the hospital to him. We both thought that was very strange. Why would the hospital be paying Jasper? Shouldn't he be the one paying the hospital to take care of me? Tom told me he was getting very concerned that Jasper was making a profit off my hospital stay. That the reason it was taking me so long to get well was that Jasper was making money the longer I was in the hospital. Tom suggested we do an experiment. He'd tell Jasper that he'd make even more money if he started helping with the transport himself. Save on hospital staff. He could take more of the grant funding they were using to study my brain. I was in such a fog, I could hardly think for myself, but Tom said not to worry—he'd think for me. The next thing I knew Jasper was at my bedside for every transport. Tom and Jasper. Over the next few days, I'd look up from my bed at both of their eyes, and even in my compromised state, I could see who was looking out for me. Who loved me. And it wasn't Jasper Carson.

I stop reading, interrupted by a loud banging noise. It takes me a moment to realize the banging is knocking. Someone is at my door.

"Sara! I know you're in there. I need to talk to you. I need to talk to you right now. Open up. It's Felicity."

Oh my God. What do I do? What should I do now? Should I let her in? Should I tell her everything?

CHAPTER 44
Holly

What did we expect to find or what did we find?

We expected to find a body. Or bones, rather. I mean a body hidden away underground wouldn't still be a body right? We expected to find a pile of bones.

Which is exactly why I did not want to go down there, if you really want to know.

But I didn't want Ava to go alone, so we snuck down there one morning.

No, it wasn't dark. It wasn't before sunrise. It was in broad daylight. I mean the rest of those lawyers were gone. They were always working around the clock, so there certainly wasn't any reason for us to sneak down there in the dark, when it could be worse. So much worse.

We crept down there quietly, because back then of course, we were still worried about disturbing Sara. We had a plan in case anyone came out the back steps and caught us. We were going to say that one of the contractors was insisting he'd left tools down in the basement and he was invoicing us for stolen property and that we were going to go down there and take pictures of the empty basement ourselves. I know—completely outlandish and not at all foolproof, but we were a little out of our minds by that point.

The building was deteriorating all around us. The black mold was back in every corner of my unit. Ava was sure there were flecks of something she feared was asbestos flaking off the ceiling beams in the unit where she slept, alone by then. Roan was on the run from the IRS and he was out of control. The only communications she received from him were threatening to take Ava to court to force her out of Easy Street, and meanwhile, IRS agents were showing up at the door to confront Ava every other day insisting they'd be back with warrants. It was like a *Law and Order* episode unfolding in the building, every day, right before our eyes. Only—there was no order.

The basement door wasn't just locked. It was padlocked. It looked like a bank vault, with this huge rusty bronze and green-colored lock taking up half the door. I took one look at it and told Ava we were probably barking up the wrong tree. But get this, she had a toolbox. A *toolbox*. And she swore she'd watched a bunch of youtube videos and now she was ready to pick the lock or something. I don't know—it was all very strange to me. She was, how can I best describe her? She was *desperate*.

She worked that lock for almost a half hour. The first screwdriver she wedged into the lock broke in her hand and created a deep gash in the middle of her palm, but Ava didn't so much as grimace. She was like a woman possessed. She told me just to keep watching up the stairwell for any sign of Sara or anyone else for that matter. And when I said, *Ava, I think we should take a break here. Bandage your hand, at least. Or get a glass of water.*

Well she glared at me, and then waved me off like I was a fool or something.

She kept on working that lock, occasionally refreshing her phone and following along some underground youtube lock picker.

When she finally broke into that padlock, we saw it.

The tunnel. It was a little anticlimactic by that point. There was nothing else down there. No bodies or bones or flammable liquids, if that's what you're getting at. No evidence that anything nefarious had happened there. Or was going to happen there.

Yes, of course, I was concerned about Ava's behavior, but I

knew we weren't actually doing anything wrong. We owned that building. We were entitled to do whatever we wanted with that building.

Paint over the mold. Break into the basement. Hide everyone's secrets. Whatever we wanted.

What was that?

Did whatever we wanted include burning the place to the ground? Yeah, sure. I'm going to go ahead and make my own objection to that question, thank you very much.

But you know what, Counselor? Let's just state the obvious here. Your client saved a lot of money with that building burning down. That's what I'm trying to help you see here. There was no environmental exclusion in that policy. I've read it cover to cover. And I've worked on environmental cases. They can cost tens and sometimes, hundreds of millions of dollars. Remediating that building would have cost you a hell of a lot more than we're asking for here. So why don't you all stop fighting us, cancel the trial and pay us what we're owed? I've already settled my medical claims under the policy as you know.

I know, we're not supposed to be talking about that medical case here. It's over. You only want to talk about the insurance fraud case you guys are trying unsuccessfully to build here.

But tell me, Counselor.

Don't you think it's time to pay up and let go of the secrets buried under Easy Street? Once and for all?

CHAPTER 45
Felicity

Felicity runs directly from the riverside meeting with Tom Clark to Sara's door. She's tired of running. She's tired of hiding. She's tired.

She bangs on the door. She hears footsteps and movement behind the door and she resolves to stand there all day and all night until Sara opens the door. She'll have to come out eventually, won't she?

The footsteps get louder and then the door opens and Felicity feels a sadness as she sees him, gray and pale and looking as unwell as she's ever seen him.

"Archie."

"Come in." Archie waves her in, and Felicity looks around for Sara but there is no one else in the apartment. No one clearly visible anyway.

Archie takes a seat on the couch. In front of him is a coffee table with a leather-bound book overstuffed with clippings and stapled pieces of paper splayed out on the table. "Sit down," Archie says as he pats the sofa cushion next to him. Felicity joins him, and asks only one more time, "Archie, where's Sara?"

"Sara's gone, Felicity," Archie sighs.

"Gone?"

"Well, for now. Hopefully, forever, but I'm not sure that's true. She keeps coming back. It's harder and harder to make her stay away these days."

"I don't understand."

"Of course not, how could you? I've wanted to explain this to you for a very long time, but I just didn't know how. How can anyone explain to someone they love that the man you love—the man you think you love—is actually a broken person. Broken in two."

Felicity looks at him, confused, but silent, because she wants to create the safe space he seems to need to tell her everything.

And he tells her, finally. Everything.

There was terrible abuse suffered at the hands of his mother's boyfriends. His mother, Delilah Bello, did the best she could, but she, too, was a broken soul. She'd been raised by cold grandparents and then dumped on her mother's doorstep—an accused murderer—at the age of thirteen, an impactful age and time. Archie's mother, Delilah, had tried to form a bond with Agnes, but it was difficult. They didn't have a very close relationship and it created a void in her life she would forever try to fill with men and booze and drugs. The Riversedge floral shop she bought with a small inheritance from her grandparents seemed to give her great joy. The Bellos would never have approved of her exploring such a creative passion while still alive. They hated any sign that Agnes's apparent broken genes had found their way into Archie's mother, Delilah, despite the fact that they'd raised her after Jasper's death until she turned thirteen.

"The Bellos. Of course. That's why I never connected you to Agnes Carson," Felicity says.

"No. Agnes kept Jasper's name until she died. She was oddly old-fashioned in weird ways," Archie chuckles. "But my mother and I were Riversedge Bellos of course."

"So Sara?" Felicity asks gently.

"She was part of a make-believe game my grandmother and I would play when I was little. When I wanted to escape my house and everything that was going on there. I'd pretend I was someone else. It seemed innocent, really, but eventually, it was harder and harder to control.

"When my grandmother died, it became impossible. When I lost her completely and inherited this book of her trauma, well, something broke me in half."

Dissociative Identity Disorder. The diagnosis was a long time coming. Archie has been hiding it for some time now.

Felicity listens as Archie shares with her his most vulnerable pain, and she holds his hand urging him forward.

When he lived separately from Felicity, he could manage his secret. Sara would emerge on Saturday mornings, after a long work week and he'd allow her her space. She was always gone again before Monday morning.

But in the apartment building—Archie knew it would be harder and harder to keep Sara a secret. He wanted this building desperately. When he heard it was on the market again, he was obsessed with getting it back and erasing its evil legacy. He was hell bent on turning it into something beautiful—a memorial to Agnes. But Archie also knew he'd need a second unit to retreat to. He tried to talk Lou into buying a unit for investment purposes and letting Archie lease it out. But Lou didn't want anything to do with the building, so Archie had no other choice but to buy it in Sara's name. He couldn't invite an actual new buyer into the deal—he needed access to a second unit. So, Archie sold his mother's floral shop reluctantly, forged some paperwork with Sara's name on it, and plugged a hole in the problem he hoped never to confront, no matter how unrealistic that really was.

As she listens to his story, Raven's words come back to Felicity, and she finally understands what they mean..

You think there's two. But there's only one.

"It's been harder than I thought, living in this space, Felicity."

She nods. Felicity looks over at the window and sees a beautiful sculpture. It's of a woman with long stone locks painted black. From a distance it looks real. The hair even looks like it's waving in the wind. Felicity understands then that the supposed sightings of Sara have never been real.

Archie follows her gaze and nods.

"My grandmother's art is all I have left of her. A few paintings and that sculpture my mother retained even though my grandmother's friend, Tom Clark, took the rest."

"I met Tom Clark," Felicity says quietly.

"You did? But how?"

"I've been reading the articles about the trial. I have my own pain that I've never shared with you, Archie. Pain that has connected me to your grandmother in ways you cannot understand."

Felicity tells him then about the summer and the tarot card reader named Raven. She tells him about her spring and summer of grief and healing. Felicity tells Archie that she understands Agnes's postpartum depression intimately, and that she wishes Agnes—and Archie—had had a mother like hers.

She tells him, too, about finding Jay Finley, about the photo he took of Agnes and Tom and how Tom plans to will Archie all the rest of his grandmother's art as per her wishes.

Archie exhales deeply and tells Felicity he feels some relief sharing his story with her. "I'm not ready for anyone else to know yet. But when the time is right, I'll tell them, too."

"I understand, Archie. We will navigate this together now. You're not alone. You were never alone."

They sit in silence for a few moments and then Archie nods his head at the statute. His expression changes and his demeanor. Felicity realizes that she is sitting not with Archie right now, but with Sara.

Sara says, "See her? Isn't she beautiful? As far as I know—it's the only sculpture she ever did. I keep her in front of the window and I imagine my grandmother looking down into the river that she and Tom Clark hurled my no-good grandfather's body into."

CHAPTER 48
Ava

Let me help you renegotiate that book deal.

Ava couldn't believe Roan had the nerve to reach out. She'd been sleeping alone for months, fielding IRS phone calls and pop-ins, and trying to break into her own damn basement for heaven's sake.

What a ridiculous waste of time that had turned out to be.

With Holly at her side, playing cloak and dagger, Ava had broken into the basement to find, well a basement. Not a body. Not a bone. No evidence of anything whatsoever. True, she hadn't been sure what she was looking for, but the way Roan and Archie were behaving lately, she was certain they were protecting something in this old building. Something other than mercury under the floorboards and mold in the closets.

Ava was tired and she was broke. Her early inspiration that fueled the beginning pages of the novel had tapered off. She was writing a story about big law corruption that felt like every other story she'd read. She was painting Jason McKoy with broad strokes of villainhood and ditto for Roan Knight and none of it felt authentic anymore. None of it felt real.

I can't be who you want me to be.

These days, those words felt intended only for Ava herself. She didn't know who she was anymore.

Ava was surprised to hear from Roan at all, but a proposed renegotiation of her book contract felt like exactly the right reason to talk to him. Of all things that might land with her, he picked the right one. Ava had been working around the clock on the ghostwriting book deal for all of a $50,000 advance, hoping that her savings and Roan's share of the mortgage would sustain her. But with Roan facing embezzlement charges, and her own savings dwindling, Ava was starting to think she just might need Roan's help.

She agreed to meet him in the Riversedge Law Club, but only after he claimed he was getting a meeting with Nola as well. *The three of us can discuss this deal together.*

This I have to see, Ava thought and she took a break from writing, if for no other reason than to get some good inspiration for a new chapter in the book.

In the Riversedge Law Club, Ava narrated her entrance into the room as if it was a Prologue.

Nola Dyer and Roan Knight had already arrived, and they looked like old friends rather than sworn enemies. Anyone observing the two handsome characters at a round table in the corner of the marble-floored dining room would never know that Nola was representing a lawsuit that named Roan Knight. In fact, the ethics of them meeting at all could certainly be questioned if a passerby did know. Nevertheless, this was the climate and culture of the Riversedge Law Club. Hazy, blurry with a side of optimism and corruption. Illegal deals weren't made in dark alleys, Ava had learned. They were made in the glaring sunlight where no one could deny they were occurring, but no one would ever stop them from happening either.

Ava took a seat. Water glasses were emptied in front of Nola and Roan. They'd apparently been sitting there long enough to hydrate. *How much other business had already been accomplished?* Ava wondered.

"Ava, thank goodness you showed. I thought you were going to leave me alone with this mercenary." Nola chuckled to add levity to her words that sounded dark and serious.

"Well, Nola, now that we're all here, let's dive in. Why would you take advantage of Ava the way you did? A $50,000 book advance. That's laughable. You wouldn't have made such an offer if Ava was a seasoned writer."

Ava felt like she was on the far outside of a conversation into which she couldn't locate an entry point. She was suddenly embarrassed to hear Roan mocking something she'd been so proud of a few months ago.

"Well, I'm hardly a seasoned writer."

Roan jerked his head toward her and suddenly Ava felt like a small child sitting at the grown up's table. It was not unlike that first day she'd met Writer Friend in the Hamptons. When Roan and Writer Friend had mocked Ava's aspirations and naiveté right there in front of her. After Writer Friend failed to offer her a drink and looked drily at the not-so-designer label on her jacket.

"Ava, don't undersell yourself. We're here to get you what you deserve. You're acting like you never even practiced law, let alone wrote a commercially viable word. Jesus."

Nola looked back and forth between the couple and seemingly saw something that wasn't there.

"Ah, I see. Good cop, bad cop. Clever."

Ava smiled awkwardly, trying to pretend this was indeed orchestrated by Roan and Ava together.

Roan leaned into the table. "Nola, we all know you're trying to make a name for yourself. I get it. Your reputation precedes you and you cut your teeth as a paralegal at one of the best firms in the country. Barr Knoll was a legend in his own time."

"Certainly, a legend in his own mind," Nola laughed, then shifted her expression. "Listen, what Barr Knoll did right was surround himself with smart women who knew how to save him from himself. His whole career was built on stilts of fraud and ego. I'm building something very different here."

Roan looked quiet. Silenced almost.

Nola looked back and forth between him and Ava, and then leaned back in her chair. Her expression turned comfortable and relaxed.

"That said, Roan. You and I both know the case against you in particular is not so strong. Not as strong as I'd hoped it would be anyway. No one has come forward to corroborate anything the witness originally swore to, and the witness herself has recanted most of what she originally testified about. Apparently, the combination of sleeping meds and wine you both indulged in that evening did much to provide a cloud over her memory of the entire evening."

Roan looked smug. Ava was surprised at what was unfolding before her. The lunch had turned into a vindication of Roan rather than a renegotiation at all.

"What are you saying, Nola?" Ava broke the silence.

"I'm saying that I'm agreeing to a stipulation to dismiss Roan from the case with prejudice and pressing forward with the case against the real villains of Rogers Hawk.

"Nice," Roan leaned back in his seat, and Ava shook her head.

"I am going to ask you to speak out about the terrible events that have happened at that firm, Roan. An insider's perspective will really help us put a nail in the coffin."

"And you've considered my offer?"

Ava watched the two of them with confusion and mounting panic.

What offer?

"Yes, of course," Nola laughed. "I've brought the papers." Nola slapped a folder down on the table with a pen, saying, "You will be the first male attorney brought into my firm. The terms are all laid out here. Bring some of those high paying clients with you and I'll provide you a shingle to practice under. When Rogers Hawk folds, as it inevitably will, you'll want to be on the good guys' side. Or the good women's side, should I say?"

Ava watched as Roan signed the papers with a flourish, and

tried to understand what was unfolding before her.

"Ava, would you kindly witness the papers?" Nola tried to hand her a pen but Ava swatted it away.

"What about my advance, Nola?"

"What about it? You don't have to pay it back, Ava, I already told you that. Even though the publisher has decided not to publish the book after all. Too much danger of defamation claims. We don't need it now. The case against Rogers Hawk is iron tight. Roan is helping make sure of that, aren't you?"

Roan nodded and smiled, his gaze trained on Nola and away from Ava.

"Wait a fucking minute, here. This was all a big sham of a meeting. This has nothing to do with me. You two just needed a witness to your deal. Can't I at least finish the book I've been working on for months?"

"Well, Ava, you are free to write anything you want, but the mounting evidence is going to speak for itself. We no longer need to try the case in the court of public opinion, frankly. So, you know the $50,000 advance, for a still unproven novelist such as yourself, is definitely the best you're going to get here. It's more than generous, frankly. And the publisher has already indicated they are simply not leaning toward moving forward with the project."

Roan nodded. "I get that."

The server came to the table then but Ava couldn't see him through the anger clouding her vision. Roan had used her. Nola had used her. And she'd been naive enough to believe it was all real. None of it was. Nola hadn't paid Ava $50,000 for her writing or her novel in progress. She'd bought her. And Ava had allowed herself to be bought so very cheaply. By Roan as well.

Ava didn't order when the waiter arrived. She got up and unceremoniously left the table. As she did so, she narrated her exit dramatically.

The heroine left the two vacant-eyed lawyers behind as she took her leave. And as she fled the scene, she looked over her shoulder and saw their faces. They were less stunned than smug. She hated them and sorted through her mind for a list of options available to her. She chose the only one she really believed was left. She hit detonate on the bomb she'd planted under their seats, cleverly, without them knowing

And as she left the building, the whole place exploded into shards of navy blue suits and smug expressions until nothing was left but the rubble.

CHAPTER 47
Holly

Finally! We're adjourned?

What do you mean, for the day?

Don't you think you've got enough information to avoid trial and just pay us the policy limits? The fire was an accident, isn't that clear? And it also saved you a hell of a lot of money, isn't that clear as well?

Listen, I know you're all doing your jobs here, but the truth is, we were up to date on our insurance premiums. You all had more than ample opportunities to examine the building when it was still standing and your appraisal was what it was.

The building burned down, and your insurance company client owes us all a big, fat check. I certainly hope we're not going to trial over this case. I was a lawyer once too, you know. I realize it makes far more sense for your guys to settle this case for the policy limits, rather than spending any more time on lawyers and depositions.

I can't even imagine what this day has cost your client.

Excuse you, I absolutely *do* want that on the record. Miss Court Reporter you go ahead and type it exactly as I said it.

As for the rest of you—it was lovely spending the day with you, gentlemen. Good luck to you.

EPILOGUE

In the end, the case of *New York Insurance vs Easy Street Co-op* was settled out of court for the policy limits. A building that was purchased for less than a million with another $800,000 in improvements and renovations was eventually settled for its policy limits of $5.2 million. The proceeds were divided fairly—if not evenly—among the owners of Easy Street.

Archie conceded that given what he'd hid from the group about his medical diagnosis, even though he'd technically contributed twice his agreed upon share, and sold his mother's floral shop to do so, he would only take one share of the insurance proceeds. He is under new medical care for his diagnosis.

And no one could really be sorry that—given its history—724 Easy Street, formerly known at 724 East Street, was gone, and with it, a sordid history of betrayal, abuse and secrets. Archie thought he wanted the building back in the family, but living in that building was more fracturing than healing.

Nola Dyer settled her claims against Rogers Hawk, which shuttered its doors not long after the Easy Street insurance settlement, and all of its attorneys were left to find other gainful employment, except the ones who were disbarred as a result of the lawsuit. Roan Knight was dismissed from the lawsuit and went to work for Nola Dyer, Esq., after all. His wealthy clients seemed far more willing to forget his legal troubles when he went to work for a rising star female attorney. He was able to bring his large roster of clients to Nola's firm for a healthy commission paid to Nola. It seemed Nola Dyer could be bought, and that Roan Knight was still just as charming as ever.

Ava turned her novel-in-progress into a scathing commentary of female attorneys who form alliances with men to get ahead. At printing, she was still trying to get an agent to represent her. She's had 27 rejection emails but she's not throwing in the towel yet.

Felicity? She left Rogers Hawk and hung up her own shingle. It was a long overdue departure from the kind of big law litigation she was sick of practicing. Her new business cards read

Felicity Huck, Family Court Lawyer:
Repairing and saving our most precious resources—children.

And the new logo is sort of geometric and abstract. Only Felicity knows it was based on the design of a tarot card that had long ago forecasted her future.

What about Holly and Daniel? Well, Holly's symptoms seem to be in control, and her health is better than ever since the tragedy that struck Easy Street. With the proceeds of her settlement with the insurance company on her medical claims, she and Daniel rented a commercial kitchen in Riversedge with a small apartment in the back. They secured the lease after a brief honeymoon and quick elopement. They have plans for the new insurance proceeds now that the checks have finally cleared.

Daniel refused to relinquish his share of the insurance proceeds and no one even thought to ask him to do so.

In the end, only Holly, his wife, who couldn't be asked legally to testify against him if anyone asked, really knew the truth. And she'd held her own during a full day of relentless questioning by a room full of dark suits who never actually asked the one question they should have which was:

Holly Riddle, did your husband start the fire on Easy Street by lighting a match when the building was completely empty? And did he do so on purpose to save both your health and your investment?

Because even if they'd asked, Holly would have had only one response:

Objection.

Have you caught up on all the
RIVERSEDGE LAW CLUB
stories yet?

Isn't it time you #JOINTHECLUB?!

Enjoy the first Chapter of IN HER DEFENSE and
the prologue of BARR NONE

IN HER DEFENSE

CHAPTER 1
Broken Promises

"There's no i in dead."

Opal slams hard on her brakes. She's been distracted by her son's bleating in the back of the car and the thoughts swirling around in her own brain that she cannot seem to quiet. She doesn't see the car whizzing down the road until it's directly behind her as she backs out of the driveway. It's almost too late by the time she comes to a complete stop. Almost. Opal exhales loudly in relief as the driver passes her by without a collision. A close call. She'll take it.

"There's no i in dead, Mommy."

Opal closes her eyes, shaking off the near miss that has just occurred steps from their front door. Ever since the nearby bridge construction began a few weeks ago, the previously quiet street she lives on with her son, CJ, has been overrun by traffic. Her road wasn't supposed to be an official detour route. Would-be bridge goers are supposed to travel the long way around

Wolff Pond and then past Hemingway Park, until they get to that hole-in-the-wall bakery, the one with the melt-like-butter-in-your-mouth croissants, and then they are supposed to make a hard right-hand turn that will lead them to a road that bypasses the bridge construction. But they don't, because no one ever does what they are supposed to do.

"There's no i in dead, Mommy. Why aren't you listening to me? We need to fix this poster. I can't take it to school like this, Mommy."

No one does what they are supposed to do. Not even me. Especially not me. Opal thinks as she shifts the car into park.

"Mommy—"

Opal leans hard on the horn in a delayed act of frustration, even though the car that had come out of nowhere is now, well, nowhere to be seen.

CJ sits quietly for a moment in response to the horn that has been meant for him.

Remorsefully, Opal turns around and looks at the forlorn poster in her son's lap. Photographs of a makeshift herb garden in various stages of growth and death are plastered in a crooked line and while they are upside down from her vantage point, Opal can still see them clearly, having looked at the photos every day over the last week or so. She can't unsee them now if she tries. The last photo in the line shows a particularly gruesome sight of a brown and rotting rosemary plant set in a kitchen windowsill pot and cared for with nothing but misguided optimism. Opal has never had a green thumb. She bought the rosemary because she read somewhere that "rosemary means remembrance" and things had turned a corner. Things in her life were so good, so positive, so different, that *finally,* she wanted to *remember.*

So she'd bought some rosemary at the local hardware store, planted it next to the basil and mint that was growing unchecked on her windowsill and crossed her fingers.

Of course, the tide has turned quickly. She no longer wants

to remember—not the rosemary plant nor anything else that has come crashing down on her in the last twenty-four hours. But CJ has gone and made that dead rosemary plant the center-piece of his damn science poster.

Opal has been so embarrassed by her son photographing her failings as a home gardener for his third-grade life cycle homework, she hasn't noticed the misspelling in the short but true caption that she sees now as her son flips the poster toward her. The final caption is upside down for him but right side up for her. He points to it ominously as Opal nods at its solemn wrongness.

This plant is dead.

Opal faces forward again, leans on the steering wheel, and tries to come up with a new game plan for the morning.

Why is he noticing it for the first time this morning? Why now?

In order to make it on time, they have to be at school in exactly – Opal leans over and checks the car clock to confirm the dire straits they are in—*21 minutes.*

She didn't think they'd run late today. After all, CJ finished the project days ago, and left it on the dining room table, where no one ever ate, and that served only as the holding ground for homework and bills and cookies they wanted to hide from com-pany. Even though she's been mortified by the photos, Opal has been so proud of CJ for being on top of things. For getting his homework done. For doing it carefully and neatly (albeit embar-rassingly calling out his mother's lack of a green thumb and reckless optimism). For all the times she's passed that poster with a mixture of pride and embarrassment over the last few days, she hasn't noticed the typo, but now that she has—now that *he* has—there simply is no time to fix it.

CJ *needs* to be at school on time this particular morning. Or rather, *Opal needs* CJ to be at school on time today: for a number of reasons, not the least of which is that Opal wants to be alone for the remainder of the day. A rare day off and she already knows she's going to need the stolen time.

After all, she doesn't want the police to show up in front of CJ to question her about a dead body.

On the other side of Hemingway Park, Ingrid DiLaurio and her son, Drake, are heading to Cosie's Bakery for a croissant on a cheat day from Ingrid's intermittent fasting. She wants something soothing and buttery today. Especially today. The wide openness of the day is unsettling, and Ingrid wants to be prepared.

She parks her car a block away from the bakery and shields her eyes from the early morning sun as she gets out, realizing too late that she's forgotten her sunglasses. Cosie's is always packed, but on Tuesdays the small storefront overflows, following a dark Monday: the only day all week that the bakery is closed. On their walk from the car, Ingrid and Drake encounter a sea of faces hurrying to and from the bakery. A hand or two goes up toward them in recognition. Ingrid exchanges one nod and two smiles. The rest of the faces overlook her and her son blankly. It always takes Ingrid by surprise how few people really know her; or at least how few *acknowledge* knowing her when she is out and about the town, despite having lived here for over a decade. Riversedge, New York is an impostor of a small town; with the posh setting, upscale mom and pop retail shopping, very few chain stores, not one McDonald's in its city limits, and an enormous brick-face library built after a year-long capital campaign, the town of Riversedge makes an elaborate pretense of *wanting* to be a small town. Riversedge has a charming tree-lined Main Street, and an annual Memorial Day parade and just one each of a firehouse, police station and post office, but still, it lacks the small town feel you'd expect in a place this size.

Just four express train stops from Manhattan, Riversedge is really a city impersonating a small town. It's a suburb of New York City, with a transient population, and though it's small enough for everyone to know each other's secrets, few actually do.

While Ingrid stands in line at the bakery, holding Drake's hand, she checks her phone for recent emails and then reviews her notes for a taping scheduled later that morning. Ingrid is the host of a popular national weekly podcast, called *Too Busy to Die*, focusing on streamlining the mess in all of our lives so that we are no longer too busy to die, but instead, less busy to live. Well, that's the soundbite at any rate, and the segment to be taped this morning will cover decluttering plans anyone can tackle in a weekend, especially with spring right around the corner. Ingrid types something into her phone that she just thought of but isn't sure she will say out loud on the taping. (*"Spring cleaning" is an unfortunate term. Most people really need to do a deep cleaning weekly, and not just annually, or seasonally, or when someone dies*).

As she and Drake move slowly toward the front of the line, Ingrid reviews notes furiously and mentally prepares for the podcast taping to try to keep a few lingering and confusing thoughts about her husband, Peter, from clouding her vision. She doesn't want to stop and think about him right now. She doesn't want to think about how he's hurt her or how he's humiliated her in the worst way possible. She wants to think about her podcast taping and preparing Drake's homeschooling lessons for the next week, and about this buttery croissant that she's allowing herself to enjoy, on this one day, that she is permitted all week long.

At the front of the line finally, she orders two croissants. Drake points out a jumbo cookie he'd like to add to the order, but Ingrid smiles and shakes her head. He knows he can't win this argument. He's hardly even putting up a fight. Ingrid winks at him, a silent reward for his obedience as she turns and says, "That will be everything, thank you." The bakery clerk gives her a polite smile without a hint of real recognition and for once, this anonymity comforts, instead of pains, Ingrid. She takes her greasy brown bag from the bakery clerk, and hurries away from the crowded bakery, down the block to her car with Drake in tow, and the pair heads home to face whatever it is that is coming next.

In spite of herself, Opal stands at the dining room table, cutting and pasting a new caption for her son's poster. She knows this is all costing precious time they don't have right now. Not this morning.

CJ isn't helping. He's got a new line of questioning for Opal.

"Mommy, how many tickets will we need for the poster award ceremony?"

Opal shrugs and rocks the glue stick back and forth on the new caption. The one that no longer has an "i" in dead.

"But Mommy, I need to know, because Mrs. Bardo says everyone is only allowed 2 guest tickets."

"Ok," Opal says absent-mindedly. She would love to stop talking about this freaking poster. She bites her tongue so those particular words don't escape her. She knows CJ repeats everything she says at home to that damn high-and-mighty Mrs. Bardo. Opal bites harder. She doesn't want to say *high-and-mighty* out loud either. That's an unfortunate phrase her mother used to use and Opal hates it so of course, it jumps into her mind at the worst possible times.

"Mommy, how many will we need?"

"Hunh?" All this tongue-biting has made her forget what they are even talking about. She rubs a sore tongue alongside the inside of her teeth and tries not to think about Mrs. Bardo.

"Tickets. How many guest tickets will we need?"

"Oh. Just the one, CJ."

"Mommy, are you sure?"

Opal knows what he's thinking, of course, but she avoids his unasked question lingering in the air, until he actually asks it, making it impossible to avoid any longer without lying.

"Mommy, will Uncle Pete be there?"

"No." Opal knows her response is too quick. She backpedals just as quickly. "What I mean is ... oh, CJ ...."

Opal crouches down to CJ's level and holds up the fixed science poster as a barrier between them as she tells him the truth. "Listen, CJ, Uncle Pete's not going to be around anymore. I know you liked him and I know you hoped he'd be around for things more often. Things like the science poster award ceremony and your birthday party and other things. But he's not our family. And he's just not going to be around anymore. And it's ok."

Opal sees her son's crestfallen face as she stands up, distancing herself from his watery eyes, and in a panic, she blurts, "Hey, what do you say after school, we go to the Main Street Ice Cream Shoppe?"

CJ's face lights up instantly.

Success.

At the Main Street Ice Cream Shoppe, they have bubblegum flavored ice cream with real gumballs littering the pink frothy dessert. They serve it with a small paper cup, so you can pick the gumballs out and save them for later. It's the only gum Opal allows CJ to eat, and the promise is a treat reserved for special occasions.

Well, Peter is gone, Opal thinks, fighting hard to keep her emotions in check in front of CJ. *I guess this qualifies as a special occasion.*

"Come on, CJ. We're late. I have to write you a note and get you to school now. When I pick you up, we'll go straight to Main Street. I promise."

Opal lays the poster back down on the table, grabs a notecard out of the dining room cabinet and starts scribbling an excuse as to why CJ is late for the first time ever this entire school year. She notices her hand shaking a bit, and worries at her penmanship and what that lofty Mrs. Bardo will think and say, but she keeps on writing nonetheless. She glances up to see CJ admiring his newly fixed poster. A thick tuft of his light brown hair shoots straight up over his head locked in place by two twisting fingers. Opal's heart aches with the realization that even with the fixed poster and the promise of ice cream and the clinical description of Peter's departure from their lives, CJ is still anxious. CJ always twists his hair in his fingers when he's nervous. It's a tic he's inherited from his biological father. That and those damn almond-shaped eyes that melt her every single time she looks at her son. CJ is Christopher Junior, named for a father he never even met, and Christopher the First was a habitual hair twister, among other things. Of course, the fact that CJ has never known his father has made it all the more confusing for Opal when she sees CJ unwittingly mimic Christopher in these small ways over the years.

As she watches her son twist his hair and study his science poster, she wonders, not for the first time, if she should have given him some other name. She laments that she has given Christopher the honor of having this lovely, perfect boy named for him. She wonders if she shouldn't have given Christopher quite so much, her son's name included.

Opal holds the rehabilitated poster out to her son who takes it happily. "Come on, CJ, we gotta get to school now."

With a note explaining his late arrival in one hand, and CJ's hand in the other, Opal heads out of the house for an encore. She folds CJ and his now perfect science poster into the backseat, buckles herself into the driver's seat, and starts to back out of the driveway, only to be stopped yet a second time by a car coming out of nowhere behind her. Two cars actually. "Don't twist your hair, CJ," Opal says nervously, glancing at CJ in the rearview mirror, as both police cars pull up alongside her in her own driveway. As she gets out of the car, she tells CJ to "stay put."

A tall, lean man who fills out his police uniform quite nicely gets out of the first car, and Opal nods hello to him. She recognizes him as Officer Tim Connors, who shows up at the hospital now and then on official business, where Opal works as a nurse, a step up from the department store makeup counter, which was her first job when she arrived in this town, and a giant step up from the other jobs she's worked since then, too. Tim Connors has a warm smile. The kind that disarms you instantly. *He must be a very good cop*, Opal has thought on occasion when she's seen him at the hospital. *I bet he can smile a confession out of nearly anyone.* And indeed, it's that disarming smile that he greets Opal with. Which must be why she responds to him with a sentence she will later wish she hadn't said out loud. "Oh. I was sort of expecting you guys." After she says it, Opal looks down at the ground in surrender.

A few minutes later, Officer Tim reads Opal her rights and then arrests her for the murder of a man named Peter DiLaurio and takes Opal away in handcuffs with her little boy in the other squad car following them. At a red light, Opal looks over her shoulder and catches a glimpse of her son in the back seat of the car behind her, with pain and shame in his eyes – or is that her own mirrored back at her? He is twisting that tuft of hair furiously. Opal wonders where his science poster is. Did he remember to bring it with him? Can she somehow get it to school so all his hard work is not for nothing?

Opal knows CJ must realize that she has broken her promise about Main Street Ice Cream. But he can't realize yet that she's broken a great many other promises as well.

At home, the police are in Ingrid's driveway. She exhales loudly, and Drake grunts nervously.

"It's ok, Drake. Mommy's going to go talk to the police officers. You stay in the car and let Mommy talk to the police, ok?" Drake says nothing in return but this isn't unusual. Drake rarely talks.

Selective mutism.

The diagnosis came four years ago. Peter always bragged about what a pleasure it was to have a child who wasn't too precious. A child who wasn't always interrupting his parents when they were talking to grownups. A child who wasn't always chattering away when his father was trying to unwind after a long day of work. Ingrid thought Drake was, sort of, *unusually quiet*, but what did she know? He was her first, her only, child, and she had been an only child as well. When he was two and three, Ingrid wondered if perhaps Drake would talk more when he had other options. Instead of pining about the start of school like she knew she was supposed to, Ingrid actually looked forward to the day when Drake would head off to school and find some more suitable companions than the ones he was obviously bored with at home. But it wasn't long after he started preschool that Ingrid was summoned in to talk to the teacher after classes had ended for the day and the children had all gone home. All except Drake.

"Frankly, I'm surprised you haven't sought out a professional opinion earlier than this," Mrs. Lopez said as she detailed the red flags she'd seen already in her short time of teaching Drake. Ingrid felt chided and scolded in the cold empty classroom. She found herself looking past Mrs. Lopez's head at a bulletin board made of fish and cut out laminated bubbles with the letters of the alphabet.

We are hooked on letters! The bulletin board announced.

Ingrid's eyes focused on the bubbles as Mrs. Lopez talked. She wasn't sure what she had missed and when Mrs. Lopez interrupted her thoughts with a persistent, "Mrs. DiLaurio?" Ingrid made excuses and stuttered about Drake's perceived speech issues, all the while screaming at Peter in her head.

You did this.

You made me think this was all ok.

You were so happy to have a quiet, well-behaved child.

You lulled me into a false sense of complacency.

And now our son is being labeled within weeks of starting school.

With the anger exploding inside her, Ingrid managed to keep her face calm and contrite and bring her gaze back from the bubbles behind the patronizing teacher's head. "Thank you so much, Mrs. Lopez. I'm grateful for you identifying an issue that's been bothering me for some time now. I'll make that appointment right away."

It didn't take long to get the diagnosis after that awkward meeting with Mrs. Lopez.

"Mute? But he talks. Not a lot. But he does talk. I've counted his words and he reached all his language milestones. I've recorded them in his baby book for the pediatrician." Ingrid tapped a closed book in her lap for emphasis.

Dr. Vee explained that selective mutism is a form of anxiety disorder that manifests itself in an inability to talk in certain social situations. Dr. Vee then gave Ingrid some brochures and pamphlets and the card of a psychotherapist in New York City that she said specialized in selective mutism in children Drake's age.

"It's fine, Ingrid. Lots of kids are shy. He'll grow out of it. You worry too much." Peter did everything but pat her on the head when she brought him the diagnosis, brochures and the card of the expensive psychotherapist who was, predictably, out of their insurance network. But Ingrid was armed with rebuttal information for Peter's condescension, having done her research following the appointment with Dr. Vee. Drake was not shy. He was anxious. Left unattended, this disorder would impede his development and his ability to function in school and in life. And he wouldn't just "grow out of this." It would require hard work and attention. Work Ingrid was willing to put in.

"And what about you, Peter? Are you willing to do the hard work to make our son feel comfortable enough to start talking to you?"

"Of course, I am," Peter said. He must have seen the resolve in Ingrid's eyes. Something that made him realize he wasn't going to win this argument. "Take him to the New York City shrink if you think that's what he needs. I'll do whatever it takes to help him. I promise."

Yes, he promised. But, like so many of his promises, Peter broke this one, too. As a result, Drake has only ever said a handful of words to his father. He's started to open up more to Ingrid recently, but Peter? Well, he's missed out. Drake hasn't won any father lottery, unfortunately, and Ingrid feels terrible that she has that in common with her sweet son.

As Ingrid closes the car door behind her in the driveway, the officer who's been waiting for her, takes his hat off and addresses her, "Ma'am? Are you Mrs. Ingrid DiLaurio?"

She nods, wordlessly.

"Ma'am, I need to talk to you. Maybe we could go inside?"

Ingrid shakes her head. "No, whatever it is. Please go ahead and tell me. My son is in the car, and I just need to know."

"Ma'am, I'm very sorry to tell you but your husband, Peter DiLaurio, was found, well, deceased, late last night, outside a property on the corner of 35th and Russell."

Looking up at the officer, who does indeed look sorry to tell her this, Ingrid is suddenly overcome with grief that the opportunity for Peter to make good on any of his broken promises is now officially over. Especially to Drake. Her eyes fill up with tears. A million words fill her brain, but she can speak none of them.

Is this what it is like for Drake, then? Wanting to say words but not able to find the breath or the energy to utter them?

The words continue to ricochet in her head. Letters and syllables and sounds that can't quite find a way to come together, no matter how hard she wills them to.

"We have a suspect in custody," the officer says while Ingrid is still waiting for the words to travel from her brain to her mouth.

The effort of trying to talk ceases then. There is a black weightless stillness and Ingrid leans all the way into it.

And later when she comes to and learns that Opal Rowen is in custody for her husband's murder, Ingrid will be relieved, even glad. Not that her husband is dead, or that this particular woman is across town in custody for his murder, but that Ingrid collapsed before she had a chance to say the words that were finally, at long last, making their way to the tip of her tongue right before she passed out.

She will be glad she didn't ask the officer, "Am I under arrest?" Because if she had found those words and asked that question, she might now be a suspect in her husband's murder instead of Opal Rowen.

BARR NONE

PROLOGUE

"I wish I was dead."

"Jesus, Ruth. What kind of thing is that to say?"

"Oh come on, don't get all Dr. Phil on me. I'm just—come on—look around you. This is what we're working for. It's exhausting. We're working our tails off billing clients like crazy so Barr Knoll can pay for this ridiculous mansion overlooking the water and filled with ugly expensive decor. Even in the bathroom for heaven's sake. Like this. What in the hell is this?"

Ruth turned Cassandra so her friend could face the sculpture she was questioning head on. Half dog, half spider, it was hideous in form and color. A dingy, horrible shade of gray clay that somehow managed to clash with every single thing in the room despite being completely colorless.

Cassandra laughed and shielded her eyes as if she'd seen

something bright. Or disgusting. Which she had.

"Why, Ruth, it's art, of course. You'd know that if you had any class."

"Oh sure, you're the one who followed me in here to bum a cigarette like we're teenagers in high school instead of over-priced Manhattan lawyers. And now you want to talk about class."

Ruth and Cassandra were camped out in the bathroom of their boss, sharing a Marlboro and each taking turns to wave the smoke up into the ceiling fan in the oversized marble and sub-way-tile-lined bathroom that was arguably nicer (that art, though!) and definitely bigger than the Hell's Kitchen apartment the two women shared with their third roommate, Tricia.

Ruth had been babbling about a nonsense legal case she was working on at their shared law firm when she suddenly launched into the lament about filling their boss's pockets with money with their own back-breaking work. Barr Knoll headed up the most prestigious law firm in New York City. Hell, maybe even in the country. Ruth and Cassandra were always being told how lucky they were to work at a place like Barr Knoll. They'd been "lucky" enough to work there for nearly five years. And each woman had thoughts about the "lucky to work there" sentiment every time they heard it.

"I feel badly that we deserted Tricia. Do you think she's ok?" Casandra tried to hide the concern and guilt behind a too-loud chuckle that turned into a cough as she sucked in a quick hit off the dwindling cigarette.

Ruth ignored the real meaning behind Cassandra's question. "I mean, she is going to have to fend off that server with the never-ending shrimp tray on her own."

Cassandra whispered then, looking over her shoulder like they were somewhere more public than Barr Knoll's Riversedge New York mansion bathroom. "Ruth, don't make any more off-hand comments about wanting to be dead. You know what that does to my heart."

"I know. And I'm sorry. I'm in a much better headspace now. Don't worry. I'm over all that. I'm good as new. Cross my heart."

There was some more banter between the women, and then they flushed the cigarette butt down the bidet. Cassandra pumped a few sprays from the bottle of lavender eucalyptus she assumed their host set out on the marble counter specifically for vices like theirs, as Ruth continued waving the last smoke rings up toward the fan.

Cassandra kept her eyes on the smoke disappearing into the holes of the ceiling rather than on Ruth as she spoke the quiet truth that still burned. "I know. And I'm not nearly as worried about you anymore as I once was. Now I'm just worried about *her*."

ACKNOWLEDGEMENTS

Thank you, thank you, THANK YOU, to my extraordinary publisher, Nancy Cleary of Wyatt-MacKenzie Publishing. Ten years of making literary magic with you! I am so very grateful for your kindness, tenacity, and the faith you have always put in me.

Thank you to Liza and Ginger, agents extraordinaire at Liza Royce Agency, for believing in these characters and this series. Your zeal and creativity keeps me going!

Thank you to my lawyer friends and colleagues through the years who have been no small part of the stories I write now. My years as a lawyer were filled with joy and chaos and inspiration and I am so grateful for all of it.

Thank you to my family, parents, and siblings, Uncle Steve and Aunt Sharon, and all the rest of you, who continue to root for me, my characters, and my stories.

Thank you to my writing community whose generosity continues to astound and delight. Especially my Tall Poppy Writers and Heather Christie, as well as Robert Rotsein, Tosca Lee, Rektok Ross, and Lindsay Cameron for the early reads and gorgeous reviews.

And finally, thank you to my children, Paul, Luke and Grace, my greatest chapters of all!